"But where will you stay?"

"With the three of you in the apartment," Mitch retorted bluntly. "It'll be cramped, but it's only a temporary measure, and I'll be out of town a lot—which is why I need you to live here at the Social Club. You can handle whatever comes up while I'm gone."

Stunned, Phoebe could only stare at him. He was serious. He actually expected her to move in with him—a man she'd known for all of twenty-four hours—just because he'd offered her a so-called job! Did he think she was so destitute that she would do *anything* for money?

"Let me get this straight. You're offering me a job, but I have to live with you. And just what exactly would you be paying me for? The duties you already described, or something a little more, shall we say…intimate?"

Dear Reader,

Happy holidaze! The holiday season always does pass in a bit of a daze, with all the shopping and wrapping and partying, the cooking and (of course!) the eating. So take some time for yourself with our six Intimate Moments novels, each one of them a wonderful Christmas treat.

Start by paying a visit to THE LONE STAR SOCIAL CLUB, Linda Turner's setting for *Christmas Lone-Star Style.* Remember, those Texans know how to do things in a *big* way! Then join Suzanne Brockmann for another TALL, DARK AND DANGEROUS title, *It Came Upon a Midnight Clear.* I wouldn't mind waking up and finding Crash Hawken under *my* Christmas tree! Historical writer Patricia Potter makes a slam-bang contemporary debut with *Home for Christmas,* our FAMILIES ARE FOREVER title. Wrongly convicted and without the memories that could save him, Ryan Murphy is a hero to treasure. Award winner Ruth Wind returns with *For Christmas, Forever.* Isn't this the season when mysterious strangers come bearing…romance tinged with danger? Debra Cowan's *One Silent Night* is our MEN IN BLUE title. I'd be happy to "unwrap" Sam Garrett on Christmas morning. Finally, welcome mainstream author Christine Michels to the line. *A Season of Miracles* carries the TRY TO REMEMBER flash, though you'll have no trouble at all remembering this warm holiday love story.

It's time to take the "daze" out of the holidays, so enjoy all six of these seasonal offerings. Of course, don't forget that next month marks a new year, so come back then for more of the best romance reading around—right here in Silhouette Intimate Moments.

Seasons Greetings,

Leslie J. Wainger
Executive Senior Editor

Please address questions and book requests to:
Silhouette Reader Service
U.S.: 3010 Walden Ave., P.O. Box 1325, Buffalo, NY 14269
Canadian: P.O. Box 609, Fort Erie, Ont. L2A 5X3

Linda Turner

Christmas Lone-Star Style

Silhouette®

INTIMATE™ MOMENTS®

Published by Silhouette Books

America's Publisher of Contemporary Romance

SILHOUETTE BOOKS

ISBN 0-373-07895-1

CHRISTMAS LONE-STAR STYLE

Books by Linda Turner

LINDA TURNER

began reading romances in high school and began writing them one night when she had nothing else to read. She's been writing ever since. Single and living in Texas, she travels every chance she gets, scouting locales for her books.

Prologue

When the phone rang at two-thirty in the morning, it was a given that the news wasn't good. It never was in the dark of night. Instantly awake, Mitch Ryan rolled over and snatched up the receiver. "Hello?"

"Mitch! Thank God you're home! I was afraid you were gone on one of your business trips and I didn't know how I was going to reach you—"

At the sound of panic in his aunt's voice, Mitch felt his gut clench like a fist. Alice Truelove was one of those rare people who went through life with an easygoing grace that he couldn't help but admire. When other people were running around losing their heads, she could always be counted on to keep hers and remain calm. Something had to be very wrong for her to be rattled.

Sitting up, he switched on the bedside light. "It's all right, Alice," he said quietly. "I'm here. What's wrong?"

"It's Glen," she choked. "He's had an accident. Emily just called."

At the mention of Alice's daughter and her husband, Mitch's lean face settled into grim lines. "How bad is it? Was Emily with him? What about the baby?"

"No, they were both at home. Dear God, I don't know what I would do if they'd been with him! A trucker ran a red light and hit Glen broadside, just three blocks from their house."

Mitch swore softly. "How badly is he hurt?"

"He's got a broken leg and a fractured shoulder, but that's not the worst of it. His head went through the window, and there could be brain damage," she said tearfully. "I have to go, Mitch. With the baby and everything, Emily needs me."

That went without saying. Emily was one of Mitch's favorite cousins, and he knew that she didn't deal well with anything that even resembled a crisis. She needed someone to lean on, to turn to when there was trouble, and with her husband out of commission for God knew how long, not to mention a two-month-old baby to take care of, the only support group she had left was her family—her mother most of all.

"Do you want the jet? I can have it fueled up and in San Antonio within a couple of hours. You can be in L.A. by the time the sun comes up."

Some of Alice's panic subsided at the quick offer, and she sighed shakily. "Thank you, dear. I knew I could count on you to help me calm down, but I won't need your plane. I've already called the airlines and made a reservation for a seven-thirty flight in the morning. I just don't know what to do about the Social Club. I may be gone a while, and that could be a problem."

"The only thing you need to worry about right now is Emily and Glen," Mitch assured her. "You stay as long as they need you. The Social Club's been there for over a hundred years. It's not going anywhere while you're gone.''

''But you wanted me to get started on the remodeling of the attic,'' she reminded him, ''and I haven't even had time to talk to an architect about it yet. And what about the tenants? I can't just leave them there with no one in charge. What if there's a problem—or an emergency? And who'll collect the rent? Someone has to be there.''

''Get a temporary to take over for you,'' he suggested. ''Or a management service to handle things until you get back.''

''There isn't time. And I can't turn the keys over to just anybody. They need to be interviewed and have their references checked, and I can't do that from California.''

As far as hints went, it was a fairly subtle one—for Alice. She wanted him to fly to San Antonio and take care of things until she got back. Swallowing a groan at the thought, Mitch's first instinct was to tell her to forget it. Old man Applebee, a business nemesis, was up to his usual tricks. Mitch couldn't leave Dallas right now without risking a major financial setback.

But he knew how Alice felt about the Social Club. How the whole family felt about it, in fact. Back in the days after the Civil War, Gertrude Ryan, his widowed great-great-grandmother, started the Lone Star Social Club in her house on the banks of the San Antonio River. There, cowboys in town from the cattle drives could meet nice women in a socially correct setting, and for a number of years, Gertrude Ryan was not only wildly successful, but the talk of the town. But then social clubs went out of fashion and she was eventually forced to put the house on the market. It was sold to a Yankee, and for many years the family had talked of getting it back.

So when the old Victorian house came on the market over a decade ago, he hadn't hesitated to buy it. Located right in the heart of downtown San Antonio on the River Walk and on the verge of being torn down, it was a sound business venture he couldn't pass up. He'd bought it for a song, restored it and turned it into eight unique apartments.

Right from the beginning, there'd never been any question in his mind whom he would ask to live there and act as caretaker and manager. Alice had always loved the house and knew its history as well as she knew the lines on her own hand. So Mitch wasn't really surprised that on her list of worries, the Lone Star Social Club would be right behind a family emergency. If he didn't fly down there and make sure the right person was hired to look after the place while she was helping Emily in L.A., she'd worry about it until he did. And she had enough on her plate as it was.

"Don't worry about the Social Club," he scolded. "Right now, your main concern is Glen and Emily. Go out to L.A. and stay as long as they need you. I'll take care of things in San Antonio."

"Personally? You're going to fly down here?"

"Just as soon as I clear up a few business matters," he assured her. "Then I'll look around for someone to take over for you until you get back. And don't worry—it'll be somebody you'd approve of yourself, not a management company. Okay?"

"But what about the remodeling? You shouldn't have to put it off just because I have to take a leave of absence. While you're there, why don't you go ahead and have an architect draw up some plans? You could handle that better than I could anyway."

Resigned, he sighed. "Okay, sweetheart. I'll talk to an architect, a contractor, whatever you want. Now will you go to L.A.?"

Pleased, she laughed, and for a minute, she sounded

like her old self, the one who never worried. "First thing in the morning. Thank you, dear. I knew I could count on you. You're always so sweet."

Applebee and any number of business associates in Dallas would have laughed at the idea of anyone calling him any such thing. Ruthless? Yes. Sharp as an executioner's blade? Without a doubt. But sweet? Only with those he cared about. "Go to L.A., Alice," he said dryly, grinning. "The Social Club will be well taken care of while you're gone."

Chapter 1

Mitch had never seen anything like it in his life. The front porch of the Lone Star Social Club was so packed with people that the crowd spilled down the steps and into the yard. Elbow to elbow and wedged tighter than too many teeth in a small mouth, strangers jockeyed for position and refused to budge so much as an inch as they fought to be the first through the front door.

Drawing up to the curb before the front walk, the cab driver glanced over his shoulder at Mitch and arched a brow at him. "You sure this is the place you want to go, mister? That looks like a pretty nasty crowd to me. Somebody inside giving away free lottery tickets or what?"

His eyes narrowed dangerously on a tall, skinny hippie-type who just then stepped out of the house clutching an antique beveled mirror to his chest like they were connected at the belly button. Mitch swore softly. "I don't know, but I mean to find out."

Shoving the fare and a tip into the driver's hand, he

grabbed his suitcase and pushed open the rear passenger door. Seconds later, he was shouldering his way through the crowd. "Excuse me, please. Let me through. I just need to get around you—"

"Hey, no cuts!"

"Wait your turn, mister! We were here first."

"I don't know who you think you are, buddy, but I've been waiting two hours to get in this joint. If you think you can just waltz in here and push in front of everyone, you're crazy. The line starts at the curb."

Angry mutterings and dirty looks hit him from all sides, but he ignored them and pushed determinedly on. Grudgingly, people gave way, but not without telling him first what they thought of him. By the time he reached the porch, he felt like a new recruit who had just run his first gauntlet at boot camp and was lucky to still be in one piece.

But if he thought the group in the yard was a tough bunch, he soon discovered that the one on the porch gave a whole new meaning to the word unmoving. Digging in their heels, their faces as rigid as stone when he asked them to move, they just stood there like the blocks of granite at Stonehenge.

Exasperated, he snapped, "What the hell is going on? I own this building and if somebody doesn't tell me damn quick what you people are doing here, I'm calling the police."

"The police!" an older woman in the crowd gasped indignantly. "Why, I never! You just try that, young man, and you're going to find yourself up to your ears in law-suits! For your information, we're here for an estate sale. One that's advertised in this morning's paper," she added smugly. "Read it yourself if you don't believe me." Slapping him in the chest with the classified section, she jabbed at the column where the ad was printed: Estate

Sale. Lone Star Social Club, Apartment 2C. Thursday, 9 to 6.

Taking the crumpled paper from her, Mitch ground his teeth on a curse. In her late-night phone call Tuesday night, Alice had mentioned that old Lindsay in 2C had died at the beginning of the month, and that his family still had to remove his things from the apartment before the new tenants moved in next week. She'd warned him that he'd have to get the place cleaned, but she hadn't said a word about an estate sale.

Because, Mitch felt sure, she never would have allowed such a thing. Alice was as protective as a mother hen when it came to the Social Club, and with good cause. In spite of the fact that the old Victorian gingerbread had been divided into apartments, it still had common rooms for the tenants. And those rooms were decorated with priceless antiques and knickknacks, just the type of things that could easily disappear when there was a crowd of strangers in the house looking for a treasure.

No, he told himself, he didn't care that Lindsay's heirs had placed an ad in the paper, he'd bet the grandfather clock in the foyer that they hadn't told Alice a thing about it. And if that was the case, he was shutting them down just as soon as he could get upstairs and have a talk with whoever was in charge of the damn sale.

"That may not be worth the paper it's written on," he warned the older lady as he stepped around her.

Determined to get some answers, he was prepared to shove his way through the rest of the mob, but this time he was grudgingly allowed to pass. Then, just as he crossed the porch to the front door, the whole house seemed to shudder and groan. Inside, a man shouted a warning that was abruptly followed by what sounded like a small explosion. A woman shrieked, then everyone seemed to be yelling.

Swearing, Mitch pushed open the front door just as all hell broke loose. A pipe had broken in the ceiling and cold water gushed down on the crowd in the foyer like Niagara Falls. They pushed and shoved and screamed, but with so many people packed into the entrance hall waiting to get upstairs to the sale, it was impossible for all of them to avoid the icy spray. Still, they tried. And in the process, a birdlike old woman was knocked to the floor.

"Watch it!" Mitch roared.

No one heard him. And there was no way to get to the woman. Anxious to escape the deluge, the yelling and shouting crowd turned en masse toward where he stood just inside the front door. He either had to let them carry him with them outside or get trampled in the rush. Left with little choice, he chose the former.

The throng on the porch, however, didn't want to give way and lose their place in line to get inside to the sale. One man pushed another and they nearly came to blows. Mitch had never see anything like it in his life. Grown men fighting over some old furniture in a damn estate sale! And all the while, the Social Club was flooding like a sinking ship about to go under. Muttering curses under his breath, he pushed and jostled his way through the horde of bodies until he was finally able to burst free in the yard. The shutoff valve for the water was near the curb, and it only took him seconds to find it and cut off the water.

In spite of that, Mitch knew the crisis was far from over. People were still angry and frightened, and inside, the old lady who had been flattened by the crowd was probably still on the floor. She might be injured badly. Not even bothering to consider whether he'd be able to fight his way through the mob again to get to her, he rushed around to the back and slipped inside through the garden entrance.

The overhead shower from the broken pipe had slowed to an occasional drip, but water covered the floor in the entrance hall and was slowly seeping toward the downstairs apartments. Mitch hardly noticed. The elderly woman had managed to move to the stairs, where she sat on the second step, but she was soaked to the skin and obviously in some pain. Pale and drawn, she sat hugging herself, shivering in spite of the fact that the heater vent was blowing almost directly on her.

Quickly shrugging out of his jacket, Mitch slipped it around her shoulders, then, uncaring of the water on the floor, knelt down in front of her. "I'm Mitch Ryan, ma'am, the owner of the building. That was a nasty fall you took. Are you all right?"

Sniffling, she nodded and told him her name was Elizabeth Randolph. "I feel like such an old fool," she confided as she wiped at the tears that trailed down her wrinkled cheek. "One second I was trying to figure out what had happened, and the next, everyone was running like the devil himself was after them. My legs just seemed to go out from under me."

She sounded so mortified that Mitch couldn't help but smile. "You're lucky you weren't trampled. I don't think that anyone even noticed you. Everyone was pretty intent on clearing out of here."

"Just because of a little water." She sniffed indignantly. "Did they think they were going to melt or something if they got a little wet? Lord save me from idiots— I never did have much use for them. Well, I need to go home and change out of these wet clothes. I must look a sight."

She started to rise, only to wince as she shifted to get her feet under her. What color there was in her cheeks drained away, and with a quickly stifled groan, she sank back down onto the stairs. "I'm all right," she gasped, as Mitch frowned in concern and quickly moved to help her. "My old bones just get stiff when I sit too long in one position. Give me a second. I'm just fine."

"Yeah, and I'm the Good Fairy," Mitch retorted, scowling. "You hurt your hip, didn't you?"

Her chin went up a notch. "I didn't break it."

"Maybe not," he replied, "but it's obviously hurting you. I'm calling an ambulance."

"Oh, no! Really, it's probably just a bruise. Please don't go to a lot of fuss."

Taking her hand, he patted it consolingly and gave her a smile that had been winning him arguments with the opposite sex since he was old enough to talk. "Mrs. Randolph, you are a guest here at the Social Club, and it's my responsibility to make sure that you don't leave here injured."

"But I'm not!"

"If it's all the same to you, I'd feel better if a doctor verified that. Just so I'll be able to sleep tonight without worrying about you. You wouldn't want to be responsible for keeping me awake tonight, would you?"

Flustered, she stuttered, "Well, no. Of course not, but it seems silly to waste good money on a doctor when I'm just a little shaken up."

Considering the fact that, at thirty-six, he had more than enough money to retire and live in luxury for the rest of his life, it was all he could do not to laugh at her objection. Instead, he only smiled and said, "Don't worry about the money—I have insurance for just such situations, so I will, of course, pick up all your medical bills. The most important thing, though, is to make sure that you're all right. Don't you agree? You wouldn't want to have problems with this as you get older because you didn't have it checked out now, would you?"

Put that way, she could do nothing but give in. "Well, no. Of course not."

"Good. Then I'll call for an ambulance." With no further argument, he pulled his cell phone from the pocket of his jacket, which was still around her shoulders, and quickly punched in 911 before she could change her mind.

The paramedics were there in record time, traipsing through the water in the foyer without so much as blinking an eye. After a quick examination, they expressed doubt that Mrs. Randolph was seriously hurt, but they did recommend a trip to the hospital for X rays just to be sure. So they strapped her to a stretcher and rolled her out through the now silent and respectful crowd on the porch, but not before Mitch got her address and phone number and promised to check on her later in the day.

The second the ambulance drove away, the people began pressing forward again, reminding Mitch that he still had several problems to deal with. No one in the house could have their water turned back on until a plumber was called and the broken pipe repaired. Damage from the break was all around him. The antique rug was soaked and the cherrywood grandfather clock, which had been in the family longer than anyone could remember, was standing in an inch of water. When everything dried out, the wallpaper in the entrance hall and stairwell would no doubt have to be replaced, as would the old pine flooring if it warped. Silently sending up a prayer, he thanked God that Alice wasn't there to see it. She would have been in tears.

The most immediate problem, however, was the sale going on in apartment 2C. That was something he could put a stop to in ten seconds flat. With his steel-blue eyes shining in a way that would have had his business associates quaking in their shoes, he started up the stairs.

* * *

Drawing up to the curb, Phoebe Smith put the transmission of her old, cranky Ford in park and turned with a smile to the two kids who sat beside her on the bench seat. Everything they possessed was crammed into the U-Haul trailer hitched to the back. "This is it, kids," she said, motioning to the huge Victorian house that sat before them like a well-dressed old lady in all her finery. "What do you think?"

His eyes as round as silver dollars, her nephew, Robby, gasped, "For real, Aunt Phoebe? This is where we're going to live? Wow!"

"It looks like a castle," Becky, too, was admiring. "Does it have a fairy godmother like in *Cinderella?*"

Chuckling, Phoebe reached over and hugged her niece. Lord, the girl was a child after her own heart! At the age of six, in spite of everything that had happened to her, Becky still believed in fairy tales, and if Phoebe had her way, she still would when she was forty. The world needed people who believed in the magic of happily-ever-after.

"I don't know, honey," she replied. "I didn't see one when I rented the apartment, but fairy godmothers are kind of shy—they don't show themselves too often. That doesn't mean they're not around and doing their good deeds," she quickly assured her. "I like to think that ours led us to this house."

Robby rolled his eyes. A year older than his sister, he considered himself far too mature to believe in such baby stuff. "Yeah, right. So where's Prince Charming?"

That was a question Phoebe had long since stopped asking herself. Grinning, she shut off the motor. "Princes, charming or otherwise, are in notoriously short supply right now, but fairy godmothers are another matter. Trust me, big guy, they're out there. You just can't see them."

Pushing open her door, she turned to grab one of the boxes stuffed into the back seat. "C'mon, let's check the place out. Everybody grab something."

She didn't have to tell them twice. Excited, they both snatched their duffel bags from the back seat, then raced for the wide, inviting veranda that wrapped all the way around the Social Club. "I get first dibs on which bedroom we get!"

"You can't! Aunt Phoebe said we have to share the biggest one."

"Then I get to pick where my bed goes before you do because I'm the oldest."

"That's not fair! I can't help it if I'm the baby."

Arguing good-naturedly, they disappeared through the mansion's front door, which was standing wide open, before Phoebe could even lock the car. "Hey, guys, wait up!" she called after them. "You don't even know which apartment it is."

Eager to explore, they weren't concerned about a detail like that. By the time Phoebe stepped into the entrance hall, they'd already reached the top of the stairs and darted down the hall, oohing and ahhing over everything they saw.

Following them, Phoebe couldn't help but smile. God, she loved them! They were her brother Frank's kids and all she had left of him now. When he and his wife were killed in a car accident early last year, it was decided that the children would stay with their maternal grandparents in New Orleans, since that was where their home and roots were. Phoebe would have loved to have them, but the kids' security was more important than her wishes, so she hadn't considered asking for custody. Then, just last week, the kids' grandmother, Louise Mallory, had called to tell Phoebe that her husband had had a heart attack and she could no longer care for the children. Phoebe had exactly five hours' notice before she picked the kids up at the airport.

She'd never thought to turn them away. They were blood, family, a last link with Frank, and she welcomed them with open arms. She was an aunt, however, not a mother, and not equipped to take care of kids on a full-time basis. Their unexpected arrival in her life, with virtually no warning, created a whole host of problems, not the least of which was a place to live. Her old apartment had certainly been big enough, but it was restricted to adults only. The second day she'd had the children, the apartment manager showed up on her doorstep asking questions. By the end of the day, she was served with an eviction notice.

At that point, she panicked. If she hadn't had the responsibility of the kids, she'd have been more level-headed—at least, she hoped so. But then again, she wouldn't have been in the predicament if it hadn't been for the kids. Haunted with terrible images of the three of them being thrown out on the street, she'd raced over to the apartment office and explained the situation, but nothing she'd said had mattered. Rules were rules, and children weren't allowed in the complex.

Financially, she hadn't been in any position to move. That's when her own fairy godmother had stepped in. She'd stopped at the grocery store the following morning on the way to work, and there on the bulletin board was a sign for an apartment to let. She called about it the second she got to work, explained the situation to Mr. Percy, the landlord, and was thrilled when he told her that considering the circumstances, he would be willing to let her slide on the security deposit, if she could come up with the first and last month's rent when she signed the lease. Skipping lunch to check out the apartment, she'd taken one look at the place and fallen in love with it. By the time she returned to work, she had a signed lease in her pocket and Mr. Percy had the last of her savings.

Eventually, she hoped to be able to get a house so the kids would have a yard to play in, but for now, watching their excited faces as she caught up with them and unlocked the door to the apartment, she knew she'd done the right thing. There was a magic to the Lone Star Social Club that would take their minds off the loss of their parents and the upheaval in their lives. They'd already smiled and laughed more in the last few minutes than they had in the five days she'd had them, and for that, she was heartily grateful. If they could find happiness here, she was prepared to stay forever.

"Wow!" Robby exclaimed suddenly from the bedroom he'd darted into. "This room is *round!* Come look, Aunt Phoebe."

Grinning, she stepped into the open doorway. "It's called the tower bedroom, sweetie. I thought you and Becky might like to share it."

His face lit up like a Christmas tree. "You mean it? It's really ours? We can move our stuff in and everything? Right now?"

"Right this very minute," she laughed.

"All right!" Taking off like a shot, he ran for the stairs. "Let's get my dinosaur collection first. I know right where I want to put it!"

It had been a hell of a day. With a groan, Mitch sank into the chair behind Alice's desk in her office. Lindsay's heirs had been more than a little antagonistic when he shut down their estate sale and gave them exactly two hours to get the rest of the old man's things out of the apartment. They'd tried to argue, but since they'd taken advantage of Alice's easygoing nature and hadn't bothered to pay the rent when it ran out last week, they were technically trespassing and they knew it. They'd finally, grudgingly, left an hour ago, taking everything that wasn't bolted down with them.

The apartment would still have to be cleaned, of course, before the new tenants, a middle-aged couple from Houston, moved in next week, but that was the least of his problems at the moment. While the Lindsay heirs were stomping up and down the stairs, carrying out furniture, the plumber finally arrived to repair the broken pipe. He'd pried up the floor in the kitchen of apartment 2B, taken one look at the old fixtures, and started shaking his head. He could, he'd told Mitch, repair the break, but it would only be a stopgap measure. The pipes were old and should have been replaced years ago. Until they were, there would be more breaks, not to mention a heck of a lot of water damage.

Too late, Mitch knew he should have bitten the bullet and replaced the pipes when he'd bought the place ten years ago and renovated it, but he was assured the plumbing would hold up another fifty years. So much for promises, he thought wryly. This couldn't have happened at a worse time. He didn't want to start any major renovations unless he or Alice was present, and he'd never intended his stay in San Antonio to be anything but temporary. He'd only planned to stay a couple of days, just until he found someone he—and Alice—could trust to oversee the Social Club while she was in L.A. Back in Dallas, Applebee was no doubt having a field day, taking advantage of his absence to cause all sorts of headaches for him, businesswise. The quicker he got back, the better.

But could he actually walk away from the Social Club knowing the pipes could explode any minute?

Trapped, he knew he couldn't. Aside from the fact that he'd never hear the end of it from Alice, the house wasn't just another business venture that made him money. It was a legacy of the past that had a personality all its own, and the day he'd bought it, protecting the family heritage became his responsibility. He couldn't turn his back on that now just because Applebee was causing problems for him in Dallas. Somehow, for the next little while, he'd have to divide his time between the two cities. He hoped that none of his business ventures suffered because of it.

Which meant he would still need someone to take over Alice's duties and oversee things whenever he was called away to Dallas, he thought as he pulled the phone book from the bottom drawer of Alice's desk. He'd call one of the employment services and see if they could send over a few candidates tomorrow.

Flipping through the yellow pages, he was just deciding which employment agency to use when he heard someone in the entrance hall. Normally, he would have figured it was one of the tenants, but he had left the front door open so the hall could dry out, and anyone could walk in. Especially since the ad for that damn estate sale was still in the paper.

Swearing, he dropped the phone book back on the desk and strode over to the front door of Alice's apartment. Jerking it open, he stepped into the hall just as a woman and two children started up the stairs, the three of them struggling to maneuver a twin-bed frame around the bend of the landing.

"Do you think the place is haunted, Aunt Phoebe?" the boy was asking in excited whispers that seemed to echo eerily in the hall. "It's an old house. There could be ghosts—"

"In our room?" the little girl squeaked, horrified. "Will they hurt us?"

"No, honey," the woman quickly assured her. "There're no ghosts in your room or anything else that will hurt you. We're all going to be very happy here."

Suddenly shifting her attention to the boy, she said, "Watch the wallpaper, honey. We don't want to tear it."

Frowning, Mitch watched them proceed up the stairs and couldn't believe his eyes. They were moving in! he thought, stunned. But the only empty apartment in the house was 2C, and that had already been leased to the Johnsons, who were moving in next week. And from what Alice had told him, the couple was middle-aged and had no children. That, in no way, shape or form described the woman on the stairs. Young and pretty, she wasn't even close to middle-aged. In fact, he doubted that she was even thirty.

His rugged face set in stern lines, he stepped to the foot of the stairs and scowled up at her. "I don't know who you are, lady, but you've got some explaining to do. What the devil do you think you're doing?"

Chapter 2

Startled, Phoebe nearly dropped her end of the bed frame. Glancing over the banister down at the foyer below, she quickly took in the unexpected sight of the man glaring up at her like some kind of fierce gatekeeper at the entrance to a castle. Tall and rangy, his blue eyes as sharp as lasers, he was, she was sure, a good-looking man when he wasn't scowling like an ogre. And all his anger seemed to be directed solely at her, which made no sense. All she was doing was moving in, and she couldn't see how that was any concern of his. After all, it wasn't like she and the kids were hauling furniture up the stairs in the middle of the night and waking everyone in the house. It was four o'clock in the afternoon, for heaven's sake!

So maybe he works the graveyard shift and this is the middle of the night for him, her conscience pointed out reasonably. He's a neighbor, Phoebe. Granted, he's not the best welcoming party you've ever had, but cut him some slack and try to get along. Remember—you have to set an example for the children.

Wide-eyed, Robby and Becky turned to her expectantly, waiting to see how she was going to handle the situation. Forcing a reassuring smile, she carefully set down her end of the bed frame and glanced down at the man who still glowered suspiciously at them from the foyer down below. "We're moving in, of course," she said lightly. "I'm Phoebe Smith and this is my niece and nephew, Becky and Robby. We're the new tenants in 2C."

Whatever response Phoebe was expecting, it wasn't the low curse he bit out. "I don't know what kind of game you think you're playing, lady, but you can just haul your stuff back down the stairs and get out of here before you find yourself in more trouble than you can handle."

Stunned, she blinked. "I beg your pardon?"

"You heard me," he said impatiently. "Spare me the fake surprise. We both know you haven't rented 2C. You couldn't have. It's already been rented to the Johnsons. They're scheduled to move in next week."

"But they can't!" she cried. "I've already rented it!"

He snorted, unconvinced. "Yeah, right. And when was that?"

"Yesterday. I met with the landlord—"

"What time?"

He threw questions at her like darts, and she had to stop a minute to think. "Eleven!"

"You couldn't have," he said flatly. "She left for L.A. yesterday morning at seven-thirty."

He sounded so sure of himself that if she hadn't known better, Phoebe might have believed him. But she knew for a fact that the landlord was a man—she'd met with him herself yesterday when he'd shown her the apartment. Whoever this guy was, he obviously didn't know what he was talking about.

"I'm sorry," she said stiffly, "I don't know who this

woman is you're talking about, but you're mistaken. The landlord is Mr. Percy. He lives down the hall in apartment 1B and he already knows we're moving in today.'' The matter settled as far as she was concerned, she turned back to Robby and Becky and determinedly lifted her end of the bed. "C'mon, kids, let's get this upstairs. If we're going to get everything inside before dark, we're going to have to hustle.''

Unable to believe her audacity, Mitch growled, "If you take another step up those stairs, I swear I'm calling the police.''

"The police!'' she gasped, indignant. Her hazel eyes flashing, she dropped the end of the bed again, this time to dig in her purse. "I don't know who you think you are, mister, but I have a lease. Signed, sealed, and delivered. Just give me a second to find it, and we can settle this once and for all.'' Muttering under her breath, she finally found what she was looking for and stomped down the stairs to wave it under his nose. "See? It was signed yesterday and gives me permission to move in today. So if you'll excuse me, I'm going to do just that.''

She did, indeed, have a lease. Written on plain white typing paper, it was simply done and appeared legitimate. The only problem was it was nothing like the legal document that all tenants of the Social Club were required to sign before they were allowed to move in.

Was she trying to pull a fast one or was she the unwitting victim of a scam herself? Mitch studied her face. Over the years, he'd dealt with his fair share of cheats and con artists, and they'd all looked him right in the eye and lied through their teeth. This woman made no attempt to avoid his gaze, but his gut told him she wasn't lying. There was too much hostility in her hazel eyes.

Resisting her efforts to snatch the bogus lease back

from him, he asked, "How much did you give this Percy fellow when you signed this thing?"

"The usual, of course," she snapped. "First and last month's rent. Not that it's any business of yours," she amended, shooting him a hostile look as he held the document out of reach. "Dammit, give me that!"

"Oh, I intend to," he assured her smoothly. "After the police take a look at it."

"Call the police if you want! I told you—"

"This isn't worth the paper it's written on," he told her quietly. "I don't know who this Percy jerk is or how he got into 2C to show you the apartment, but he had no authority to rent you anything."

"But he lives in 1B—"

"The landlord does live there," he agreed. "But she's a woman, and her name is Alice Truelove. She's my aunt. My name is Mitch Ryan and I'm watching over things while she's in L.A. for a family emergency. If you don't believe me, knock on any door in the building. All the tenants will tell you the same thing."

She didn't want to believe him—he could see the struggle going on in her expressive eyes as they searched his, the denial she wanted to cling to—and he sympathized with her. He hadn't forgotten the times he'd been taken in by a good liar. It hadn't happened to him often, but it wasn't a pleasant feeling.

"Look, why don't you come in the office while I call the police?" he suggested. "You need to report this."

It was that, more than anything, that seemed to convince her he was telling the truth. What little color there was left in her cheeks drained away, and with a nearly silent moan, she sank down onto the bottom step of the stairs. "Oh, God, it's true! Now what are we going to do?"

* * *

Just about every penny she had was gone.

Unable to think of anything but that, Phoebe was still sitting on the stairs ten minutes later when a detective arrived and introduced himself as Sam Kelly. "I used to live here," he informed her as she rose to her feet and shook his hand. "I understand from Mitch that you had some trouble with a scam artist renting you an apartment here at the Social Club."

She nodded numbly. "Apparently so. He said he was the landlord. His name was Percy."

She gave him a description of the man. "I had no reason not to believe him. He buzzed me up to the apartment when I arrived and already had a lease there for me to sign. I did think it was a little odd that he was showing the place before the other tenants had moved out, but he assured me he had their permission and they would have their things out by the time I was ready to move in. And they did. The apartment *is* empty."

"The tenant died three weeks ago and the rent expired last week," Mitch said. "His family was in the process of having an unauthorized estate sale this morning when I arrived. People were coming and going all over the place, taking God knows what out of the house, so I shut it down and the family got everything out by noon."

"The tenant died?" Phoebe gasped. "Mr. Percy said he had bought a house and was giving up his lease."

Not surprised, Sam Kelly nodded. "Apparently Percy—and that's only one of the names he's used—has said a lot of things. And not to just you, Ms. Smith," he assured her. "Over the last four months, he's pulled this same scam a number of times. He watches the obits in the paper, finds out where the deceased lived, and rents out their apartment to as many prospective tenants as he can line up before the family finds out what's going on.

How did you hear about the apartment here at the Social Club?''

''I saw an ad on the bulletin board at the grocery store,'' she said simply. ''Normally, I wouldn't have looked twice at it, but I needed a place and it looked like a legitimate ad. And when I called the number listed, the receptionist answered, 'Lone Star Social Club.' I had no reason to be suspicious.''

''Do you remember the phone number?'' She didn't, but she still had the number in her purse and dug it out for him. He quickly jotted it down and the address of the grocery store where she'd seen the ad. ''Was the receptionist a woman?''

Surprised, she said, ''Yes! How did you know?''

''Our boy uses the same MO every time and he has a female accomplice. They never place an ad in the paper— that would be too easily traced—and they usually list the phone number of the deceased in the ad if the phone hasn't been turned off.''

Straightening from leaning against the doorjamb, observing the questioning, Mitch said, ''So what happens now? Apparently, nothing was stolen except the rent money, and that was in cash. How are you going to track the jerk down without a paper trail to follow?''

''I'll check with the grocery store manager and see if he knows how long the advertisement has been on his bulletin board and who put it there. He probably won't know anything about it, but sometimes people have to check with the store office before they're allowed to put anything on the bulletin board.'' Shutting his notebook, he tucked it into his jacket pocket. ''It's a slim hope, but it's one of the few leads we've got. And then there's always the phone company. Other than that, there's not much I can do.''

''But what about the obituaries?'' Phoebe asked, frowning. "If this guy restricts himself to just renting dead people's apartments, why can't you just watch the obituaries and figure out where he's going to strike next?"

It was a logical question, one that the detective unfortunately had an answer for. "It's not that simple. Even if we had the manpower to check out the obits every day—which we don't—the department just couldn't afford it. Not when there's no way to anticipate when or where this guy's going to strike next. He's been known to go as long as six months without pulling one of these scams, then hitting twice within one week. The only way he's probably going to get caught is if he just screws up."

Alarmed, Phoebe felt her heart drop to her knees. "So what are you saying? You're not even going to try to catch him? What about my money?"

"Cash is almost always impossible to recover," he said simply, regretfully. "Your best bet is to just write it off as a loss and go on with your life."

"But you're talking about nearly a thousand dollars!"

He winced. "I know. It's a hell of a lot to ask a person to turn their back on, but I'd be as big a jerk as the creep who did this to you if I let you think you were ever going to see that money again. It's gone, Phoebe. It was lost to you the minute you traded cash for a worthless lease and walked away."

Deep down inside, a part of her had known—the second Mitch Ryan convinced her his aunt was the real landlord of the Social Club—that she was never going to get her money back, but she hadn't wanted to believe it. She was an optimist right down to the tips of her toes—always had been and always would be. In the face of adversity, when nothing but trouble and sorrow seemed to lie ahead, she'd always before found comfort in the sure knowledge that with time, everything would work itself out.

But not this time. How could it? She had two children

to support, no apartment, and she'd just been swindled out of every dime she owned.

"So that's it," she said flatly, her eyes stark with despair. "You've done all you can do."

"I'm sorry," the detective said gruffly. "No one hates this kind of thing more than I do, but the sad truth is there's not a hell of a lot the police can do about scam artists. Not unless we're just lucky enough to catch one in the act, and that doesn't happen very often." Taking one of his business cards from his pocket, he pressed it into her hand. "Call me in a couple of days. By then, I'll have had time to follow up any leads I might get from the store manager on who put that ad on the bulletin board."

She nodded, but they both knew there would be little point in calling. He'd already told her everything she needed to know. Her money was gone. Nothing else mattered.

The future loomed before her and the children like a dark, bottomless pit, and though she tried to tell herself they were going to be all right, she couldn't quite bring herself to believe it. Nightfall was only two hours away, and she didn't even know where they were going to spend the night. There were several shelters around the city that would take them in, but just the thought of being that desperate, that destitute, brought the sting of tears to her eyes and the slump of defeat to her shoulders. Dear God, how had she let this happen?

Mitch Ryan thanked the detective for coming and showed him out, but Phoebe hardly noticed. Lost in her painful musings and growing panic, she wasn't even aware of how their sudden change in circumstances affected the children until Robby spoke up. Seated halfway up the stairs, where he and his sister had sat as quiet as mice during the entire conversation with Detective Kelly, he asked in a scared voice, "Now what do we do, Aunt Phoebe? We don't get to live here, do we?"

Jerked back to her surroundings, Phoebe glanced up sharply and felt her heart constrict at the sight of him and his sister staring solemnly down at her. The mischief that invariably sparkled in Robby's brown eyes was gone and in its place was a fear that didn't belong in the eyes of a child his age. At his side, her freckles standing out starkly on her pale face, Becky was just as grim and on the verge of tears.

And she was the one who had brought them to this. They'd turned to her for stability and security, and she'd given them anything but that. Because of her, they didn't know where they would sleep tonight or tomorrow or the night after that. They'd lost their parents, were separated from their grandparents by illness and distance, and now they didn't even have a roof over their heads. She didn't blame them for crying—she wanted to cry herself.

But when she started up the stairs to them, the smile she forced for them was playful and teasing. "Hey, guys, why all the long faces? There's been a little bit of a mixup, but—" she assured them as she crouched down in front of them and enfolded them both in a fierce hug "—just wait. You'll see. We'll find another place just as nice as this one."

Standing just inside the front door, Mitch watched her hug the kids again, then tickle them until they collapsed in a giggling heap against her. Another man listening to her musical laughter might have been seduced by the pretty picture, but the last time he'd been taken in by a woman's smile, it had cost him more than he cared to think about. That wasn't a mistake he intended to make again.

That didn't mean he wasn't sympathetic. He was. He would sympathize with anyone who suddenly found themselves in her position. But he was a realist and could easily predict what was coming next. Any second now, she would look around for someone to bail her out of her predicament. It was just the nature of women, especially those with children in tow, to play the helpless female whenever things got rough. It was genetic.

However, if the lady thought *he* was about to charge to her rescue like some kind of misguided knight, she'd find out soon enough that she was sadly mistaken. His armor was back in Dallas, tarnished, battle-scarred and retired from service. He didn't run rescue missions anymore.

Or get taken in by big, sad eyes, he reminded himself. But he couldn't forget the look on her face when she realized that she'd turned next month's rent over to a con man. Stricken. There was no other way to describe it.

Guilt twisted in his gut, annoying him no end. He wasn't responsible for the mess she was in, he thought irritably. He wasn't the one who'd scammed her, and he certainly wasn't the one who'd given her a lease, bogus or otherwise. If he started taking in every stray and her pups who'd fallen on hard times, the Social Club would be packed to the rafters.

But instead of turning to him with a helpless look when she heard his footsteps on the wood floor of the entrance hall, she released the kids and turned to look down at him with a composure that surprised him. He'd expected tears. "We'll be out of your hair just as soon as we can get our things loaded back into the U-Haul," she informed him coolly. Dismissing him, she turned back to the kids. "Okay, guys, you ready? Lift!"

He should have been thrilled. Instead, he found himself perversely aggravated. Where the hell did she think she was going? She'd just lost a bundle of money and an apartment, and she didn't seem the least bit concerned about it. So why was he? He supposed she'd go back to wherever she came from and make some kind of deal with her old landlord when it came time to pay next month's rent. Either way, it wasn't any of his business. She was nothing to him and after today, he'd never see her again.

He should have returned to Alice's apartment and left her to her task. Instead, he found himself starting up the stairs toward her, scowling all the way. "Here—let me help you with that. It's too heavy for the kids."

It was an instinctive offer—he'd been raised in a family of women, who had taught him to always lend a hand to a woman or child who needed his help—but she reacted as if he'd just insulted her. Lightning-quick, her chin set at a proud angle, she moved to block his path. "That won't be necessary. We got it up here by ourselves. We can get it down."

Standing two steps above him, her hazel eyes level with his and snapping fire, she gave him a look that dared him to lay so much as a finger on her possessions. At any other time, Mitch would have laughed. The lady obviously didn't know who she was messing with. She was barely five foot two and slender as a ballerina—if he had a mind to, he could snatch her up and haul her downstairs as easily as a sack of potatoes. Then they'd both see how tough she was.

But he'd always been a sucker for a dainty woman, and his gut clenched at the thought of touching her. Swearing silently at himself, he retorted, "What you're going to do if you're not careful is fall and break your pretty little neck. That'd be something for the kids to see, wouldn't it?"

"I'm not going to do that."

"You're damn right you're not. Because you're going to let me help you. Or call a mover. The choice is yours."

He saw in an instant that she wasn't a woman who cared for ultimatums. She stiffened, her mouth compressed with rebellion, and for a second, he actually thought she was going to cut off her nose to spite her face and call a mover. For one damn bed! But there was such a thing as carrying pride too far, and she obviously knew it.

Giving in with little grace, she grumbled, "I don't know why you're making such a fuss. I've moved lots of times without anyone's help, but have it your way. It's your building. Which end do you want?"

"Yours."

She knew what he meant. He wanted her to move to the opposite, lighter end of the bed so he could take the heaviest part when they started down the stairs. It was a logical suggestion and, she was sure, not intentionally suggestive. But the second the single word was out of his mouth, he realized as well as she did what he had said. Blue eyes that she would have sworn didn't have so much as a glint of humor in them were suddenly warm with amusement, and with no warning whatsoever, her cheeks were on fire.

In the pregnant silence, Becky, watching the confrontation from four steps up, glanced at her brother and said in a whisper that seemed to echo to the rafters, "Why is Aunt Phoebe's face so red? Is she mad?"

Mortified, Phoebe wondered wildly if it was possible to die of terminal embarrassment right there on the spot. Quickly averting her gaze from Mitch's sudden devilish grin, she choked, "No, honey, I'm not mad. Why don't you and Robby go up to the apartment and get your duffel bags? Then you can load them in the car just as soon as Mr. Ryan and I get the bed back in the U-Haul. We're going to have to find a place to stay tonight, and it's getting late."

Robby immediately challenged Becky to race him up the stairs, and they both took off. Her cheeks still flushed,

Phoebe quickly took their place at the opposite end of the bed frame and bent to get a grip. All business, she nodded for him to proceed. "All right. Ready when you are."

But instead of lifting his end and backing down the stairs with it, he just stood there, frowning at her. "What do you mean, *you have to find a place to stay tonight?*" he demanded. "Aren't you going back to your old apartment?"

"No."

"Why the hell not?"

"Because it's an adults only complex," she said simply, and set down her end of the bed. She didn't know why she bothered to give him an explanation—it really wasn't any of his concern—but she found herself telling him about how the kids came to live with her. "My landlord gave me one week to find another place," she concluded. "I thought I had."

"But surely if you explained to him—"

"It wouldn't do any good. He already found another tenant."

That was it, end of story. Leaning down again to grip the bottom edge of the bed frame, she arched an eyebrow at him when he again made no effort to lift his end. "I thought you were going to help me move this thing."

"I thought you had somewhere to go," he retorted, scowling at her as if her homelessness was her own fault. "What are you going to do?"

Confused, she scowled right back at him. "Don't worry about me. This isn't your problem."

She spoke nothing less than the truth. Just because she had been conned out of just about every penny she owned in his building didn't mean he was in any way responsible for what happened to her or the kids. After all, it wasn't as if he'd participated in Percy's little scam—he hadn't known anything about it. So why was he so concerned about what she did when she left the Social Club? Anyone would have thought he'd be glad to see the last of her.

When she said as much, he looked at her as if she'd just insulted him. "Maybe I don't like the idea of throwing a woman and two kids out in the street when it's getting dark," he snapped. "I like to think I'm not that much of a louse."

"But you're not throwing us out," she pointed out reasonably. "We don't belong here. If some other stranger had wandered in here by mistake, you would naturally expect them to leave. That's what we're doing. Why do you have a problem with that?"

It was a good question, one he didn't have an answer for. And that frustrated the hell out of him. Regardless of how difficult the question was, he was a man who seldom had problems coming up with an answer. But with this woman he didn't even know, he didn't have a clue why he couldn't let her walk out the door. He just knew it would be a mistake.

"Damned if I know," he said honestly. "I guess because I feel partly responsible. If the jerk who scammed you hadn't been able to get in here in the first place, you wouldn't be homeless right now."

"But that's not your fault. After all, it's not like this is the first place Percy has pulled this particular little job. He obviously has no trouble breaking into other people's apartments."

"Maybe not, but that doesn't change the fact that you have no place to go tonight." And that, more than anything, ate at him. He could just see her and the kids sleeping in the car tonight and he wasn't letting that happen.

Making a snap decision, he said, "Look, the way I see it, we both have a problem. You don't have an apartment, and I've got an empty one that needs to be cleaned before the new tenants move in next week. Granted, I could pay a cleaning service to do that for me, and you could go to a hotel tonight if you absolutely had to. But why should you do that when you could stay here, just for the cost of cleaning the apartment?''

''You mean we could stay for tonight?''

He shrugged. ''The Johnsons won't need it until next Thursday. As long as you're out before they show up, I don't see any reason why you couldn't stay until then. That would give you some time to look for another place without feeling like you had to take the first available thing that came along. *If* you don't mind cleaning the apartment, of course.''

It was a fair deal, one that benefited them both. Still, Mitch half expected her to turn him down. The women he knew in the corporate world wouldn't have considered cleaning someone else's apartment, even if doing so would put a temporary roof over their heads. Sharp and cunning, they would have been more inclined to try to sweet-talk him into letting them stay for nothing.

Phoebe Smith, he was glad to discover, didn't practice those kinds of wiles. In fact, he didn't know whether to be flattered or insulted when she apparently didn't even consider trying to charm him. Instead, she made a rapid decision. Abruptly stepping around the bed frame, she took two steps toward him and held out her hand. ''We have a deal, Mr. Ryan. Thank you for the offer. I promise the kids and I will stay out of your way over the next couple of days and leave the apartment spotless when we move out.''

Taking her hand, he shook it firmly. ''Fair enough. We might as well take this bed frame back upstairs, then. If you're going to be here a week, you're going to need it.''

In spite of the fact that they were going to be there less than a week, he offered to help her carry her bed up, too, but she couldn't see the sense of that. The kids would share the one bed and she planned to stretch out on the floor in her sleeping bag.

"This'll be fine," she assured him. "It'll be simpler to leave most of the stuff packed in the U-Haul—I'll rent it for a few more days, and I'll camp out on the floor. It isn't as if it's for the rest of my life."

He looked as if he wanted to argue, but he obviously thought better of it. "All right. If that's the way you want it. I'll leave you to unpack your things."

The kids let out a whoop the second the door closed behind him, delighted that they were getting to stay. Grinning, she cautioned, "It's just for a week, guys, okay? Don't start thinking of this place as home. As soon as I can manage to work something else out, we'll be moving on."

She might as well have saved her breath. "Can we have a fire in the fireplace, Aunt Phoebe?" Becky asked with wide-eyed innocence. "There's wood and everything already in it. Please?"

"We can roast marshmallows after supper," Robby added eagerly. "And make s'mores! It'll be just like at camp."

Rolling her eyes, Phoebe groaned. They were in love with the place and they hadn't been there thirty minutes! How was she ever going to move them out without breaking their hearts? "I don't think we need a fire tonight," she hedged. "We've got to unpack and cook supper. Maybe tomorrow night."

She tried to dampen their enthusiasm by pointing out that the social club didn't have a playground like a regular apartment complex and there probably weren't any kids for them to play with, but nothing she said fazed them. Chattering happily, they helped her bring in the bare essentials they would need for the next couple of days, then followed her all over the apartment as she did a hasty cleaning. They hardly touched their supper, then it was bath time. They were so excited, she never expected to be able to get them to bed by their regular bedtime, but it had been a roller coaster of a day, and they were worn out. Their heads hardly hit their pillows before they were both out like a light.

The silence in the apartment was sudden, complete, welcoming. Sighing softly, Phoebe couldn't help but smile. She was crazy about the kids, but they were ceaselessly energetic and they loved to chatter. She realized she would probably come to treasure times like this, when they were in bed and the quiet of the evening gently settled around her.

But tonight, of all nights, she knew she had no reason to be at peace. Yes, they had a roof over their heads, thanks to Mitch Ryan. And a quick call to the U-Haul leasing agent had—for a nominal fee, thank God!—bought her another week before she had to return the trailer. After that, however, her luck would run out. A week from now, there was no telling where the Smith family would be. Any sane person would have been poring over the classifieds in the paper, looking for another apartment. But she'd worried enough for one day. Tonight, she was going to take a bubble bath.

How long she soaked in the tub, she couldn't have said later. The water was still warm, however, when she thought she heard the front door to the apartment open. Startled, she sat up straight in the water, listening, her heart thundering. She'd forgotten that she had to block the front door with cans and noisemakers, to wake her in case Becky walked in her sleep.

Swearing, she rose, dripping, to her feet and snatched up a towel. Dear God, what had she been thinking of? Louise, the kids' maternal grandmother, had warned her about Becky's sleepwalking and the need to set up some kind of alarm system. Worried, she'd diligently set up the cans each evening for the last week, just in case Becky felt unsettled about the changes in her life, but until now she'd slept peacefully through the night. Phoebe had an awful feeling that had just changed.

Sick at the thought, she hurriedly pulled on her nightgown. She was still struggling into her robe when she rushed into the kids' bedroom. Robby lay dead to the world at one end of the bed. At the other end was Becky's pillow. She was nowhere in sight.

"Oh, God!"

Frantic, Phoebe quickly searched the rest of the apartment, but it was empty and the front door was standing wide open. Rushing out into the hall, she thought she heard the sound of a door opening quietly downstairs at the back of the house, and her heart stopped dead in her chest. Dear God, Becky had gone outside! Out into the cold and the dark, wearing nothing but a thin flannel gown. Asleep, she wouldn't be aware of the dangers of downtown San Antonio at night, and not just from someone who might wish her harm. The river ran right behind the house. In most places, it wasn't more than four or five feet deep, but Becky was only six years old and small for her age. If she fell in, she could easily drown.

Swallowing a sob, Phoebe ran for the stairs.

Chapter 3

Seated at the old rolltop desk in Alice's office, Mitch frowned down at the screen of his laptop computer and tried to make sense of the business proposal he'd spent the last hour working on. In its current state, he admitted in disgust, it was the worst plan he'd ever come up with. Amateurish and half-baked, it didn't make a hell of a lot of sense, and it was all because he couldn't get the little brunette in 2C out of his head. When he should have been thinking about sales figures and projected profits over the course of the next few years, all he could think of was the love and laughter that had lit her face as she sat on the stairs and tickled her niece and nephew. And this after learning that she was homeless and that she'd just lost a considerable amount of money! Any other woman he knew would have been crying, or, at the very least, raging at the Fates. Instead, she'd found a way to laugh, and for the life of him, he couldn't figure out how. He knew she was aware of just how dire her circumstances were—he'd seen the panic in her eyes—but by the time he'd helped her get that damn bed into the apartment, she'd acted like she didn't have a care in the world. And for some reason, that grated on his nerves. Dammit, she should have been worried!

Outside, the wind raced around the house, moaning and stirring up fallen leaves, as a cold front charged through the city like a freight train headed for the border. A few minutes before, the moon had been shining down on the lovers strolling hand in hand on the River Walk, but now it had disappeared behind gathering storm clouds, and the night had suddenly become dark and ominous.

Tree limbs groaned and cracked and scraped against the eaves, and somewhere in the house, a door slammed. Knowing how the electricity had a tendency to go out during a storm, Mitch quickly saved what he was working on and shut down his computer. He should, he supposed, haul in the antique wicker furniture on the back porch before it started raining. Alice always worried about it getting wet, and if something happened to it, he'd never be able to replace it. It had been her mother's, and it meant more to her than a safe full of diamonds.

Dragging on a jacket, he headed for the back door and stepped out onto the darkened porch just as lightning slashed across the night sky. Thunder seemed to crack right over his head. Instinctively, he ducked…and thought he caught sight of someone in the garden. Stiffening, he searched the darkness, convinced his mind was playing tricks on him. The temperature had dropped twenty degrees in the last ten minutes and any second now, the storm was going to come down on the city like the vengeance of God. Only a fool would be walking in the garden.

Then lightning flared again, for a split second stripping away the darkness like a photographer's flash. And there, caught in the eerie gray light of nature's electrical display, were Phoebe Smith and her niece, in their nightclothes, looking for all the world like they were out for a Sunday stroll in the garden. If he hadn't seen it with his own two eyes, Mitch would have never believed it.

"What the hell!"

Furious, he strode toward them. The woman was crazy. Certifiable! She had to be. Only a nutcase went for a walk in a thunderstorm. And she had her niece with her, for God's sake! What was she doing? Trying to get them both killed?

Muttering curses, he had every intention of reading her the riot act, but she never gave him the chance. She glanced up and he saw both distress and relief written on her pale face. "Oh, thank God!" she breathed in a voice that was barely above a whisper. "Please tell me you know something about sleepwalking! I don't know what to do. I've been trying to get her back into the house, but I'm afraid I'll wake her up and I've always heard you're not supposed to do that. But if I don't get her inside soon, it's going to start raining and she'll wake up anyway."

Her teeth were chattering…and she was shaking like a leaf, which wasn't surprising since the wind seemed to be blowing straight from the Arctic and she had nothing on but a light gown and robe. And she was barefoot, dammit! So was her niece. But unlike Phoebe, Becky seemed totally unaware of the change in the weather despite her thin gown. Her expression was blank, and, amazingly, she was asleep with her eyes open. When thunder boomed overhead, not so much as an eyelash flickered in response.

Swearing, he shrugged out of his jacket and quickly, carefully, settled it around the little girl's shoulders. "How long has she been out here?" he asked gruffly.

Hugging herself, Phoebe blinked back tears. "I don't know. Maybe ten minutes. She and Robby were both in bed asleep, so I took a bubble bath. I was in the tub when I heard the front door open. By the time I got dressed, she was outside. Do you think we should wake her?''

Mitch studied the child through narrowed eyes, then shook his head. ''No. She'd probably be spooked if she woke up and found herself outside, especially in this weather. If she's scared of thunderstorms, she'd really be freaked. Let's see if we can get her back to the porch.''

By unspoken agreement, they flanked Becky, then Phoebe reached out and gently nudged the little girl toward the house. ''C'mon, honey,'' she said softly. ''It's time to go back to bed.''

Becky gave no sign that she heard. But when Phoebe gave her another little push in the middle of the back, she stepped toward the porch without an ounce of hesitation and walked through the door Mitch hastily pulled open for her. In a trancelike state, she walked up the stairs and into apartment 2C as if it had been home all her life. Her bed was just as she'd left it—with her pillow at one end and her brother at the other. Ignoring Robby, she crawled in at the end where she'd left her pillow, stretched out, and closed her eyes. Just as the storm finally broke outside, she sighed in contentment and relaxed into peaceful sleep.

If she hadn't been so afraid of waking her, Phoebe would have laughed. The little minx! If she could sleep through the storm rattling the walls, she could sleep through anything.

Glancing up, her gaze met Mitch's and she saw that he was obviously thinking the same thing. Amusement glinting in his eyes, he exchanged a slow grin with her just as thunder cracked three times in succession overhead. Phoebe knew that if Mitch hadn't come to her rescue, she'd probably still be out there trying to get Becky inside and soaked to the skin by now.

His thoughts obviously mirroring hers, his gaze dropped, reminding her that she wore nothing but a thin gown and robe. Granted, she was covered from her neck to her ankles, so it wasn't as if he could see anything. But the second his eyes slowly lifted back to hers, she felt his awareness that she was naked underneath her nightclothes.

And with no effort whatsoever, he stole her breath.

Fighting the need to cross her arms over her breasts, she told herself that if she acted nonchalant, he would, too. But her heart did a funny rollover in her chest and her throat closed tighter than a fist. She couldn't for the life of her manage a single word.

Caught in the heat of his gaze, she would have sworn time ground to a stop. Then he blinked, the warmth abruptly disappeared from his eyes, and she couldn't be sure she hadn't imagined the entire incident. "Looks like she's not going anywhere else tonight," he said coolly, "but you might want to barricade the front door just in case."

Her throat still thick, she said stiffly, "Yes. Of course. Thank you for your help."

"No thanks necessary. I'm just glad we got her inside before the rain hit."

With a nod good-night, he took his leave with the graceful stride of a man who seldom if ever lacked confidence in himself. Watching him, Phoebe never knew that his heart was pounding just as hard as hers.

The morning dawned clear, bright and cold. A brisk wind still blew out of the north, but the clouds were gone and the only sign of last night's storm was the puddles in the street. Becky didn't appear to remember her little walk in the garden the night before. As perky as she usually was in the morning, she chatted happily all the way to school about the field trip her class was taking to the zoo later in the week.

Jealous, Robby snorted disdainfully as Phoebe pulled up before the front door of the elementary school. "The zoo's for babies. There's nothing there but a bunch of dumb old animals, anyway."

Biting back a grin, Phoebe put the transmission in park and turned to face him with a pretended frown of disappointment. "Well, darn! That's too bad. Grandma Louise told me she was going to send you some mad money you could spend anyway you wanted. I thought maybe you might want to spend it at the zoo and park. You were the one who said you wanted to ride the ponies in the park, weren't you?"

That got his attention. His eyes as big as saucers, he gasped, "You mean it, Aunt Phoebe? Really?"

"Well, of course I mean it." She laughed. "Of course, if you think the zoo's for babies—"

"No. No! I want to go!" Launching himself at her, he gave her a fierce hug, then turned and scrambled out of the car.

Rolling her eyes like a woman three times her age, Becky said, "How come boys are so goofy, Aunt Phoebe?"

"I don't know, honey," she admitted, laughing. "When I figure that one out, we'll both have it made in the shade."

Twenty minutes later, Phoebe arrived at work, still chuckling over the incident. Her smile, however, faded the second she stepped through the doors of Wainwright Pharmaceutical. She'd worked there for three years, and she had to admit that she was treated fairly enough. Oh, she could have used a raise, but couldn't everyone? No, she had no complaints about Wainwright. As a secretary to one of the vice presidents, she knew she had it better than most. It just wasn't what she wanted to do for the rest of her life. She wanted to be a writer, and somehow taking dictation wasn't the same thing.

Greeting Larry, the guard at the gate, she headed upstairs to her office and dreamed of the day she could walk in and give her notice. For all she knew, it could be as early as tomorrow. She'd written some children's stories for the family, but it was in mysteries that she planned to leave her mark on the literary world. She'd already written one, which was currently circulating through the different publishing houses in New York, and she had every reason to believe that it would eventually sell. It had been rejected by two of the top mystery publishers in the business, but she was far from discouraged. She'd received very nice letters from the editors who had read the manuscript, and they'd both been very encouraging. So she'd sent it to a third publisher, then started writing a second manuscript. It was, she knew, only a matter of time, before all her hard work paid off.

In the meantime, though, she still had a job to do, and she did thank God for it, especially now that the kids had come to live with her. Like most people in their early thirties, her brother and his wife had never thought that they would die so young, so he and Karen had only had the most basic of insurance policies. After their funeral and bills were paid, there was nothing left for the kids. If she hadn't had a decent-paying job, Phoebe knew she still would have found a way to take them, but things would have been much rougher than they were.

She'd just hung up her jacket when her boss, Ned Grisham, stepped into the open doorway that connected their two offices. A man of average height with a plain, good-natured face, he was usually smiling. But not this morning. His normally ruddy complexion was gray, the look in his eyes more than a little lost.

Alarmed, she stepped toward him. "Mr. Grisham, what's wrong? Are you sick? Here…sit down while I call the nurse—"

"No!" Taking the phone from her, he hung it back up. "I'm all right," he assured her when she frowned at him searchingly. "Really. I'm not going to drop dead at your feet or anything like that. I've just had something of a shock."

"What kind of shock? Is it Janice? Has something happened to her?"

At the mention of his wife, he gave her a sad, defeated smile that scared her to death. During the three years she'd worked for him, she'd never seen such a look on his face. "No, it's not Janice or the kids or anything at home. Please…come into my office and I'll tell you all about it."

Bewildered, her heart pounding with a dread she couldn't explain, she followed him into his spacious office and dutifully took a seat in one of the two chairs angled in front of his desk. She expected him to take his own chair, but he moved restlessly to the window, where he stared blindly out and seemed to totally forget that she was even in the room.

If Phoebe needed any further evidence that something was horribly wrong, she got it when he finally turned to face her and she saw the tears in his eyes. Alarmed, she moved to his side, her own eyes stinging in sympathy. "Please tell me what's wrong, Ned," she pleaded. "I can't help if I don't know what the problem is."

"I started working here right out of college," he said simply, "and never wanted to go anywhere else. Oh, I know I probably could have made more money somewhere else, but I never did like the idea of jumping from job to job in search of the almighty dollar. The working conditions were great, the salary was acceptable, and I was content to stay put and work toward retirement.''

Shaking his head as if he couldn't believe his own stupidity, he laughed without humor. ''It never entered my head that I might not get to stick around that long.''

Startled, Phoebe gasped, ''Are you saying you've been fired?''

''Not just me,'' he said grimly. ''There was a board meeting last night, and it was decided to terminate all the vice presidents.''

''*All* of them?''

He nodded. ''Letters were waiting for each of us on our desks this morning. We didn't even get it from the big guy himself.''

''Oh, Ned, I'm so sorry! No wonder you're so upset! Have you told Janice yet?''

''I called her right after I read the damn letter. It was, needless to say,'' he added with a wry grimace, ''not the kind of surprise she expected on her birthday.''

''Her birthday! Oh, she must be devastated.'' Her heart breaking for both of them, she wished there was something she could say to make the hurt less, but there wasn't. ''I don't understand how Mr. Wainwright can justify this,'' she said, frowning in confusion. ''I know the company's downsizing, but you don't get rid of your best employees just to improve the bottom line. Not if you want to have any kind of decent business left. Maybe if you talked to him—''

''Talking won't do any good. The board's made its decision, and we're stuck with it. That includes you, Phoebe.'' At her blank look, he said gently, ''If there are no vice presidents, then there are no secretaries to vice presidents. I'm sorry, but it looks like we've both been eliminated.''

Stunned, she didn't remember moving, didn't remember reaching for her chair. Suddenly she was sitting again in front of his desk and had no idea how she'd gotten there. She stared up at him in shock. "You're firing me?"

He winced, then nodded, his mouth pressed flat into an angry white line. "Believe me, I didn't have any choice in the matter. There isn't a man on the board who had the guts to look you and the other secretaries in the eye and tell you that you got caught in the fallout, so I had to be the one to do it. Spineless cowards," he muttered bitterly. "I don't know how they sleep nights."

Feeling like she'd just been flattened by an eighteen-wheeler that came out of nowhere, Phoebe hardly heard him. Fired. How could she be fired? She was a responsible, dependable employee who never even took a sick day unless she was almost dead. Over the course of the three years she'd worked there she'd only been late once, and that was just last week, when she had to enroll the kids in school—

Her thoughts ground to a halt at that, horror curling sickeningly into her stomach. The kids! They looked to her to protect them, to provide for them, to keep them safe and warm and out of harm's way. And now, not only did she not have a home for them, she didn't have a job. Dear God, what was she going to do?

"Phoebe? Are you all right?"

If she hadn't been so sick at heart, she would have laughed. All right? She was homeless, jobless, and closer to hopelessness than she'd ever been in her life. And it scared her to death. She wasn't a person who lost faith. Even when her brother and his wife were killed, she'd managed to take comfort in the thought that God, in his infinite wisdom, found it fitting to take together two people who loved each other so much. But this...this made no sense. There was no silver lining, no rhyme or reason, no explanation for the run of bad luck she'd had over the course of the last week and a half.

If she'd been the self-centered type, she would have asked *Why me?* and never given a thought to the fact that she wasn't in this mess alone. But that wasn't her nature, and she only had to see the disillusionment in Ned's eyes to know that the change in their circumstances had hit him every bit as hard as it had her.

For both their sakes, she pasted on a smile and determinedly squared her shoulders. "Well, I can't say I feel like dancing a jig or anything," she replied in a weak attempt at humor, "but I was looking for a job the first time I came in here. I guess it's only fitting that I'll be looking for one when I walk out for the last time. I suppose the firing's effective immediately."

"Actually, it's not," he said, surprising her. "I think the board was afraid of bad press so they're giving us until Friday to get out. I know that's not much notice, but it could have been worse. And you have vacation time coming to you, of course. Take the rest of the week if you'd like to look for another position. You know I'll give you an excellent reference."

She'd never doubted that for a moment. Thanking him, she knew that the sooner she hit the pavement, the better, but when she drove out of the employee parking lot a short while later, she literally didn't know where to turn. She felt like a child who'd been given permission to play hooky and didn't know what to do with her time. Where did she go from here?

Three hours later, she was still asking herself the same question. Everywhere she went, she was told the same thing. Companies either had no openings or they weren't hiring until the first of the year. Considering that it was nearly the middle of November, she understood why a business would want to wait until after the holidays to hire new personnel, but that didn't help her situation any. She needed a job now!

In growing desperation, she went to an employment agency, but the positions she found listed there paid dismal salaries. She could have gotten any one of a number of those, but that would have meant she'd have to take a second job at night just to make enough to get by. If she'd had only herself to consider, she wouldn't have ruled that out as an option. But she couldn't leave Robby and Becky with full-time baby-sitters. They'd been through enough already.

Disheartened, disillusioned, she walked out of the employment office without a clue what she was going to do. Twenty minutes later, she braked to a stop in front of the offices of I Spy Private Investigators. Owned and operated by her friend, Dana Winters, it was the one place where she knew she *wouldn't* find a job. But if anyone knew what was going on in the city's business world, who was hiring and firing and up to their eyeballs in industrial espionage, not to mention playing around on their wife, it was Dana. She made it her business to know.

Pulling open the front door, she stepped inside to find Dana on the phone. "Yes, ma'am," she said into the phone as she shot Phoebe a quick, surprised smile of greeting. "I'm a licensed private detective. I can find out just about anything you need found, from friends you've lost touch with to the driver who crashed into your fender while you were in the grocery store." With a wave of her hand, she motioned for Phoebe to take one of the chairs in front of her desk, then arched a brow at a question from the woman on the other end of the line. "Unfaithful husbands? Yes, ma'am, I've been known to track down my fair share of them. But it's too delicate a job to discuss over the phone. Why don't you come into the office this afternoon and you can give me the particulars. Around four? That'll be fine. I'll see you then.''

Hanging up, she leaned back in her chair, her green eyes sharp and knowing as they swept over Phoebe. ''Why aren't you at work? What's wrong?''

Not surprised that Dana immediately sensed she was in trouble, Phoebe didn't even try to pretend there was nothing wrong. They'd been best friends since fourth grade and had always been able to read each other like a book.

''The board met last night and decided to trim the budget by eliminating all the vice presidents,'' she said bluntly. ''The secretaries—and yours truly—got caught in the cross fire.''

Outraged, Dana straightened like a poker. ''They *fired* you? Are they out of their minds? You're the best thing that ever happened to that damn company!''

Phoebe had to laugh about that. No matter what the situation, she could always count on Dana to be in her corner. ''Oh, yeah, I made a big impression on the board members—I doubt there's one of them that even knows my name. The firing wasn't personal, Dana.''

''It damn sure was,'' she countered hotly. ''You're out of a job, aren't you? That makes it personal.''

''Nowadays, everything comes down to the bottom line. The board answers to the shareholders, and profits are down, so they decided to look at management and see who could be eliminated. It was just my misfortune that I work for management.''

Still disagreeing, Dana shook her head in wonder. ''You never cease to amaze me, girlfriend. You're the one out of a job, yet you're making excuses for the jerks who canned you. So what are you going to do?''

''I was hoping you could tell me who might have an opening. I hit the employment agencies this morning, but no one seems to be hiring until after the holidays, and I can't wait that long. I'm in trouble, Dana.''

Puzzled, Dana frowned. ''Don't you think you're being a little negative here? I know you've got the kids to think about now, but it's not like you're destitute. You've got your savings and a roof over your head—''

''No, I don't,'' Phoebe cut in quietly. ''That's why I'm in trouble.'' Feeling like a fool all over again, she told Dana about the fiasco at the Lone Star Social Club. ''I still can't believe I was so stupid. I didn't check his references or anything.''

''And why should you?'' Dana demanded, jumping to her defense. ''He appeared to be the landlord. He was in the apartment, for God's sake! Why would you be suspicious of him?''

She shrugged. ''I don't know. I guess I just thought I'd know a crook when I saw one. Instead, I gave him almost every penny I had and now I don't even have a place to stay to show for it. If it hadn't been for Mr. Ryan's generosity, the kids and I would have had to go to a shelter last night.''

''You could have stayed with me and Troy,'' Dana said quietly. ''The apartment's a crackerbox, but we do have a guest room you could have used. And it wouldn't be forever…and once we finish building the house, there'll be plenty of room for all of us.''

Not surprised that Dana would take in her and the kids just like that, Phoebe smiled and shook her head. She appreciated the offer, but there was no way she could accept it. The slab for Dana's dream house had just been poured that week. It would be months before it was finished and there was no way she could impose on anyone, even her best friend, for that long. No, this was her problem, and she would deal with it.

"You know I can't do that," she replied. "Troy would have a stroke."

"He would not! He loves you like a sister!"

"And what man wants a sister around when he's still practically on his honeymoon?" she quipped, grinning.

"We're not on our honeymoon. That was weeks ago."

For the first time in hours, Phoebe laughed. "And now you're an old married couple? Yeah, right! I've seen you two together, remember? You can't be in the same room together for five minutes without touching. The last thing you need right now is me and my tribe moving in with you."

The fact that it was true didn't make it any easier for Dana to accept. "But where will you go?" she cried, frowning. "Damn it, Phoeb, I'm worried about you! You can't expect me to just stand around with my hands in my pockets while you and the kids get tossed out into the street."

"Nobody's tossing us out," she assured her. "I've made arrangements with Mr. Ryan to stay at the Social Club for the rest of the week, so it's not like we're camping out on the sidewalk or anything. And by the time we do have to get out, I hope to have something else lined up."

"How? You don't have any money, and even if you got a job tomorrow, you couldn't make enough in a week to put anything down on an apartment. And with everything we've got tied up in the house, I don't have any to loan you." Swearing, she reached for the phone. "I'm going to call Troy. There must be something we can do to help—"

Without a word, Phoebe leaned forward and took the phone from her. "No," she said quietly. "I didn't come here for a loan or a place to stay or to worry you to death. I just need a job. Who's hiring?"

Her frown fierce, Dana started to argue, only to give in with a sigh of disgust. "You always were stubborn as a post."

Far from insulted, Phoebe only grinned. "You taught me everything I know."

"Of course I did," she chuckled. "That's what friends are for."

Scribbling a list of names down on a yellow legal pad, she tore off the sheet and handed it to her. "Try Morton-Barker first," she suggested. "I did a little surveillance work for them a couple of weeks ago and caught one of the secretaries to a vice president helping herself to company funds. Word is she's going to be indicted next week. I haven't heard if they've hired anyone to replace her yet, but ask to see Morton himself and mention my name. I don't know if it'll help or not, but it won't hurt."

Nodding, Phoebe folded the list and carefully stored it in her purse. It was a start. That was all she asked.

Mitch didn't know how Alice handled her job without going quietly out of her mind. By noon, it seemed like everyone in the building had a problem that they expected him to solve for them. If it wasn't a lost key or squeaky floors, it was a nightclub across the river playing music until all hours of the night. And then there was the upkeep on the old building. A heater vent in 2A was blowing nothing but cold air and the hot-water heater in 1D was on the blink. He'd called in the necessary people to make the repairs, then met with three different plumbers to discuss replacing every pipe in the place. He hadn't gotten any written bids yet—those would be in the mail by the end of the week—but the verbal estimates were daunting. And on top of all that, he was on the phone to Jennifer, his secretary in Dallas, trying to keep tabs on what Applebee was up to while he was gone. There was no question in his mind that he needed to get back to Dallas, and damn quick. But like it or not, he knew now that he couldn't turn the running of the Social Club over to some impersonal management company until Alice returned. The house was too old and fragile and had too much historical significance. A member of the family needed to be there to make sure that repairs were done correctly, and he, unfortunately, was the only one available.

Stuck between a rock and a hard place, there was nothing he could do but accept the inevitable and try to make the best of it. If he couldn't go to his office, then he'd bring his office to San Antonio. Getting on the phone, he called a local office equipment company and arranged to have a computer, fax, and laser printer delivered. Another call to an Internet service got him on the Web by the time the computer was delivered, and by two, he had a complete office set up in Alice's apartment and was interviewing prospective secretaries sent over by the employment agency.

With everything set up and ready to go, finding a temp to answer the phone and deal with the Social Club's minor problems while he was busy handling more important business shouldn't have been all that difficult. He knew he could be demanding, but he didn't think asking a secretary to be computer-literate and friendly on the phone was asking too much. Evidently, though, it was. None of the four women he interviewed was right for the job. Two didn't know how to send E-mail, and a third didn't know the difference between the Web and Jack Webb. The fourth could have done anything he wanted without missing a beat, but she had the sourest disposition of anyone he'd ever met in his life. Frustrated, he was considering calling a different employment agency when there was a knock at the door to Alice's apartment.

Wondering which tenant had a complaint now, he irritably got up and went to answer it, only to find himself face-to-face with Phoebe Smith. He hadn't seen her since last night, not since he'd caught her in the garden in her nightclothes, and it wasn't until now that he realized just how much that image had stuck in his mind. She was dressed for work in a businesslike black print dress and sensible heels, but all he could see was her in that damn flannel nightgown and robe.

"What do you want?"

He knew he sounded rude and wanted to kick himself when she flinched, but, dammit all, there was something about her that just seemed to rub him the wrong way. That didn't, however, excuse poor manners. Pulling the door open wider, he said stiffly, "Sorry about that—it's been one of those days. What can I do for you, Ms. Smith? Is something wrong with the apartment? The heat's not working? Or are the pipes rattling? Just tell me what it is and I'll try to get someone in to fix it."

Confused, she frowned as she stepped past him into the apartment. "Nothing's wrong…at least not with the apartment."

So something was wrong somewhere else, he deduced with a silent groan. Why wasn't he surprised? Yesterday, the lady had had nothing but one problem after another. Why should today be any different?

His mouth curling cynically, he lifted a mocking eyebrow. "So what's the problem this time? It can't be your niece sleepwalking in the garden again—it's too early. So what is it? Did you park in a loading zone and have your car towed or what?"

"Actually," she said with a candid honesty that amazed him, "I lost my job. I just wanted you to know in case you heard the kids talking about it and thought I'd try to renege on the terms of our agreement. You don't have to worry. We'll still be out of here before the Johnsons move in, as promised."

Chapter 4

A smart man wouldn't have gotten involved. He would have thanked her for keeping him apprised of the situation, then shown her the door. After all, he didn't know her, and didn't want to know her. If she had a tendency to wander into his thoughts at will, it was only because she was a beautiful woman, and he appreciated that. But she also seemed prone to one disaster after another, and he had enough headaches to deal with as it was. The last thing he needed or wanted was another one.

But instead of wishing her luck in finding another position, then sending her on her way, he heard himself ask, "What exactly do you do?"

"I'm a secretary," she replied. "Why? Do you know someone who's hiring?"

No, he told himself. He damn well didn't. But the idea had already taken root, and even as he cursed it, he knew he couldn't let it go. He didn't believe in coincidence. Things happened for a reason, and he'd learned a long time ago not to question what fate threw in his path.

He scrutinized her through narrowed eyes. "I might. Why were you fired?"

"I wasn't!" she snapped, stung. "The company's downsizing and my position was eliminated. If you don't believe me, call my boss. He lost his job, too."

"I just might do that," he retorted. "What's his name?"

"Ned Grisham. He is—was—vice president of sales."

When she rattled off the number, Mitch lifted a skeptical brow. "You were the private secretary to a vice president?"

Once again, her eyes sparked fire. "I wouldn't lie about something that can be so easily checked, Mr. Ryan. Now if you'll excuse me, I have to pick the kids up at school. There's no point in sending them to day care after school now that I'm not working."

Her cheeks bright with color, she walked out with her chin up and her back ramrod-straight. Watching her, Mitch told himself he was a fool for even considering hiring her. The lady had a real talent for getting under his skin. Five minutes. That was all it seemed to take for them to lock horns.

But he needed a secretary, dammit! And if she'd worked for the vice president of a company, as she claimed, she was more than qualified to handle any work he threw at her. Just because she had a knack for setting his teeth on edge didn't mean they couldn't work together. At least she had a brain that appeared to be in working order, which was more than he could say for the Einsteins he'd interviewed earlier in the day. And she stood up for herself—he liked that in a secretary. He wanted someone who could work alongside him and who had the gumption to make executive decisions on her own when she had to. Phoebe Smith could do that.

If she was going to work for him, though, she needed

a place to stay. And he needed her close at hand, prefer-
ably in the building, so she could take complete control
of things whenever he had to make unexpected trips to
Dallas. The only problem was that once the Johnsons
moved into 2C, there would, to put it simply, be no more
room at the inn. Every apartment at the Social Club was
rented.

She would have to find somewhere else to live…unless
he let her move into Alice's apartment with him.

Immediately, his common sense rejected the idea. Had
he lost his mind? Phoebe Smith was a stranger. He'd
known her for all of twenty-four hours, and what he knew
about her was hardly reassuring. She seemed to attract
trouble like the plague, and for all he knew, she could be
the kind to take advantage of any man stupid enough to
be taken in by her hard-luck story.

And then there were the kids. They appeared harmless
enough, but the truth was, he didn't know a thing about
rug rats. And the apartment was hardly set up for more
than one or two people at the most. There were only two
small bedrooms. The four of them wouldn't be able to
turn around without running into each other.

But Phoebe would be right there, day and night, to as-
sist him or the tenants with any problems that came up.
And now that she'd lost her job, she could start work as
soon as she finished cleaning the Johnsons' apartment. He
could hand the responsibility of the Social Club over to
her and turn his attention back to his own work. He'd be
there, of course, for any major decisions that had to be
made, but she could handle anything else that cropped up,
including overseeing not only the renovation of the attic
but the more immediate problem of the plumbing repairs.
The more he thought about it, the more he liked the idea.
Maybe it was time he gave her old boss a call.

* * *

His brown eyes dancing with wicked laughter, Robby stuffed the rest of his peanut-butter-and-jelly sandwich in his mouth and forgot he wasn't supposed to talk with a full mouth. "You should have seen Mr. Foster when the monkey jumped on his head in the lunch room and grabbed his wig, Aunt Phoebe. He was so mad, his eyes sort of bugged out and he turned this funky shade of purple! It was awesome!"

Phoebe shouldn't have laughed. Sneaking a pet monkey into school and allowing it to snitch a teacher's toupee was a serious matter, and she should have warned Robby not to ever think of pulling that kind of stunt himself. But he was such a natural storyteller, mimicking everything the monkey did, that she could just see the portly teacher, who took himself far too seriously, gasping in outrage.

"Stop!" she choked. "You're killing me!"

"That's what Mr. Foster said," Becky chimed in, giggling. *"Somebody get this monster off me! He's killing me!"*

That sent Phoebe off into another gale of laughter. She loved this part of the day, when she could sit down with the kids and hear about their day. At her old apartment, they had quickly established a routine of sitting at the kitchen table for a snack while she started supper. That hadn't stopped just because most of their things, including her battered but sturdy table, were still in the U-Haul moving trailer parked out in front of the Social Club. With a trusting acceptance that only made her love them more, the kids had made do with lawn chairs and folding snack trays and didn't seem to care that they didn't know where they were going to be living next week.

"Remind me never to buy you two a pet monkey," she teased as they finished their snacks. "Okay, what's on the agenda for homework? Becky, how are you coming with your spelling? And what about that library book of yours, hotshot?'' she asked Robby. ''Don't you have a book report due tomorrow?''

''Can't we watch cartoons first?'' Becky pleaded. ''Please?''

''Just for a half hour?'' her brother wheedled. ''Then we'll do our homework. I'll even help Becky with her spelling.''

They looked up at her with such innocent, hopeful faces that if she hadn't known better, she would have sworn that they'd never watched cartoons a day in their life. Her lips twitching, she said, ''I swear you're both going to grow up to be con artists. Go on. Watch your cartoons. But only thirty minutes!'' she yelled after them as they whooped and ran for the living room and her small, portable TV. ''Then it's time to buckle down and get to work.''

She wouldn't, she knew, have to hound them about their school work. They were both smart as whips and really liked learning. Usually, she didn't even have to remind them about their homework. As soon as their favorite cartoon went off, they always turned off the TV without being told and finished whatever worksheets they'd brought home with them.

Sending up a silent prayer of thanks that their parents had taught them such good study habits, she reminded herself that she had work of her own to do. She'd promised to clean the apartment in exchange for staying there, and except for the quick once-over she'd given the kitchen and bathroom last night when she and the kids had moved in, she'd hardly begun. One look inside the blackened oven and she knew she had her work cut out for her.

When there was a knock at the front door of the apartment ten minutes later, she was up to her elbows in hot, sudsy water and cursing what looked like twenty years' accumulation of dirt and grime on the small, apartment-size stove. Not surprisingly, the kids didn't answer the door. When they were engrossed in their cartoons, the space shuttle could have landed right next to them and they never would have noticed.

"I'm coming," she muttered when whoever was at the door knocked again. "Geez, give me a second—"

Her words trailed off at the sight of Mitch Ryan standing on her threshold, his clenched fist already raised to knock again. She hadn't forgotten how rude he'd been to her earlier, that he'd all but accused her of lying about her work experience. And every time she thought about it, she fumed. *No one* had ever accused her of lying before, and she didn't like it. She didn't like it at all!

Glaring at him, she made no move to open the door wider and invite him inside. "You don't seem the type of man who associates with liars, so I assume this isn't a social call," she said tartly. "Are we disturbing the neighbors or what?"

If she'd wanted to touch a nerve, she had the satisfaction of knowing she'd done so. Irritation flickered in his blue eyes like lightning before a storm. But instead of retorting icily, the way she half expected, he surprised her by mockingly marking off an imaginary point in the air.

"Score one for you, Ms. Smith," he drawled. "Would it help if I explained that I spent the morning interviewing women who claimed to have the same skills you do? Three out of four of them barely knew how to turn on a computer, let alone operate one. On a good day, I'm not the most trusting of souls. By the time you knocked on my door, I would have doubted the Pope himself."

As far as explanations went, it was a good one. He'd had a rough day and she'd caught him at a bad time. He didn't appear to be the type of man who bothered to explain himself very often, and she supposed she should have been grateful that he'd taken the time to do so to her. But nothing, not even a rotten day, excused rudeness.

Her smile as sardonic as his, she crossed her arms over her breasts and leaned a shoulder against the doorjamb, her eyes coolly meeting his. "If that's an apology, Mr. Ryan, I'm afraid you left out a few words. Like *I'm sorry.* You should try them. They have a nice ring to them."

Amazingly, he laughed. "I was getting to that. *I'm sorry.* There. Now can I come in? I'd like to talk to you."

The charming smile he flashed her was free of mockery and lit up his usually stern face with devastating effect. Her eyes drawn like a magnet to his mouth, Phoebe felt something shift deep inside her, something that shook her to the core. Stunned, she told herself she could not be attracted to Mitch Ryan. It just wasn't possible. If her heart was doing cartwheels in her breast, it was because he'd surprised her by actually acting civil.

Standing her ground, she shook her head. "I don't think so. I'm busy cleaning the stove, and frankly, I can't think of a thing we need to talk about that hasn't already been said."

Amused, he cocked a teasing brow at her. "Do I make you uncomfortable, Ms. Smith?"

"No, of course not!"

Her answer was a little too quick, his blue eyes a little too knowing. Flustered, she warned herself that this was a man she'd be wise to be wary of. He was attractive and sophisticated and all too aware of the effect he had on women. Scott Calvin, the only man she'd ever given her heart to, had been much the same way. She'd known the second she met him that he was out of her league, but thought she could handle him and the way he made her feel. She'd been wrong.

She was smarter now, though—she no longer ventured out into water that was over her head. And Mitch Ryan definitely swam with the sharks. Knowing that, she should have been immune to his brand of charm, but standing there, caught in the trap of his gaze, she could not deny that he had only to turn that devilish smile of his on her to make her go weak at the knees.

Disgusted with herself, irritated at him, she let out her breath in a huff. "Look, I don't know if you're having a slow day or what, but I really don't have time to stand here and amuse you. So if you've really got something to say to me, spit it out so I can get back to work."

Her tone held just the right amount of studied indifference to send the most persistent of men packing, but it didn't so much as dent Mitch Ryan's hide. Grinning, he said, "We're a mite touchy today, aren't we? I guess getting fired can do that to a person."

"I *wasn't*—"

"Fired," he supplied for her, chuckling. "Yes, so you've said. And as it happens, your old boss verified that."

"You called him?"

"I generally check out the people I hire."

If there'd been a chair nearby, Phoebe would have dropped into it. "I beg your pardon?"

"You heard me," he said dryly. "I need a secretary and you're a secretary who needs a job. According to Ned Grisham, you're conscientious and dependable and given the chance, you could have run Wainwright Pharmaceutical with one hand tied behind your back. That's what I need. Someone who can take the initiative and handle things without me having to constantly tell them what to do. I want to begin remodeling the attic into another apartment, and all the plumbing in the building needs to be replaced, but my business interests take up a lot of my time. Your duties would include supervising all repairs as well as lining up an architect and contractor for the remodeling, then seeing that the construction gets under way as soon as possible. I would also expect you to handle whatever problems crop up with the tenants, too, since I'll be traveling back and forth between here and Dallas.''

"But what about your aunt? Won't she be back soon? Surely she wants to be involved in the remodeling.''

"She had hoped to be," he replied, "but there's a good chance that she won't be back until after the first of the year.'' He told her about Glen's accident and his extensive injuries. "Luckily, there was no brain damage, but the doctors expect him to be laid up for quite a while. They have a two-month-old baby girl, and there's no way Emily can handle her and Glen without some help. Alice will stay as long as she's needed, but she's as anxious as I am to start the remodeling. So if you're asking if the job is a temporary one, the answer is yes. But it's not something that's going to end today or tomorrow. You can count on being here at least until Christmas, possibly longer.''

Christmas. To someone else, being guaranteed work just until the holidays might not have sounded like much. But from the moment Ned had told her she was out of a job, the one thing Phoebe had not allowed herself to think about was Christmas. How could she even think about buying Christmas gifts for the kids if she didn't have a job?

"You'd have to live here at the Social Club," he continued, "but that would be one of the requirements of the job, so there would, of course, be no rent.''

"But I thought all the apartments were rented," she said, frowning in confusion. "The Johnsons—''

"Will still move in next week," he assured her. "I was talking about Alice's apartment. You and the kids can bunk down at her place while she's gone.''

"But where will you stay?''

"With the three of you in the apartment," he retorted

bluntly. "It'll be cramped, but it's only a temporary measure, and I'll be out of town a lot—which is why I need you to live here at the Social Club. You can handle whatever comes up while I'm gone."

Stunned, Phoebe could only stare at him. He was serious. He actually expected her to move in with him—a man she'd known for all of twenty-four hours—just because he'd offered her a so-called job! Did he think she was that destitute, that desperate, that she would do *any-thing* for money?

Straightening away from the doorjamb, she said with a dangerous silkiness, "Let me get this straight. You're offering me a job, but I have to live with you. And just what exactly would you be paying me for? The duties you already described or something a little more, shall we say…intimate?"

It was, she thought furiously, a legitimate question, but suddenly *he* was the one who looked like he'd been insulted. His blue eyes steely, he said coldly, "I'm going to pretend I didn't hear that. But just for your information, I don't have to stoop to taking advantage of a woman who's down on her luck to get sex. All I have to do is pick up the phone."

It was no brag, just fact. There were any number of women in his life, and he was cynical enough to know that it had nothing to do with his looks. It was a sorry fact of life that he could have been as ugly as homemade soap and still had just about any woman he wanted because of the balance of his checkbook.

His jaw rigid, he gave her a hard look. "So are you interested in the job or not? I've given you the terms. Take it or leave it. At this point, it makes no difference to me."

It was well known in business that he who cared the least won. As she hesitated, Mitch tried to convince himself that he really didn't care if she turned him down flat.

She wasn't the only decent secretary in the city. If he had to, he'd hound every employment agency in town until somebody found him an acceptable temp to take over for Alice.

But instead of rejecting him outright and slamming the door in his face as he expected, she observed him consideringly. ''If I were interested—and I'm not saying I am,'' she said quickly, ''it would only be under certain conditions.''

Even as the words popped out of her mouth, Phoebe wondered what in the world she was doing. Successful, cynical men like Mitch Ryan were a law unto themselves. Strong, type A personalities, they believed in the bottom line and were convinced that most people would screw you if you gave them the chance. They guarded their business every bit as aggressively as they did their hearts, and that could make for impossible working conditions.

Especially considering her own personality. In most cases, she was easygoing; she didn't like to draw lines in the sand. Mitch, on the other hand, was a man who was extremely sure of himself. If push came to shove, her personality would be the one that would be run over.

Still, he was offering her a job *and* a place for her and the kids to stay, rent-free. That wasn't something she could dismiss lightly. Her grandmother had always told her that sometimes the worst things that happened to you turned out to be the best, and there was a distinct possibility that this was one of those times. If fate had led her to the Lone Star Social Club, she'd be a fool to pass up this possibility.

''I'm not an unreasonable man,'' he told her. ''Name your terms and I'll tell you if I can live with them.''

Praying she wasn't making a mistake, she straightened her shoulders. ''Since the children and I will be sharing a room, we'll take the biggest bedroom.''

He nodded. "I agree. I'd already thought of that. Anything else?"

"Yes. Since we'll all be sharing the kitchen and living room, you can't go around like you have the place to yourself. You'll have to be fully dressed whenever you're not in your bedroom."

Considering the fact that they were strangers and she had children to protect, she thought her request was a logical one, but he seemed to find it vastly amusing. His eyes glinting with wicked laughter, he said with a straight face, "Once I finish work for the day, I usually strip first thing, but I guess I can be convinced to keep my clothes on. I wouldn't want to shock the kids or anything."

Another time, she would have laughed. But all too easily, she could see him undressing at the end of a long day, and the image startled her. Color flying in her cheeks, she said shortly, "See that you don't. And it isn't as if we're going to be imposing on you forever. As soon as the remodeling of the attic is completed, the kids and I can move in there."

"I don't have a problem with that."

"Good. Then you shouldn't have any objection to us living there rent-free for the next six months if I can get the work completed ahead of schedule. It will get us out of your hair and compensate me for the extra hours I'll have to put in in order to get things finished ahead of time. Until then, of course, my things will have to be put in storage. You can pick up the bill as part of my salary."

Unable to believe her own daring, Phoebe braced for rejection. She knew it was an outrageous request, but it never hurt to ask. All he could do was say no. And in the silence that stretched between them, she was sure he was going to do just that.

But instead of an outright refusal, he said, "I was prepared for the project to take three months. If you can get it finished by Christmas, the apartment's yours until the first of June.''

''Rent-free,'' she stressed.

His lips twitching, he nodded. "Rent-free, Ms. Smith. Is that all?''

A wise woman would have stopped while she was ahead. After all, he'd already agreed to more than she'd dared hope for. She had a job, a place for her and the kids to stay at least through the holidays, possibly until next summer. She should have been satisfied, but a cloud of butterflies stirred in her stomach just at the thought of sharing an apartment with him. Such an arrangement could, she knew, turn out to be a disaster if they didn't work everything out beforehand so there would be no mis-understandings. But Lord, it was hard! How did a woman look a man in the eye and tell him not to get any ideas about her when he hadn't shown the least bit of interest in her as a female?

Heat climbing in her cheeks, she blurted out, "Just for the record, I'm not agreeing to any hanky-panky.''

Any hope that he would let that pass with just a nod of agreement died a swift death. His expression as solemn as a judge's, he lifted an eyebrow over a twinkling eye. "Hanky-panky, hmm? Would you care to define that?''

She wouldn't, she told herself as she suppressed a smile. But he didn't make it easy for her. He was daring her to enjoy the outrageousness of the discussion, and it was all she could do to keep a chastising frown firmly in place. "I wouldn't have thought I'd have to spell it out to a man of your vast experience,'' she replied smoothly. "You just keep your hands to yourself and we'll get along fine.''

"I'll try to restrain myself,'' he assured her dryly. "So do we have an agreement?''

"Not quite yet.'' On a roll, she held up her hand and

started counting additional conditions off on her fingers. "Don't be dragging in at all hours of the night—the kids and I will try not to disturb you and it's only fair that you do the same. I won't pick up after you or wash your clothes. I don't mind doing the cooking, but in return I expect you to do the dishes when you're home for meals. We'll split the rest of the housework."

When she marked off her last finger, she looked him dead in the eye. She'd never been more serious. "If you have a problem with any of this, you'd better speak up now. Because once we move in, all conditions are carved in stone."

Impressed and amused, Mitch couldn't help but admire the lady's spunk. She didn't have two nickels to rub together and would have been homeless if it hadn't been for him, but did she let that stop her from laying down the law? Hell, no!

Without a moment's hesitation, he held out his hand. "Then we have a deal. Shall we shake on it?"

She didn't want to—he could see the doubts in her eyes and in the way she stared at his outstretched hand as if it was some kind of trap about to snap shut around her fingers. But one thing she wasn't, he was discovering, was a coward. Squaring her shoulders, she placed her hand in his.

The moment their hands touched, something seemed to spark between them like static electricity. Something that made his heart jump and his stomach clench and his fingers instinctively tighten around hers. Taken aback, he frowned down at their joined hands and tried to convince himself he'd imagined the whole thing. But he wasn't imagining the sudden hammering of his pulse or her soft, nearly silent gasp as she slowly, carefully, pulled free of his touch. Her eyes wide and wary, she glanced up at him, and even a blind man could have seen she was thinking the same thing he was. What had they gotten themselves into?

Over the course of the next week, Phoebe lost track of the number of times she woke up during the middle of the night wondering what had ever possessed her to agree not only to work for Mitch, but to live with the man once the Johnsons showed up to claim their apartment. It was never going to work. How could it? They were strangers, from two different worlds. And the apartment, while more than adequate for his aunt, was very, very small for four people, even if two of them were children. Within minutes of moving in, they'd probably all be at each other's throats.

Dreading it, she readily admitted she was more than a little nervous about the move. Thankfully, she had the cleaning of 2C to distract her. Over the next few days, as she scoured the place from top to bottom and tried not to think about what would happen when she finished, time ran out and the Johnsons were scheduled to arrive the following morning.

Still, she put the move off all day. Last-minute items had to be taken to the public storage Mitch had arranged for her, the U-Haul trailer had to be returned and she had to vacuum the apartment one last time before she left it for good for the Johnsons. By the time she picked up the kids from school and treated them to an after-school snack at McDonald's, she could no longer postpone the inevitable. When they arrived back at the Social Club, all she and the kids had to do was carry their personal items into Alice's apartment.

Her heart pounding, she told herself that her nervousness had nothing to do with Mitch. She would have been apprehensive about moving in with any man she barely knew. But when she unlocked the front door of Alice's apartment with the spare key Mitch had given her, she couldn't forget the way his fingers had felt closing around hers when they'd shaken hands after she'd agreed to work for him. For hours later, she hadn't been able to forget the warmth of his touch.

Since then, she'd come to the conclusion that she'd imagined the sparks that had seemed to jump from his hand to hers. That didn't, however, stop her knees from trembling as she stepped into the apartment. Unconsciously, she braced for that first moment when she would come face-to-face with him. Silence, however, was her only greeting.

"It's awfully quiet, Aunt Phoebe," Robby whispered loudly as he peeked around her into the apartment. "Is Mr. Ryan here? Maybe we should come back later. He might get mad if we come in while he's not here."

"It's okay, honey," she assured him. "Mr. Ryan gave me a key, remember? He's in and out a lot with business meetings and stuff, so we'll just make ourselves at home. Our bedroom is the one at the back, off the kitchen. Let's check it out. And remember," she called after him and Becky as they darted off toward the rear of the apartment, "we don't touch anything that doesn't belong to us. We're guests and it's important that we respect other people's property. Okay?"

"Yes, ma'am. Don't touch. We'll remember."

"Wow! Look! Bunk beds!"

"I get the top!"

"That's no fair. I'm the oldest. Aunt Phoebe!"

Hardly hearing their squabbling, Phoebe hurried after them, frowning. "What bunk beds? Mrs. Truelove has bunk beds in her guest room?"

"Yeah, and they're red!" Becky said excitedly. "Look, Aunt Phoebe, I can stand on the top one and not even touch the ceiling! Isn't that cool?"

For an answer, Phoebe quickly swept her down off the top bed and set her back down on the floor. "Keep that up, Miss Priss, and you'll be sleeping on a sleeping bag on the floor. At least you can't fall off that."

Turning back to the red metal beds, Phoebe took one look at them and knew they were new. And only one person could have bought them. Mitch. But why? Alice's bed was queen size, and the kids didn't take up that much room. She'd been more than prepared to sleep with them for the short while they would be in this apartment. After all, if she could finish the remodeling of the attic early, it wouldn't even be two months.

Robby, never one to miss an opportunity to pull rank on his sister, said hopefully, "Does that mean I get to sleep on the top bunk, Aunt Phoebe? *Please?* I won't stand up on it. I promise. Only little kids do that kind of goofy stuff."

Grinning, Phoebe ruffled his hair. "Nice try, cowboy, but I know a line when I hear one. If I let you sleep up there, you'd be swinging from the chandelier the second I turned my back on you, and you know it."

His dimples flashing impishly, he didn't deny it.

"Anyway, maybe I want to sleep up there," she told the two kids. "Have you thought about that? Huh?"

They giggled, and just that easily, they were distracted, their argument, for the moment, forgotten. They explored the apartment, respectfully kept their hands behind their backs whenever they spied a particularly enticing treasure of Alice's that they wanted to explore, then reluctantly settled down to do their homework while Phoebe started supper. By the time the three of them sat down at the kitchen table to eat, Mitch still hadn't put in an appearance.

Two and a half hours later, the kids had taken their baths and, after much discussion, had decided that they would trade off sleeping in the top bunk every other night. A flip of a coin decided that it was Becky's lucky night. After much grumbling from Robby, they finally both went to sleep.

Silence fell softly, gradually, like snow in the forest, as the grandfather clock in the foyer quietly counted off the hours. Usually this was the most treasured time of the day for Phoebe, when her chores for the evening were done and she could turn her attention to her book. But even as she set up her old electric typewriter on the kitchen table, she didn't think there was much point. Not tonight. Her surroundings were too unfamiliar, the apartment too quiet. And, try as she might, she kept watching the clock and waiting for Mitch. Where the devil was he?

Irritated by the thought, she said sternly, "That's none of your business. You're not the man's keeper. If you want to worry about something, worry about your heroine in this chapter. She's in a hell of a mess."

She shouldn't have been able to concentrate. She was prepared to stare at the half-finished page she'd left in her typewriter and see nothing but Mitch Ryan's face. But the words reached out and grabbed her, and with gratifying swiftness, her fingers were soon flying over the keys. Lost in the story an hour later, she never heard Mitch's key in the lock.

Chapter 5

It wasn't often that Mitch put one over on Applebee. The old man was too sharp, too slick. He'd been wheeling and dealing before Mitch had been born, and he didn't let anyone beat him at his own game without putting up a fight. When Mitch heard he was angling to buy three struggling radio stations in south Texas, he checked into the situation, discovered the old man was on to a damn good buy, and put in a bid of his own. Less than an hour ago, he'd met with the owner at a hotel on the River Walk and learned that not only had he gotten the bid, but he'd cut Applebee out of the running by a mere five thousand dollars.

That more than made up for the grocery chain the old man had stolen out from under his nose last month, Mitch thought with a grin as he let himself into Alice's apartment. Five grand was pocket change to Applebee—he'd kick himself for not upping the ante when he had the chance. God, what he wouldn't give to be a fly on the wall when the old goat got the news!

Grinning, he felt like celebrating, and if he remembered correctly, Alice kept a bottle of wine in the pantry for special occasions. This more than qualified. Whistling softly to himself, he headed for the kitchen.

It wasn't until he spied Phoebe sitting at the scarred old oak table, frowning at a typewriter that looked like it was straight out of the Stone Age, that he remembered she and her rug rats had been scheduled to move in that day. In the mad rush to outmaneuver Applebee he'd completely forgotten.

His absence obviously hadn't stopped her from making herself at home. Wearing jeans, an oversized, faded red sweatshirt and some kind of fuzzy socks on her feet, she had papers scattered all over the table and a cup of hot chocolate close at hand. As he watched, she propped her feet on the chair opposite her, closed her eyes and went perfectly still. Seconds later, her fingers began to fly over the keys.

Amused, he silently crossed the room to take up a position directly across from her. She never noticed when he leaned back against the counter and crossed his arms over his chest. He meant to tease her the second she opened her eyes, but as his gaze wandered over her, he couldn't help but notice, not for the first time, that the woman had an old-fashioned English-rose prettiness about her that she didn't even seem to be aware of. There was no artifice to her, nothing calculated. Her makeup had faded hours ago, and her hair could have used a comb. Still, she was beautiful, and he couldn't figure out why.

It had to be her skin, he decided. It had a creaminess to it, a translucence, that made a man just want to reach out and touch to see if it was as soft as it looked.

Suddenly realizing he was tempted to do just that, he pushed away from the counter with the intention of getting the hell out of there, but he'd waited too long. She opened her eyes and gasped at the sight of him standing right in front of her. "What are you doing?"

Caught watching her, he actually felt a blush steal into his cheeks. He'd never felt more like an idiot. Scowling, he snapped, "I was about to ask you the same thing. I came in here to get a drink. What *are* you doing?"

It was, he thought, a logical question, one that certainly shouldn't have produced a blush, but that's exactly what it did. Avoiding his gaze, she ripped out the sheet of paper in the typewriter, then began to gather the other pages spread out on the table around her. "I'm writing a book," she said stiffly. "A murder mystery."

Although he was momentarily surprised, he didn't know why he hadn't figured out sooner that the lady was the creative type. In spite of the fact that her former boss had done nothing but sing her praises when he'd talked to him, she wasn't like the other women he knew in the business world. She didn't have the tough outer shell that you needed to climb the corporate ladder, that single-minded ambition and cunning that a woman had to have to compete with a man.

Instead, she had an innocent naiveté to her that the women of his world had lost years ago. Now he knew why she'd been such an easy mark for that Percy jerk who'd swindled her out of her rent money. She was a dreamer, an eternal optimist. She had to be if she actually thought she could beat the odds and get published.

He could have told her that her chances were slim to zero, but he would have been wasting his breath. Dreamers never cared about the odds—they were more interested in fairy tales and happily-ever-afters. Cynics like himself knew there was no such thing.

"I didn't know you were interested in writing. Have you had anything published?"

Phoebe smiled slightly at the question, not surprised

that he had asked it. He was, after all, a man who focused on the bottom line. He would never understand that half the fun of one day being published was the challenge of getting there. "Not yet," she said. "But it's just a matter of time."

Suddenly remembering that he had missed supper and she was taking up most of the kitchen table, she quickly jumped up to unplug her typewriter and return it to its case. "I didn't mean to hog the table. If you're hungry, there's leftover chicken from supper in the refrigerator. Oh, and I forgot to thank you for the bunk beds for the kids. I don't know why you did it, but they were thrilled."

"It was nothing—they needed a place to sleep that didn't take up a lot of room, and that seemed like the best solution. You don't have to put your things away," he said, frowning as she gathered up her manuscript. "I've already eaten. I just felt like celebrating and remembered Alice kept some wine in the pantry."

Plugging Phoebe's typewriter back in, he stepped over to the pantry and grinned at the small wine rack attached to one wall. There was only one bottle in it, but one was all he needed. "Here we go," he said as he turned back to face her. "A chardonnay from one of the Fredericksburg vineyards. Can I tempt you to join me?"

She didn't have much of a head for alcohol and told him so. "But don't let me stop you. What are you celebrating?"

"Outsmarting a damn clever old goat," he said with a grin as he found a wine glass in the cabinet and poured himself a drink. "It isn't often that I get a chance to put one over on Harold Applebee. He's usually too smart for that."

Amused at how pleased he was with himself, Phoebe couldn't help but notice that whoever this Applebee character was, Mitch spoke of him with what almost sounded like affection. Which was surprising since the other man appeared to be some kind of business adversary.

Sinking back down into her chair, her brows knitting in a frown, she studied him curiously. "Is he a friend? I know that sounds stupid—people don't usually go around outsmarting someone they consider a friend—but you sound like you admire him."

"I do," he said promptly. "He taught me everything I know about business. But he's not a friend. At least, not anymore," he qualified, as his smile faded. "He tried to pressure me into marrying his granddaughter and I refused. We haven't spoken since."

Phoebe couldn't imagine anyone pressuring Mitch Ryan into doing anything he didn't want to do. She barely knew him, but she could see that he was a man who would be as immovable as Gibraltar if he felt strongly about something.

"You didn't love her?" she asked quietly. "Or you didn't appreciate being pressured?"

"I'm not the marrying kind," he retorted flatly. "I told both Lisa and Harold that at the beginning. They both thought they could change my mind."

If she'd been looking for a relationship, Phoebe would have been wise to take his warning to heart. But she'd been there, done that, bought the T-shirt, and sold it at a garage sale. Her heart was still bruised from the beating Scott had given it, and the last thing she wanted was a man in her life. Especially one like Mitch Ryan. If he didn't believe in marriage, he didn't have any romance in his soul, and hers was overflowing with it.

Relieved to discover that they were as different as night and day, she said, "My grandmother used to say that you can save yourself a lot of heartache if you just listen to what people are saying when they tell you who they are—

and don't try to believe they are the person you'd like them to be. That's a mistake I try not to make.''

Short of telling him flat out that he didn't have to worry about her getting any ideas about him, she couldn't have been any clearer. One look in his steely blue eyes, and she knew she didn't have to spell it out. He wasn't a stupid man—he'd gotten the message.

They started working together the very next morning. With the kids in school, they had the apartment all to themselves, and in the silence that engulfed them, things could have been awkward. After all, it was an intimate setting, and the fact that they were sharing the apartment was hardly the norm between a boss and his secretary. Mitch wouldn't have blamed Phoebe if she'd been uncomfortable, but she proved to be every bit as professional as her former boss had claimed she was. All business, she did whatever he asked of her without complaint, and anyone seeing them together would have thought that they'd worked together for years instead of a matter of hours.

And things only improved the next day and the day after that. Like Jennifer, his secretary in Dallas, she didn't need supervision or direction to do her job. She dealt with all the tenants' problems and the plumber who arrived to start installing new pipes, began researching architects and contractors for the attic remodeling job, and still managed to handle whatever work he needed her to do for him. And with an intuitiveness that unnerved him, she began to anticipate his needs before he did.

He was, he knew, damn lucky to have her. She was just what he'd been looking for, someone he could leave in charge whenever business took him back to Dallas. And although he'd been a little apprehensive about sharing the apartment with her and the kids, his fears had proved to be groundless. The kids were settling in nicely, and they were all learning one another's quirks and oddities with good humor. Things couldn't have worked out better if he'd planned them himself.

A wise man would have been sending up a silent prayer of thanks to whatever angel had sent her to the Social Club in search of an apartment. Instead, his gut was telling him he never should have hired her, let alone let her move in with him. And he'd learned a long time ago to pay attention to his gut.

She was, he thought irritably as he unobtrusively watched her type a letter for him, a woman he found impossible to ignore. And he couldn't for the life of him say why. She didn't flirt with him, very seldom spoke of anything but business during working hours, and even dressed in power suits and business clothes as if she were going to an office every day. Still, there was something about the way she moved, an unconscious seductiveness, that was far more enticing than the slow, knowing smiles and flirtatious batting of eyelashes that women had been using since time immemorial to get a man's attention. Half the time, she acted like she didn't even know he was in the same room with her.

And he was, he was discovering to his growing irritation, a man who didn't like to be ignored. Especially by a pretty woman.

Disgusted with himself and in need of some space, he growled, "I want that mailed as soon as you finish it."

Her eyes on the computer screen and the document she was working on, she saved the letter, then punched in the appropriate keys to print it out. "I'll walk down to the box on the corner. Pickup's not until one, so it will go out today."

"It'll go out even quicker if you take it out to the main post office," he retorted. "I'll handle things here while you're gone."

That got her attention. Surprised, she turned to look quizzically at him. "I didn't realize this was that important. Do you want me to overnight it?"

What he wanted, dammit, was thirty to forty minutes when he didn't have to smell the subtle, bewitching scent of her perfume. What the hell was it, anyway? "No," he said coldly. "I just want it sent out as soon as possible, and the quickest way to ensure that is to drop it off at the main post office. If you have a problem with that, I'll do it myself."

That was a totally unnecessary remark—he knew it the second the words were out of his mouth and he saw her eyes widen with a quick flash of hurt. Feeling like a louse, he wouldn't have blamed her if she'd snapped back at him, but she had, he was discovering, too much class for that. A blank look he decided he hated dropped over her face, and with no expression whatsoever, she handed him the finished letter to sign. "That isn't necessary. That's what I get paid to do, and we're nearly out of stamps anyway."

He should have apologized. He usually didn't take out his bad moods on his employees, and he'd never before had a problem admitting when he was acting like a jackass. But there was just something about the stiff way she held herself that rubbed against his nerve endings like shards of glass. Scowling, he added his signature to the bottom of the page and shoved it back at her. "If we need any other supplies, get them while you're out."

She all but snapped him a salute. "Yes, sir. Will there be anything else, sir?"

His eyes narrowed at the drill-sergeant treatment, but he only shook his head. "No. Don't forget to keep track of the mileage on your car so I can reimburse you for the gas."

Phoebe was tempted to tell him to keep his damn gas

money, but she was using her car for his business, and fair was fair. Just because he was in a foul mood about something and taking it out on her was no reason to cut off her nose to spite her face. After all, she wouldn't even be driving to the main post office if it wasn't for him.

Folding the letter, she slipped it into the envelope she'd already addressed, grabbed her purse, and rose from the worktable he'd set up for her use. ''I'll keep a running tally and turn it in to you at the end of each week,'' she said coolly. ''I should be back within an hour.''

Her chin held high, she sailed out and told herself she was glad to have a little time to herself. When she'd agreed to their arrangement, she hadn't stopped to think that by living and working in the same apartment, she would never get away from the office. Or her boss. She couldn't turn around without running into him. And there were times, like now, when tempers became more than a little frayed, and she couldn't explain why. Everything would be fine, they'd both be working at individual projects without complaint and even share the computer without the least ill will. Then his eyes would meet hers, she'd get this funny feeling in her stomach, and suddenly they'd both be sniping at each other like a couple of kindergartners arguing over the same swing on the playground.

It was just too much togetherness, she decided as she reached her car in the parking garage down the street. They couldn't, like most bosses and employees, go home to their separate apartments at the end of the day, not when their bedrooms were just across the hall from each other. They even took turns sharing the same bathroom, for heaven's sake, and if anything was guaranteed to create tension between a man and a woman, it was that! They both just needed some space, and lots of it.

Maybe she'd take the kids to the library after supper and spend the evening there, she thought as she unlocked her car and climbed inside. Mitch and the kids had gotten along fine, but a break would probably do everyone some good.

Distracted by her thoughts, she absently placed the key in the ignition and turned it. Nothing happened. Frowning, she jiggled the key and turned it again, with the same result. Other than the soft click the key made when she turned it, there was no sound at all.

Muttering a curse, she leaned her head against the steering wheel with a low moan. No! This couldn't be happening. Not now! She'd known the starter was going out, but she'd kept putting off getting it fixed, hoping she could make it last until after Christmas, but it looked like her luck had just run out. And it couldn't have happened at a worse time.

"Damn!"

Now what was she supposed to do? She didn't have the money for a new starter, and there was no way on God's green earth that she was going to ask Mitch for an advance on her salary. Not after everything he'd already done for her. She'd just have to find another way. After all, it wasn't as if she was completely penniless. She did have some cash—at least enough for a good used part. All she had to do was call a few junkyards and see if she could find one.

Given the circumstances, the last thing she wanted to do was return to the apartment to make the calls and have to explain to Mitch that she had another problem. If he didn't already think that she needed a keeper, he would after this, but there was no way she was going to be able to keep this to herself. Not only did she have to use the phone in the apartment to make the calls, she was going to have to ask him to drive her to wherever she ended up getting a rebuilt used part. Groaning at the thought, she headed back to the apartment.

When she stepped inside the door, he was studying the same quarterly reports he'd been working on all morning. His eyebrows rose at the sight of her. "That was quick. Did you forget something?"

Reluctantly, she told him about the problem she'd been having with her starter. "I should have had it fixed last month, but to tell you the truth, it was working so well that I forgot about it. Now it looks like I don't have any choice."

"What's it doing?" he asked, setting the reports down on his desk and pushing to his feet. "Maybe I should take a look at it."

"Oh, no!" Horrified at the thought of him doing another favor for her, she quickly moved to her work area and reached for the phone book. "Thank you, but that's not necessary. I know what the problem is—it's the starter. It's been on its last legs for months—I guess it finally decided to give up the ghost. If you want to help, though, I'd appreciate it if you'd give me a lift to the junkyard."

Sure he was going to regret asking why, Mitch couldn't control his curiosity. "And why would I do that?"

"Because that's where I'm going to get the part."

"Of course," he replied dryly. He should have figured as much. From the moment he'd met her, she'd done nothing but constantly surprise him with the way she solved problems—he didn't know why this time should be any different.

Leaning back in his chair, he surveyed her with barely concealed amusement. "So you're buying a used part. And who are you going to get to put it in for you? No self-respecting mechanic at a dealership will do that. They'll charge you for a new one."

"I know. That's why I'm not taking it to the dealer. I'll do it myself."

She was so serious, he couldn't help but laugh. He could just see her decked out like a grease monkey, trying to figure out where the starter even went. "Sure you are. And then you're going to change the plugs and tune it up, right? C'mon, Phoebe, quit kidding around. We both know you don't know one end of a motor from another."

It was the wrong thing to say to a woman who obviously prided herself on being able to do just about anything. Casting an ironical glance at him, she said, "Wanna bet?"

Enjoying himself, he grinned. "Make it easy on yourself."

"I intend to," she retorted. "How about the price of the starter? I'll buy it, then you reimburse me when I put it in correctly."

"Only if I get to watch. I'm not going to let you sneak off and let some man put it in for you."

Insulted, she sniffed. "I don't have to cheat to win. So is it a bet or not?"

Rising to his feet, he extended his hand. "You're on, hotshot."

If Mitch hadn't seen it with his own two eyes, he never would have believed it. Other women would have cringed at the grease and grime of the junkyard and turned up their nose at anyone who worked there. But not Phoebe. Oh, no. She greeted the guy who ran the place like an old friend, talked shop with him, then argued good-naturedly with him over the price of the *new* starter she needed. When they finally came to terms on what they both considered a fair price, they were as chummy as if they'd known each other for years.

Intrigued in spite of himself, Mitch warned himself not to be taken in by the lady's gift of gab. Maybe she did have the ability to talk to just about anyone, which in itself was a damn valuable asset, but that didn't mean she knew squat about auto mechanics. Used-car salesmen could do the same thing, and most of them couldn't tell a carburetor from an alternator.

Heading back to the Social Club, he took his eyes away from the traffic long enough to shoot her a considering look. "That was some pretty good wheeling and dealing you did back there. Where'd you learn to bargain like that?"

Pleased at the compliment, she grinned. "I come from a long line of horse traders."

"And here I thought you were going to say you came from a long line of mechanics. Then I would have really been worried. Just for the record, I don't like to lose."

That was something she'd already figured out for herself. The man gave a whole new meaning to the word *competitive*. Far from disturbed by that, she only chuckled, her hazel eyes twinkling. "Then I guess you're not going to enjoy paying up, either. Of course, if you wanted to concede defeat now, I might be convinced not to say 'I told you so.' Then again, I might not. I've got a feeling you don't lose very often and a woman's got to take her victories where she finds them."

"Talk's cheap," he retorted. "I think you're bluffing."

"Better men than you have made that mistake," she tossed back. "Go ahead—stick by your guns. That'll just make the winning that much sweeter. Oh, and by the way, you can pay me in cash. Then I won't have to make an extra trip to the bank."

She was nothing if not cocky. Not sure if he wanted to laugh or strangle her, Mitch drove into the garage down the street from the Social Club and was lucky enough to find a parking space two over from her car. "Okay, Miss Smarty-Pants, put your money where your mouth is. Let's see you do your stuff."

He didn't have to tell her twice. Taking a small tool box from the trunk of her car, she immediately set to work, and within sixty seconds anyone with eyes could see that she knew what she was doing. When Mitch bit out a short curse, she looked up at him with a grin that was every bit as mischievous as her nephew's. "Did I happen to mention that I took an auto-mechanics class in high school so I could spend some time with this boy I had a crush on? We never actually dated, but we spent a heck of a lot of time together under the hood of a car. If I had to, I bet I could build one from scratch."

She probably could, the little minx! "How convenient that you didn't feel the need to mention that vital bit of information until now," he drawled.

If he expected to make her feel guilty, he failed miserably. She only laughed and returned her attention to removing the old starter. "Nice try. And when was the last time you told old man Applebee everything you knew when you were both going after the same company?"

"That was business."

"So is this. Anything that involves money is business to me. Granted, this is only pocket change to you, but a buck's a buck. And it's not as if I didn't warn you," she dared to remind him with a cheeky grin. "I gave you the chance to concede defeat, if you'll remember correctly. Now I get to say 'I told you so.'"

"I wouldn't be so quick to count my chickens if I were you," he warned silkily. "You haven't gotten this pile of bolts running yet. And watching a teenage grease monkey work on a motor when you were just a kid isn't the same thing as doing it yourself years later."

Not the least disturbed, she chuckled, "Oh, ye of little faith." Tossing the old starter into the back floorboard of her car, she reached for the new one and quickly began to install it.

A brain surgeon couldn't have had surer hands. She knew exactly what she was doing and didn't seem the least concerned that she was getting filthy. She had taken the precaution of pulling on an old pair of coveralls, but that didn't protect her hands from the oily grime. Her nails were soon dark with it, and when she unconsciously scratched at her cheek, she left a long black smudge from her cheek all the way to the curve of her jaw.

He was normally a fastidious man, especially when it came to women. He liked a lady who enjoyed being a female. That didn't mean she had to be dressed to the nines all the time, just that she had to look and feel and smell feminine. So when he watched Phoebe attach the last wire to the starter and straighten out from under the hood, smelling of grease, her face and hands in need of a good scrubbing, the last thing he expected to feel for her was desire. But she was delightfully full of herself. She flashed her dimples at him and he felt the punch of her smile like a fist right in his gut.

And she never even noticed. Cocking her head at him, she said, "Do you want the honor of firing her up or shall I?"

The only thing he wanted to fire up right then was her, and the realization stunned him. What the hell was wrong with him? The lady was working for him and they had an agreement. That made her off-limits, and he was a man who never had a problem respecting boundaries. A deal was a deal, and he'd given her his word. He wouldn't go back on it.

But his word had never before been so difficult to keep. Curling his hands into fists to keep from reaching for her, he shook his head. "You go ahead. It's your vehicle."

Grinning, she slid into the driver's seat and inserted the key in the ignition. A split second later, the engine roared to life, accompanied by the sound of her laughter as she bounded out of the car. "Yes! I knew I could do it!"

You'd have thought she'd just won the damn lottery instead of a measly twelve bucks. Her hazel eyes fairly sparkled with triumph and she was so pleased with herself she could hardly stand still. Unable to take his eyes off her, he fought the need to smile. There was, he told himself ruefully, nothing worse than a winner who rubbed your face in your defeat with a spontaneous victory dance that made you want to laugh out loud.

Damn her, why did she have to be so different from every other woman he knew? He could have handled someone cool and sophisticated, who not only knew all the rules of the game, but wasn't above using her feminine wiles to bring a man to his knees. But Phoebe was neither cool nor sophisticated and wouldn't know a feminine wile if she tripped over it. How was he supposed to deal with a woman like that?

Delighted with herself, she sashayed up to him and held out her hand. "I believe you owe me twelve dollars, Mr. Ryan. Would you like your 'I told you so' before or after you pay up?"

He didn't mind eating a little crow, especially when he was in the wrong. If he'd been thinking straight, he would have told her to go ahead and have her fun at his expense, then paid her what he owed her. But his gaze got hooked on her teasing smile, on the sweet, tempting curve of her mouth, and even as warning bells clanged in his head, he knew he was going to kiss her. There wasn't a doubt in his mind that he would regret it later—the lady would make sure of that—but there was no way he could walk away from her when she was smiling up at him so prettily. Just once, he assured himself. He had to taste her just once to satisfy his curiosity. Then he'd be able to finally put her out of his head.

"Later," he growled, and took her hand to pull her into his arms.

"Mitch! What—"

With a touch as light as the brush of the morning dew on a magnolia blossom, he pressed a long, lingering kiss to her lips. Just once. That was all he allowed himself, but damn it was hard to step back and let her go! The second his mouth touched hers, she gasped softly and the sound rippled through him like the thunder of a summer storm. Before he thought to note the danger, he wanted her more than he wanted his next breath.

He couldn't have been more stunned if she'd tripped him and beat him to the ground. He controlled his passions—they didn't control him. But there was no question about it—his heart was beating out a wild rhythm in his chest, and she hadn't even kissed him back! And that rhythm only intensified when he drew back to glare down at her. Her eyes were closed, her lashes thick fans against her cheeks, and on her face was an expression that could only be described as transfixed. It was all he could do not to haul her back into his arms and kiss her all over again.

Then her eyes opened and focused on his face, and she blinked like someone coming out of a daze. "Oh, God!"

Keep it light, he told himself, and drawled, "Not quite, but I'm flattered that you think so."

Flustered, she blushed as red as a cranberry. "I didn't mean…you're not…dammit, I said no hanky-panky!"

"*That* was hanky-panky?"

"Yes! And you agreed," she reminded him hotly as her temper started to simmer. "You promised to keep your hands—and your mouth—to yourself! Or was that just lip service to get me into the apartment? I wouldn't have thought you were that kind of man, but I've been wrong before."

That stung. "It was just a kiss—"

"An unwanted kiss," she began.

That was as far as she got. "Watch it," he growled. "If it was so unwanted, why didn't you just say no? Or push me away? You had to know that's all it would have taken to get me to back off."

Caught in the trap of his hot, steely gaze, she was forced to acknowledge deep inside that he had a point. But if he thought she was going to stand there and admit that she'd wanted him to kiss her, he wasn't nearly as sharp as she'd thought he was.

"What I know is it's not going to happen again," she snapped. "If you've just got to kiss somebody, then go pick a woman off the street. I'm not interested. I'm not looking for a man. I don't want one. You got that? Have I made myself clear?"

"Perfectly," he replied coolly. "The next time you want me to kiss you, you'll let me know."

Frustrated, Phoebe could have screamed. How could such an intelligent man be so incredibly dense? "What part of no didn't you understand? There isn't going to be a next time, dammit!"

"If you say so."

"I do," she ground between her teeth. "That's what I've been trying to tell you. Just stay away from me. Keep your hands and your mouth to yourself, and we'll get along just fine."

Not giving him a chance to respond, she snatched up her tools and deposited them in the trunk of her car, then grabbed her keys and stormed back to the Social Club to clean up. If her heart was still racing and her cheeks embarrassingly warm, it had nothing to do with that kiss. She was just irritated. She didn't lose her temper often, but when she did, it took her a while to calm down. She just needed some space, some time to herself to put the whole incident out of her mind. Remembering the errands she still had to run, she sent up a silent prayer of thanks. If she was lucky, she wouldn't be back until after she picked up the kids from school.

Maybe by then, she'd be able to look Mitch in the eye without remembering the taste of his mouth on hers.

Chapter 6

As she unlocked the front door to Alice's apartment, Phoebe knew she'd taken the coward's way out. She'd waited to collect the kids from school before returning to the apartment because she couldn't bring herself to face Mitch again without having the kids there to diffuse the inevitable tension that was bound to spring up between them the second they came face-to-face. So she'd lingered over her errands, dragging them out, buying herself time until school let out. In the end, though, she'd procrastinated for nothing. The apartment was deserted, and at her work area was a note from Mitch. In a bold hand, he explained that he'd had to fly back to Dallas to take care of some business that he had to handle personally, and he didn't know when he'd be back.

Reading the few instructions he'd left for her, Phoebe couldn't help but feel things had worked out for the best. She'd never expected to be attracted to him, and she was sure that he hadn't planned that kiss between them any more than she had. It had just happened, and she had to believe it was because they were practically living in each other's pockets and working so closely together. She just needed a break from him to put things back in perspective. By the time he returned, she'd wonder what she'd ever seen in the man.

Or at least, that was what she told herself. But that night, after the kids were in bed and she settled down at the kitchen table to work on her murder mystery, the apartment seemed strangely empty without him. Her mind had a tendency to wander to Dallas, and she found herself wondering what he was doing and who he was with. With seemingly no effort on her part, her hero's hair turned from blond to black and his eyes from green to sharp, cold blue. Irritated with herself, she changed everything back, but it didn't help. In the silence of the apartment and her own thoughts, she could hear his footsteps in the hall and the deep rumble of his voice as he said good-night to the kids.

She couldn't get him out of her head and she didn't like it. He had no right to nag her this way, dammit! He probably hadn't given her a second thought since he'd walked out of the apartment, and if she was wise, she'd do the same thing.

She tried, she really did, but every time she let her mind drift the least little bit, he stole into her thoughts like a thief in the night. Giving up in frustration, she went to bed, but he walked through her dreams like he owned them, and her sleep was anything but restful. By morning, she could cheerfully have killed him.

Annoyed with him and herself, she had no intention of spending the day mooning over the infuriating man. She had work to do, work she was getting *paid* to do, and she wasn't going to let him interfere with that even if he was the one doing the paying. So as soon as she returned to the Social Club after taking the kids to school, she grabbed her sketch pad and a pencil and hurried up to the attic to see what ideas she could come up with for the remodeling project.

Mitch had shown her around the old attic ballroom several days after she and the kids moved in and discussed the changes that would need to be done in order to transform it into a luxury apartment, but Phoebe had never been up there by herself before. Reaching the top landing, she didn't bother with a light, but stood in the shadows, absorbing the peace of the place, the quiet that seemed to vibrate in the very air.

The Lone Star Social Club had a well-known history in the city, and anyone who had lived in San Antonio for any length of time had heard the stories about the place. Just about every tenant she met had a story, an anecdote, a tale that had been passed on by Mitch's Aunt Alice, and they all sounded like they just happened yesterday.

For the first time, Phoebe understood why. In the attic, tucked under the eaves where grand balls had taken place long before the turn of the century, time hadn't touched the house at all. The morning sun streamed in through the dormer window on the east side, highlighting the rich patina of the old oak floor. Countless cowboys had danced across that floor, holding their ladies at just the proper degree of closeness, and the wood still bore the scars of their boots. Outside, the twentieth century raced by, but inside, wall sconces that looked as if they had been designed by Edison himself decorated the walls. A flip of a switch proved that their candle-shaped lights were in perfect working order.

The scene sprang to life before Phoebe's eyes as she pictured the women in their hoopskirted dresses being twirled around the dance floor by cowboys in starched shirts and string ties, the smell of perfume and pomade mingling with the sweet freshness of the night air. Smiling, she told herself her imagination was just working overtime, but the images were as clear as if she herself had stepped back in time. Sinking down to the floor, her back propped against the newel post, she let her pencil fly over the paper.

Humming to the strains of a waltz only she could hear, she lost herself in her drawings and never noted the passage of time. One scene after another took shape on her sketch pad, beautiful, romantic etchings that were so detailed, she could only marvel at them. She'd always been able to draw, but she'd never done anything so magical before. She could almost see the couples moving across the page.

Sure she had to be getting some kind of heavenly inspiration, she finished a second sketch and started a third. This one, however, was different. The couples were gone, the party long over. Instead of a ballroom, the attic was now a romantic apartment under the eaves. Light and airy and open, a cozy breakfast nook at the east dormer opened into a white-on-white kitchen, which in turn gracefully flowed into an octagonal living area that was situated right in the middle of the original ballroom floor. To preserve the feeling of spaciousness, the only walls were on the west side of the living room, and they followed the angled roofline to create two bedrooms and an old-fashioned tiled bathroom, with a claw-foot tub, directly under the west dormer.

It was, Phoebe decided, studying the finished sketch, a thoroughly modern design that fit amazingly well in a historic setting. The original wall sconces, wainscoting, and even the glass-paned doors of the kitchen cabinetry kept the spirit of the past, while the open living areas were straight out of the present. Light, airy, and old-fashioned, it was a design that Phoebe felt sure the original architect of the Social Club would have heartily approved of.

It was also everything that Mitch had told her he wanted in a design, but she still needed his approval before she could take the sketch to an architect. She could have faxed it to his Dallas office, but she doubted that he'd want to be bothered with the attic renovations when he obviously had a business crisis to deal with. So she bided her time and waited for him to return.

When two days passed with no further word from him, she should have been relieved. She needed the time away from him to forget a kiss that never should have happened. In her wildest dreams, she never expected to miss him.

At first, she told herself it was just her imagination. How could you miss someone you barely knew? If she found herself thinking about him more than she should, it was just because she was reminded of him everywhere she looked. The computer and office equipment, most of the food in the refrigerator…all of it was his. Even the majority of telephone calls were for him. It was enough to drive a sane woman right over the edge.

Frustrated, she went out of her way to keep herself busy. When she wasn't finishing up the paperwork Mitch had left for her, she was checking the references of the different contractors she was considering for the remodeling of the attic. And in between those tasks, she was running the Social Club, which had turned out to be more time-consuming than she'd anticipated. She had to chat with tenants who just wanted to visit, and she had to keep a close eye on the plumber replacing the pipes throughout the building. Then there was the questionnaire the city had sent to all tenants on the River Walk about the new noise ordinance. Just making sense of it was enough to give her a headache, but she thanked God for it. It was hard to think of Mitch when she was trying to comprehend legalese.

The evenings, however, were the most difficult. When the kids were in bed and she was alone with her typewriter in the kitchen, she should have been able to lose herself in her writing. But it was if he'd been waiting all day to slip into her thoughts, and the moment she sat still and relaxed, he pushed past the feeble barriers she'd erected to keep him out of her head. Suddenly he was there, taking up all her thoughts, and she couldn't manage to string two sentences together without memories of him disturbing her. Disgusted, she put her typewriter away and finally called the one person she could count on to help her get her head on straight. Dana.

"Thank God!" her friend said the second she recognized her voice. "I've been worried sick about you! Where are you? Are you all right? If I hadn't been tied up on a rush case for the district attorney's office, I swear I would have come looking for you to shoot you! Don't you know better than to disappear on people who care about you?"

"I'm sorry. I know I should have called. I've got to call the Mallorys, too—I'll do that just as soon as I finish talking to you. I don't know where the time went. It's just been so hectic around here—"

"Here? Where's *here?* Blast it, Phoebe, I want a phone number where I can reach you! I haven't slept all week, wondering if you and the kids were in a shelter or out on the street, or what!"

Grinning, Phoebe chuckled. "We're fine, Mother. In fact, things couldn't be better. We're right where I originally intended for us to be...at the Lone Star Social Club."

"But...I thought the owner was only going to let you stay there a week."

''He was, but you're never going to believe what's happened.'' She told her then about Mitch's job offer and her and the kids' move into Alice's apartment. ''So you see,'' she said, ''you did all that worrying for nothing. I've got a job and a temporary place to live for now. All I have to do to make that permanent is to finish the remodeling of the attic ahead of schedule, and I don't see any reason why I shouldn't be able to do that. Things couldn't have worked out better if I'd written the script myself.''

Not quite convinced of that, Dana said, ''I don't know if I'd go that far. You don't even know this Mitch character. What if he's some kind of ax murderer or something?''

Well used to her friend's suspicious mind, Phoebe laughed. ''Then I'd be dead by now. He's not an ax murderer, Dana.''

''How do you know? Did you check him out?''

''Of course not!''

''Why not?'' Dana demanded. ''This is the nineties, girlfriend, and there's a lot of meanness out there. A woman can't be too careful. Especially when she's got two children to look out for.''

She had a point—Phoebe knew that. But her sense of fair play was outraged at the idea of investigating a man who had gone out of his way to help her. ''But he's been nothing but nice to us,'' she argued. ''And I do have some protective instincts. If he was a lowlife, I like to think I'd know it.''

''Scott was a lowlife,'' she reminded her quietly. ''And I hate to say I told you so, but everyone could see it but you. What if Mitch Ryan is another Scott?''

Instinctively, Phoebe rejected that. There was no way that Mitch was anything like Scott. Granted, they both were sharp, intelligent men with an air of power about them, but Scott was a user who would say anything, do anything, to get ahead. She knew it because he had used her. He'd started romancing her his first week on the job at Wainwright, and it wasn't until six months later that she learned he was an industrial spy from Wainwright's biggest competitor. He hadn't wined and dined her and given her the rush because he fell in love with her; it was because as executive secretary to a vice president, she had security clearance. While she'd foolishly thought he was thinking of marriage, he was just hoping to charm her into helping him steal secrets from the company. Instead, she was the one who turned him in.

"I have nothing that Mitch Ryan could possibly want," she told her friend. "And even if I did, he's not Scott. He's an ethical man who has no problem stating up front what he wants."

"He's an entrepreneur, Phoeb," Dana reminded her. "That means he plays by his own rules. I don't want to see you get hurt again. Let me do a background check. He'll never know, and I'll feel a lot better."

Hesitating, Phoebe cringed at the thought. But Dana had a point. Scott had completely pulled the wool over her eyes. And she did have to protect the kids. Mitch might be everything he appeared to be, but she really did need to know for sure.

"All right," she agreed reluctantly. "But I'm doing this under protest. God knows what I'm going to say to him if he finds out."

"He won't," Dana assured her. "Just leave everything to me."

Phoebe only snorted. That was easy for her to say. She wasn't the one who was going to have to find a way to look him in the eye when he came home.

"Well, you were right. He's not an ax murderer."

Laughing at her friend's greeting on Sunday night,

Phoebe couldn't help but be relieved. "I told you he was harmless."

"I don't know if I'd go that far," Dana replied dryly. "He's no Boy Scout. In fact, the man's downright dangerous. And I'm not just talking about business, sweetie. He's been involved with his share of women."

Dana was nothing if not good at her job, and Phoebe didn't doubt for a minute that if she asked, Dana could tell her anything she wanted to know about Mitch's sex life, right down to what he liked to wear to bed. But that was information she was better off not knowing. "Spare me the details," she said quickly, amused. "Of course he's got women coming out the wazoo. He's rich and good-looking. What's not to like?"

"Oh, God, I was afraid you'd say that," Dana groaned. "Damn it, Phoeb, don't you dare tell me you're falling for this guy! He's trouble. You hear me? Everyone I talked to said he thinks love is a four-letter word. That might be fine for some women, but you still believe in fairy tales. I'm afraid he's going to break your heart."

"But I'm not even looking for a man. You know that."

"And that's when a woman usually finds one," her friend retorted. "Just watch yourself, okay? I don't want to see you get hurt."

Phoebe assured her that wasn't going to happen. But long after she hung up, she couldn't forget the taste and feel and heat of Mitch's kiss. The time they'd spent apart had done nothing to lessen its impact.

She should have been worried sick about that, but Mitch soon proved to be the least of her problems. When Becky complained before bedtime about a stomachache, Phoebe just assumed she'd eaten too much spaghetti at supper. She loved the stuff, especially with meatballs, and she'd had two big servings. Assuring her she'd feel better in the morning, she'd sent her to bed and decided to make it an early night herself. She'd hardly fallen asleep however, when Robby woke her with the disgusted announcement that Becky had just tossed her cookies.

Dazed and still half asleep, Phoebe frowned up at him in the darkness. "Cookies? What cookies?"

"She's sick, Aunt Phoebe. She just threw up all over me!"

Alarmed, Phoebe threw off the covers and only just then heard the six-year-old retching in the bathroom. "Oh, God! I'm coming, honey! Just hold on."

Spent, as pale as a ghost, Becky burst into tears at the sight of her. "I'm sorry, Aunt Phoebe! I didn't mean to get sick. It just happened."

"Shh. It's okay, sweetheart," she assured her as she grabbed a washcloth from the linen closet and quickly wet it in the sink. "I'm not mad at you. Of course you didn't mean to get sick! You just ate too much at supper. Here, let's wash your face and get you out of those pajamas and into some fresh ones." Soothing her, she sat down on the wicker stool next to the claw-foot tub and pulled her onto her lap, only to frown in concern. "My, God, you're burning up!"

Silent tears streaming down her face, Becky leaned weakly against her. "My head hurts. Can I go back to bed now?"

"In a minute, sweetie. First we need to clean you up, then change the sheets on your bed. Do you hurt anywhere else?"

She nodded glumly as Phoebe helped her out of her pajamas. "My tummy. It aches real bad."

"I know, honey. It sounds like you've got a nasty old flu bug."

Or a stomach virus or one of those twenty-four-hour things that kids always seemed to get and she didn't know a thing about. Maybe she should call a doctor. But which one? She hadn't gotten the kids a doctor yet since they hadn't been sick since they'd come to live with her, and she could hardly call a strange pediatrician in the middle of the night. But she had to do something. Heat was radiating off Becky in waves, and she didn't even have a thermometer to take her temperature.

"How about a bath, sweetie?" she suggested. "It'll bring your temperature down and make you feel more comfortable. Then I'll change the sheets on your bed and you can go back to sleep."

"Okay," she said weakly. "But can't I have some Children's Tylenol, too?"

Standing solemnly in the open doorway of the bathroom, Robby said quietly, "That's what Mama always gave us when we were sick. She used to say it brought a fever down quicker than an ice storm."

Her heart breaking at the wistfulness of his tone, Phoebe would have given just about anything at that moment to produce his mother for him. It was at times like this, when they had no one to turn to but an aunt they had barely begun to bond with that they had to miss her the most.

"Mama always knew just what to do, didn't she? She may not be here to hold you, but she's still watching out for you. I don't have any Tylenol, but there must be an all-night pharmacy somewhere in town that delivers." Quickly filling the bottom of the tub, she tested the water to make sure it wasn't too cool, then turned back to Becky to help her into the tub. "Okay, sweetheart, in you go. Just sit in there for a minute and cool down while I call the pharmacy. Holler if you need me."

Not only did she find an all-night pharmacy, but she was lucky enough to talk to a pharmacist who had children of her own and knew exactly what Phoebe was going through. "I know it's unnerving, but these things usually aren't as bad as they seem. Just keep her comfortable and give her plenty of fluids. The Tylenol will bring the fever down, and if you're lucky, she's over the worst of the vomiting. If it gets really bad, though, or her fever sky-rockets, you might want to take her to the emergency room, but I doubt that that'll be necessary. It sounds like the flu.''

''And I was just hoping she ate too much spaghetti for supper.''

The other woman laughed. ''Sorry. No such luck. Not if she's got a fever. And I hate to be the bearer of bad news, but usually when one kid in the household comes down with this kind of garbage, the others do, too. So just get ready. Your nephew's probably already got the bug in his system.''

Phoebe groaned at the thought. ''Are you sure? He seems perfectly fine now.''

''Give it another twelve hours or so,'' the pharmacist advised sagely. ''With mine, it seems like the second one always waits until his brother is just beginning to feel better before he starts moaning and groaning and turning green.''

''But can't I give him something now to prevent it?''

''Grape juice,'' she said succinctly. ''Sometimes it works, sometimes it doesn't, but it's worth a shot. And it wouldn't hurt you to drink some yourself. You're not immune just because you're an adult, you know. If you're not careful, the kids could be taking care of you.''

Phoebe doubted that—she was one of those disgustingly healthy people who never got sick—but she thanked her for her help and promised to try the grape juice. Leaving Robby to listen for the buzzer that signaled the delivery of the Tylenol, she quickly changed the bed sheets on both kids' beds, since Becky had been sleeping on the top bed when she got sick. Phoebe then tossed the soiled sheets in the washing machine, and by the time she returned to the bathroom, Becky was noticeably cooler. But her head still ached and she complained that her stomach was hurting, and before the delivery boy arrived from the pharmacy, she was sick again.

After that, Phoebe lost track of time. She was able to convince Robby to drink a generous glass of grape juice and get him back in bed, but Becky was another matter. Her temperature started to rise again in spite of the Tylenol that Phoebe was finally able to get down her, and she just couldn't seem to get comfortable. Phoebe tried rocking her, sponging her down, singing softly to her, but nothing seemed to help. When she finally fell asleep at three in the morning, it was more from exhaustion than anything Phoebe did to make her feel better.

So tired she could barely keep her eyes open, Phoebe never remembered crawling into bed. Then the phone rang three hours later and she jerked up with a start, her heart pounding. The new tenants in 2C had no hot water. Just barely managing to stifle a groan, Phoebe promised that the problem would be taken care of just as soon as she could get hold of the plumber. It wasn't even six-thirty, and the day had begun.

After the night she'd had, Becky slept late—for which Phoebe was thankful—but Robby was fresh as a daisy and showed no sign of the bug that had knocked the stuffing out of his sister. He ate a full breakfast, chattered about a science project that was due Friday, and gave her a big hug before leaving for school with Mrs. Tucker, the neighbor across the hall who volunteered to give him a ride when Phoebe told her about Becky's illness. He'd barely closed the door behind him when Becky woke up, burning with fever.

When Mitch walked into the apartment a little before noon, he was not in the best of moods. He was, in fact, coldly furious. His flying trip to Dallas had been too little, too late. Over the last few weeks, he'd been negotiating to buy a prime piece of real estate in Dallas. He'd thought he had it all but signed, sealed, and delivered. But while he was cooling his heels in San Antonio, he'd left Applebee a clear field to work his mischief. He'd snatched the deal right out from under him without even breaking a sweat, and no amount of wheeling and dealing on Mitch's part had changed that.

Disgusted, he'd given serious consideration to calling Phoebe to tell her he wouldn't be back. Applebee was going to eat him for lunch if he left town again, and only a fool would give the old goat that kind of opportunity. But the Social Club was his family's legacy and he couldn't leave anything as important as a remodeling job in the hands of a stranger. Even if that stranger was someone as dependable and efficient as Phoebe. And then there was Alice. He didn't even want to think of facing her if something went wrong because he wasn't where he'd promised to be.

So he'd come back, but he wasn't happy about it. Knowing Applebee, he'd started planning his next attack before Mitch's plane had even left the ground.

Muttering curses at the thought, he headed straight for the computer and didn't notice the condition of the apartment until he tripped over a pile of sheets by the entrance to the laundry room. Swearing, he glanced up and couldn't believe his eyes. The place looked like it had been hit by a tornado. There were sheets and towels and dirty clothes piled everywhere, and the kitchen sink was full of dirty dishes.

"What the hell!"

What the devil was going on? he wondered, stunned. With all Phoebe had to do while he was gone, he'd known she'd be too busy with his work and the kids to do much else, but surely she'd at least had time to do the dishes and throw a few loads of clothes in the washing machine. From the looks of things, she hadn't cleaned so much as a glass the entire time he was gone.

Scowling, he strode toward the small hall that led to the bedrooms, intending to find her and demand an explanation, but just then, she stepped out of the bedroom she shared with the kids, and the words died in his throat. Her hair was pinned haphazardly on top of her head, her face devoid of makeup. She wore jeans and a faded sweatshirt that hung almost to her knees, swallowing her slender form whole. Another time, she could have looked as young as Becky, but not today. There were dark circles under her eyes and exhaustion weighed down her narrow shoulders.

Alarmed, he started to reach for her, but she looked so tired, he was afraid she would crumble if he so much as touched her. "What is it?" he demanded hoarsely. "What's wrong?"

"Becky has the flu," she said tiredly. "I'm sorry the place is in such a mess, but she's been so sick that I've hardly been out of her sight."

"To hell with the apartment," he growled. "How is she? Have you talked to a doctor?"

She nodded tiredly. "After she threw up for the fourth time, I called the emergency room at County General and was able to talk to a pediatrician. Evidently, there's this really nasty twenty-four-hour thing going around, and poor Becky seems to have it. She's not throwing up anymore, thank God, but the doctor said to expect the fever to last for at least another twelve hours. She's sleeping now, but as long as she's got fever, she's contagious, so you might think about going to a hotel for the night. Believe me, this is something you don't want to get."

If he'd had half a brain in his head, he would have jumped at her suggestion and gotten the hell out of Dodge. And not because he was afraid of getting sick—he couldn't remember the last time he'd had so much as a cold. No, his need to get out of there had nothing to do with Becky's flu and everything to do with an attraction he'd felt sure he'd put in perspective while he was in Dallas. It was a physical thing, nothing more, he'd concluded, and could easily be dismissed.

But now, seeing her so frazzled and exhausted, all he could think about was drawing her into his arms and promising her he'd take care of everything. And that scared the hell out of him. Because there was nothing so dangerous as a vulnerable woman to a man who found it easy to play the white knight.

Still, he couldn't bring himself to leave her. Not when she was out on her feet and obviously needed help. "I'm not leaving you to deal with this alone," he said flatly. "Where's Robby?"

"At school. He ate breakfast like it was going out of style this morning and seemed perfectly fine, so there was no reason to keep him home. The doctor said if he doesn't show any symptoms within the next twenty-four hours, he probably won't get it."

The phone rang then, and with a tired sigh, she turned to answer it. "That's probably Mrs. Johnson again. She called before six-thirty this morning to complain that they didn't have any hot water. I put in a call to the plumber, but he had another emergency and hasn't shown yet."

Grim-faced, he stepped in front of her to block her path to the phone. "I'll deal with Mrs. Johnson. You go to bed."

"Bed? You can't be serious! Look at this place. I've got to do some laundry. Oh, and I need to show you some sketches for the attic—"

"No, you don't. Not now." Ignoring the ringing phone, he set his hands on her shoulders and turned her toward her bedroom. "Go lie down and take a nap," he said, and gave her a gentle push in the right direction. "I'll take care of the phone and the laundry and anything else that pops up. You get some sleep so you can take care of Becky when she wakes up."

"But Robby will be home soon. Mrs. Tucker's going to pick him up at school. The pharmacist said for him to drink grape juice. It might keep him from getting sick…"

"I think I can manage to pour him a glass or two. And if we run out, I know where the store is. Okay? Now will you lie down before you fall flat on your face?"

She didn't want to. Even with her back to him, he could see her trying to gather the energy to protest. But she just didn't have it in her. Her stiff stance abruptly melted and with a quiet sigh, she gave in. "All right. But just for a little while. And don't do the laundry. I'll do it when I get up."

"Fine," he said. "Have a nice nap."

Stumbling toward her bedroom like a drunk heading for a bar and the first desperate drink of the day, she waved a hand in acknowledgement and never looked back. The second the bedroom door closed behind her, Mitch snatched up a pile of sheets and dumped them in the washing machine with enough soap to kill a truckload of germs. Then he headed for the kitchen.

Housework wasn't his favorite thing to do, but his mother had made sure her boys knew how to cook and clean up after themselves, and he set about righting the apartment with grim determination. All kinds of juices littered the kitchen counter, not to mention half-full glasses that had barely been touched, and he could almost see Phoebe trying to coax her niece into drinking first one juice, then another in an effort to bring down her triple-digit fever. She must have been frantic.

Something clenched in his gut at the thought of what she must have gone through all by herself last night. A blind man could see that she loved those kids like they were her own, but being their sole caretaker was a heavy responsibility for her slender shoulders. If he'd been there, he could have helped her or at least walked the floor with her while she worried.

Watch it, man, a caustic voice sneered in his head. You keep thinking like that and someone might think you're starting to care about the lady. And we both know better than that, don't we? Nobody's going to get past that hard shell around your heart, especially a homeless waif towing two rug rats behind her.

Scowling, he reminded himself that he didn't have to apologize to anyone for who and what he was. But as soon as he had the dishwasher loaded and running, he pulled a frozen chicken out of the freezer and started a pot of soup. When that damn little voice wondered how Phoebe would react if she knew she was the first woman he'd cooked for in a decade, he told it to shut the hell up. If he wanted to cook in his own damn apartment, it was nobody's business but his own.

In a bear of a mood, he'd just put the last load of sheets in the dryer when Robby ran in from school. Bright-eyed and excited about the grade he'd made on a short story he'd written, he could hardly stand still. "Where's Aunt Phoebe?" he asked, fidgeting from one foot to the other. "My teacher said I might be the next Mark Twain. You know—he wrote that story about those two boys…Huck and Tom? Wait'll I show Aunt Phoebe. She's really going to like my story—"

Clutching the crumpled story to his chest, he started to dart around him, only to be brought up short when Mitch grabbed him by the arm. "Hold up there, pardner. Why don't you show it to me, instead? Your Aunt Phoebe's lying down right now. I'm sure she'd love to see it later."

It was a simple enough excuse, one that shouldn't have alarmed Robby in the least. But he went as white as a sheet at Mitch's words and frantically began tugging at his arm to free himself. "Let go! She's sick, isn't she? That's why she's lying down. She's sick and you don't want me to know it!"

The accusation stunned Mitch...and explained the sudden fear in the boy's eyes. He'd already lost his parents; Phoebe was the only stability he and his sister had left in the world. If they lost her, too, they had to know they would be totally alone in the world. No wonder the poor kid was terrified. Most adults couldn't handle the thought of being alone. For a child, it had to be the most frightening thing in the world.

"C'mon, Robby, you know I wouldn't lie to you," he said quietly. "Your aunt was up with Becky most of the night. She was so tired when I came in that she could hardly see straight, so I sent her to bed. She's okay. Really."

His brown eyes searching, Robby obviously wanted to believe him, but he was too worried about Phoebe to let go of his fear. "You promise?"

"I'll do better than that," Mitch said easily. "I'll show you. C'mon."

Preceding him to the bedroom door, he motioned for the boy to be quiet, then silently eased open the door. Just as he'd promised, both Becky and Phoebe were asleep and didn't so much as stir when the door opened. Exhausted, Phoebe hadn't bothered to change and had crawled into bed fully dressed, shoes and all. She hadn't even pulled the covers over herself.

His mouth twitching into a smile, Mitch started to close

the door now that Robby had been reassured, but then his gaze locked on Phoebe's flushed cheeks and he frowned. She hadn't had a drop of color in her face when he'd sent her to bed, but now her cheeks were a rosy hue that he doubted came from sleep. Suddenly concerned, he quietly crossed the room to her bedside and gently cupped her cheek in his palm, only to swear in alarm. She was burning up with fever, too.

Chapter 7

"Phoebe? Wake up, sweetheart. You need to take something to bring your fever down."

Weighed down by a hot, heavy blanket of sleep, Phoebe vaguely heard Mitch's voice coming to her from somewhere. She shifted restlessly on the bed. It seemed like every time she closed her eyes, he was there in her thoughts, and now she was dreaming that he had called her "sweetheart." It had to stop, she told herself dully. She was so tired, and she never could find the time to catch up on her sleep. As soon as she got up from her nap, she was going to tell him to stop pestering her. A woman ought to be able to go to bed without a man taking up space in her dreams and making her want things she couldn't have.

"I know you're tired, honey, but you're burning up with fever. Wake up just long enough to take some aspirin, and I swear I'll let you go back to sleep."

Frowning, she tried to sink deeper into her dreams, but

that persistent, husky voice followed her, coaxing and prodding and refusing to be ignored. Her head starting to throb, she groaned. "Go 'way. Need sleep."

"I know. And I'll let you," he promised. "Just as soon as you take some aspirin."

Still caught up in her dream, she felt his hand on her cheek again, and it was so real that she could no more resist his touch than the tides could resist the pull of the moon. Struggling toward consciousness, she forced open heavy-lidded eyes and blinked in confusion at the sight of Mitch sitting on the side of her bed. Where had he come from? He was supposed to be in Dallas. Instead, he was there, in her bedroom, cupping her cheek and frowning down at her worriedly. And she was sick.

"What are you doing?" she asked hoarsely. "You have to get out of here. I'm contagious." She started to push up into a sitting position, but the second she lifted her head off the pillow, her stomach reacted violently in protest. Moaning, she bolted from the bed and ran for the bathroom.

Sick as a dog, she never knew Mitch was right there with her until he slipped an arm around her waist from behind and gently wiped her face with a damp washcloth. Mortified, she protested weakly, "Go away. You shouldn't be in here."

"And where else would I be?" he growled. "On the telephone wheeling and dealing while you're sick in the bathroom? I don't think so. Are you done here?"

She nodded, and in the next instant found herself swept up in his arms. Her head spinning, she clutched frantically at him. "Mitch! Put me down! I can walk."

"Sure you can," he snorted. "Look at you. You're so weak, you couldn't swat a fly if your life depended on it. Relax. I'm just carrying you to bed so you won't fall on your face in front of the kids. They're worried about you.''

"Oh, God!" she whispered. The kids. She'd completely forgotten them! Her head throbbing and her stomach still cramping, she glanced around as Mitch carried her into the bedroom, only to feel her heart clench at the sight of both kids sitting on the lower bunk. Becky, abruptly awakened from her own nap by Phoebe's mad dash to the bathroom, appeared to be on the mend and would have looked almost like her old self if silent tears hadn't trailed silently down her face. Next to her, huddled close, Robby was drawn and quiet, his brown eyes far too somber for a child who had gone laughing off to school just that morning.

"Hey, guys, why the long faces?" she teased weakly as Mitch laid her on the bed. "I'm okay. Really. I've just got that nasty old flu bug. This time tomorrow, I'll be back to my old self, so don't cry. Everything's fine."

"Then why was Mitch carrying you?" Becky sniffed. "Can't you walk?"

"Of course I can," she replied. "I was just a little wobbly and Mitch was afraid I'd fall. I'll be fine, honey, after I rest a while."

Unconvinced, Robby said accusingly, "You said you never get sick. You're not going to die, are you?"

"Oh, no, sweetie!" Horrified that he would think such a thing, she ignored her churning stomach and wobbly legs, not to mention Mitch's disapproving frown, and climbed out of bed to give them both a hug. "I'm not dying. You hear me? I'm going to stick around until you two grow up and we're all old and gray together. So don't worry about me, okay? Now, why don't we see about getting you guys a snack? Becky, do you think you could eat some Jell-O? I made your favorite—strawberry."

When the little girl nodded eagerly, Mitch said firmly,

"Come on, kids, *I'll* get the Jell-O. *You* change into your nightgown and get back in bed," he told Phoebe, and tossed her the gown she'd hung on the hook on the back of the bedroom door. "I'll be right back with some juice and aspirins, then you're going back to sleep."

If she hadn't been so miserable, she would have bristled at his high-handed manner and told him that he didn't give her orders, especially about when she went to bed. But before she could even summon the energy to open her mouth, he'd scooped Becky up, much to her delight, and hustled Robby out to the kitchen for Jell-O.

Glaring after him as he shut the door, she was half tempted to defy him and go to bed just as she was. But he was a man who didn't lack for arrogance, and she wouldn't put it past him to strip her clothes from her himself and stuff her into her nightgown if she didn't do as he said. Mumbling curses under her breath, she untied her shoes, then tugged them off, and was amazed at how much concentration it took. Frowning, she struggled out of her sweatshirt and pulled her gown over her head, but she couldn't find the strength to manage her jeans. Sighing tiredly, she stretched out on the bed and closed her eyes. Just for a minute, she promised herself. She'd just rest for a minute and work up the energy to get out of her jeans.

Mitch served the kids their Jell-O at the coffee table in the living room, turned the TV to the cartoon station, and strode back into Phoebe's bedroom without bothering to knock. He'd seen the faint flash of fire in her eyes before he'd walked out and wouldn't have been surprised to find her sitting in the middle of the bed, fully dressed right down to her shoes and openly defiant.

Instead, she'd collapsed in a heap on her pillow.

He should have been amused. Even though she'd made an attempt to change, she'd still found a way to defy him.

Her sweatshirt and tennis shoes lay where she'd dropped them on the floor by the side of the bed, but she'd obviously run out of steam when she'd pulled on her nightgown. Still unbuttoned, the enticing curve of her breast clearly visible, the gown was bunched around her waist, exposing her jean-clad hips and legs. She'd never gotten around to squirming out of them.

If she'd wanted to thwart him, she couldn't have found a better way. He either had to strip her out of those jeans or listen to his conscience nag him the rest of the evening for not helping her when she obviously couldn't help herself. It was, he decided, a terrible thing, having a conscience. It damn near made it impossible for a man to mind his own business and keep his hands to himself.

Scowling, he knew he had no choice but to do the right thing, but he damn well wasn't going to enjoy it. She was asleep, for God's sake, and sick on top of that! Only a real pervert would get any enjoyment out of stripping a woman in that kind of condition, and he hadn't sunk that low yet.

His jaw rigid, he sank down on the side of the bed and reached for the snap of her jeans. He was, he told himself, going to do this fast, then get the hell out of there. But in the sudden ringing silence of the bedroom, the sound of her zipper being lowered was like a rough growl. She was the one with the fever, but he was the one who broke out in a sweat. Swearing, he tried not to notice the softness of her skin, not to mention the lace of her panties, as he worked the jeans down her hips and thighs, but he'd set an impossible task for himself. He wasn't made of stone, and she had the most beautiful legs he'd ever seen.

Grinding his teeth on an oath, he reminded himself that he was a man of principle, then tossed the jeans on the floor. A heartbeat later, her gown was pulled down, covering her all the way to her ankles, and the sheet and comforter were tugged up over her. Relieved, Mitch glared down at Phoebe's sleeping form and didn't know if he wanted to laugh or shake her. He generally expected some kind of a reaction from a woman when he undressed her. She didn't even know he was there.

He should have left her then, but she still hadn't taken anything for her fever, and she was burning up. He hated to wake her, but he didn't see that he had any choice. A high fever was nothing to play around with. "Phoebe? C'mon, honey, wake up. I know you want to sleep, but we've got to get some aspirins down you."

She moaned and tried to turn away, but he was having none of it. Gently shaking her shoulder, he coaxed, "Just two, and then I'll leave you alone. I promise. C'mon, beautiful. Open your eyes."

She didn't want to. She fought him, whimpering, but he was as stubborn as she was, refusing to let her rest until she did as he said. Finally opening pain-dulled eyes, she cried softly, "Why are you doing this to me? Can't you see I'm sick?"

She sounded so pitiful, he winced. "I'm not trying to torture you, honey. Can't you feel how hot you are? We've got to get your fever down. You don't want to end up in the hospital, do you? Then take your medicine like a good girl. That's right," he said when she forced down the pills with a swallow of grape juice. "Just a little more juice, and then you can go back to sleep."

Afraid she would get dehydrated, he tried to get her to drink all of it, but she could only manage two more sips before she pushed the glass back into his hands. "No more," she choked, and collapsed back against her pillow with a tired sigh.

Just that little bit of effort had drained the last of the color from her cheeks, and Mitch didn't have the heart to push her further. Setting the juice on the nightstand in case she might need it later, he started to push to his feet, but he'd barely moved when she reached out and grabbed his hand. "The kids…"

"Are just fine," he assured her. "They're both eating Jell-O and watching cartoons, so don't lie here and worry about them. If you want to worry about something, worry about kicking this thing and getting back on your feet. I'll take care of the kids."

"But they're not your responsibility," she protested weakly. "I should be taking care of them."

"And just how are you going to do that when you're burning up with fever and can't even keep your eyes open?" he countered.

"I just need to rest—"

"Finally! The woman agrees with me!" he said to the ceiling, grinning. "Now that we've got that cleared up, I'm going to check on the kids. I'll be back to see if you need anything after you've had your nap."

He didn't give her time to protest, but strode out and quietly shut the door behind him, leaving it open just a crack so he could hear her if she called for help. The kids were just where he'd left them, glued to the TV. Becky showed no signs of the nausea that had tormented her all night. Her aunt, however, was another matter. Her stomach might have settled down for the moment, but she was still one sick puppy, and he had a feeling she was going to get much worse before she got better.

That prediction, unfortunately, proved to be all too true over the course of the next four hours. She was sick more times than he cared to count, and if it wasn't her stomach that was bothering her, it was her head. And to make matters worse, her fever went up and down like a yo-yo, making it impossible for her to get comfortable.

And in between caring for her, he had the kids to deal with. Robby needed help with his homework and there was supper to make, then afterwards, they both needed baths. For a logical, efficient businessman who ran multimillion-dollar companies without breaking a sweat, handling a six- and seven-year-old should have been a piece of cake. And at times, it was. When they didn't have him running in circles.

And it wasn't as if they were bad kids. They were just kids. They teased and argued, and there were moments when Robby had to only look at Becky wrong to make her squeal in protest. And as the evening grew long, those moments became more and more frequent. Attributing their irritability to the fact that Becky still wasn't feeling completely up to snuff and Robby himself might be coming down with the flu, he decided it wouldn't hurt either of them to go to bed a little early.

He'd watched Phoebe put them down for the night enough times to know the routine. They brushed their teeth, said their prayers, and then she read to them for a few minutes after she checked under the bed and in the closets for monsters. That he figured he could handle. But when he casually suggested that they trade beds with him for the night so he could keep an eye on Phoebe, both children got unusually quiet. They exchanged a speaking glance, and before he suspected something was wrong, they both started to cry.

Alarmed, he said, "Hey, it's nothing to cry about. If you don't want to, that's okay. I'll just sleep on the couch so I can hear Phoebe if she needs me during the night."

Her little face solemn and pale, Becky looked up at him with big blue eyes swimming in tears and had no idea how she broke his heart. "Aunt Phoebe's really bad sick, isn't she? Sicker than me."

"I told you she was going to die," Robby whispered to his sister. "Tommy Parker's grandmother did the same thing. She puked and puked and she died. The doctor said it was 'cause her independic thing burst inside her, but it was really 'cause she puked too much.''

Confused, Mitch frowned. "Independic thing? What's that?" Even as he asked, understanding dawned. "Oh, you must mean appendix!"

He nodded solemnly. "That's what I said."

Fighting a smile, Mitch said dryly, "I beg your pardon—so you did."

"So Aunt Phoebe's going to die?"

"No!" Becky cried angrily, punching him. "She can't! She said we'd all be old together!"

"You don't get to pick when you die!" Robby snapped back. "That's why Mommy and Daddy died in the wreck. God took 'em and he can take Aunt Phoebe if he wants to."

Suddenly realizing that they'd been picking at each other all afternoon because they were worried to death about Phoebe, Mitch fought back growing panic. He could handle cooking for them, seeing that they were washed and fed, even cleaning up after them if they were sick as dogs, but what was he supposed to say to two kids who had lost their parents, their home, even their grandparents over the course of the last year, and were now afraid they were losing the one person they had left in the world that they loved?

This was out of his league, dammit! He only saw his own nephews and nieces three or four times a year, and that hardly made him an expert on kids. He didn't know how to talk to them, how to reassure them and calm their fears, how to make them feel safe. They needed Phoebe, not him.

But Phoebe was out of commission and he was the only one around when Robby drew back his arm to strike back at his sister. "Whoa!" Quickly snatching Becky up on his lap, he frowned at Robby and drew him to his side in an reassuring embrace. "C'mon, guys, you can't hit some-one just because you don't like what they say."

"But he said—"

"Tommy's grandmother—"

When they both jumped to their own defense at the same time, he held up a hand, stopping them in their tracks. "Like I said, you can't hit someone just because you don't like what they say. Phoebe is *not* dying. If your friend's grandmother died, it wasn't because she was throwing up," he told Robby quietly. "She was throwing up because she had a bad appendix, and if the doctors didn't find that out in time, that's what killed her. Phoebe has the flu. Just like Becky did."

"And I didn't die," the little imp on his lap said tri-umphantly. "So see, you're wrong!" And with that an-nouncement, she stuck her tongue out at him.

Phoebe's early demise momentarily averted, Mitch couldn't remember the last time he wanted to laugh so badly. But Robby was puffed up like a thundercloud and still looked like he wanted to smack his sister one, and Mitch couldn't say he blamed him. If that wasn't just like a female—to rub it in when she was right!

What was needed was a quick distraction. Struggling to hold back a chuckle, he told Robby, "I noticed you have a lot of books in the bookcase in the hallway. Why don't you go pick out your favorite, and I'll read to you guys before you go to bed."

He didn't have to make the suggestion twice. Robby took off like a shot, with Becky right behind him, trying to talk him into picking out *her* favorite. Grinning, Mitch half expected him to choose something he knew his sister detested, but to his surprise, the boy selected something they both apparently liked. Returning to the living room, his brown eyes alight with eager anticipation, he handed the small book to Mitch. "This one's the best."

As the two kids took a seat on either side of him on the couch, Mitch studied the book in surprise. It was a homemade, hand-bound volume that was obviously well loved. Slightly tattered and soiled from handling, it was entitled *Professor Rat and the Case of the Lost Glasses* and written by P.S. Urant.

Snug against his side, Becky informed him solemnly, "We know what happens at the end but we won't tell you so you'll be surprised."

Amused, Mitch grinned. "I appreciate that, shortcake. I just hate it when someone spoils the ending for me."

Expecting the book to be some silly animal story that anyone over the age of nine could figure out by the end of the second page, he opened the book and began to read. By the end of the first paragraph, he was chuckling. A page and a half later, he was laughing out loud with the kids and thoroughly captivated.

The story was funny and intriguing and unlike any of the predictable children's books he'd read to his nieces and nephews. Professor Rat, the main character, had a wicked sense of humor that appealed to both children and adults, and that took no small amount of skill on the part of the writer. Not sure if P.S. Urant was a man or a woman, Mitch had to admit that he—or she—had a way with a phrase that was downright impressive.

And that didn't begin to describe the artwork. Old-fashioned, and reminiscent of Andrew Wyeth, with detail that was beautiful to behold, the pencil drawings spoke of an imagination that touched on wonder wherever it looked. There were angels magically peeking out from large, billowing clouds, and grinning wood nymphs hidden in the thick foliage of a shadowy forest. Professor Rat and his friends seemed to leap off the page, their faces brimming with personality and good humor. Without a single written word, the story could have been told with just the illustrations alone.

All too soon, the mystery of the missing glasses was solved and he reached the last page. Closing the book, he turned it over and studied the cover again. "I can see why this would be one of your favorites," he told Robby, "but it looks homemade. Where'd you get it?"

"From Aunt Phoebe," he said with a grin. "She always gives us a book for Christmas."

"She made it!" Becky piped up. "Isn't it beeeutiful?"

Mitch couldn't have been more shocked if she'd said Phoebe was a stripper at the Baby Doll House out by the airport. "What do you mean she *made* it? Are you saying she wrote it?"

She nodded, her eyes dancing happily. "Mmm-hmm. And she drawed it, too. See." Pointing to the author's name typed on the cover, she read, "P.S. Urant. That stands for Phoebe Smith, your aunt."

Stunned, Mitch stared down at the simple homonym and wondered that he hadn't seen it sooner. After all, he knew that she enjoyed writing—she spent hours every evening banging away on her old typewriter on the kitchen table. She had the drive—he'd never doubted that—but whoever wrote *Professor Rat* had a heck of a lot more going for them than mere drive. She had to see pictures in the clouds and hear the whisper of stories in the wind, then somehow transform all that to the written and illustrated page. Phoebe was a damn good secretary, but he'd never suspected she had that kind of talent and creativity.

Confused, he said, "I thought she wanted to write murder mysteries, not children's books."

"She does," Robby replied. "She just does this kind of stuff for the family and her friends every year for fun. She says when you give a gift, it should be a part of yourself, and that's what her stories are—a part of her heart. She's pretty cool, huh?''

Mitch had to agree with that. The lady was, in fact, one surprise after another. Just when he thought he had her figured out, she turned around and did something that blew his mind. And it wasn't even as if she was trying to fascinate him. She just seemed to do it naturally, and that was really starting to worry him. It was bad enough that he couldn't put that kiss out of his head. He liked everything about her, and that could only mean one thing. He was in trouble.

And there wasn't a damn thing he could do about it. Even if she hadn't had the flu, he'd given her his word she could stay there at least until Alice returned, and he had to stick by that. He didn't fool himself into thinking it was going to be easy. Because even now, when he'd seen her at her worst and she was so sick she could barely lift her head off the pillow, he couldn't forget the feel of her in his arms. God help him when she got back on her feet.

Trying not to think about that, he'd just put the kids to bed in his room and was going to check on Phoebe when the phone rang. When he quickly answered it and recognized his aunt's voice, he didn't know why he was surprised that she'd call tonight, of all nights. Alice had been trying to marry him off from the time he was twenty-five, and somehow she always seemed to know when he was thinking more than he liked to about a woman. If she found out he was actually living with one, regardless of how innocently, she'd have the wedding planned and the church reserved before he could blink.

Determined to make sure that didn't happen, he said easily, "Hello, Alice. I was just thinking about you. How's Glen?''

"That's just why I was calling, dear," she said somberly. "You know he hurt his shoulder in the accident. His doctor was hoping to avoid surgery, but today he decided he was just prolonging the inevitable. He operated this afternoon."

Mitch swore softly. "Damn. I'm sorry to hear that. How's Em holding up? She must be a basket case."

"She wouldn't leave Glen's side if she didn't have to for the baby," she said simply. "I don't know how she's kept from falling apart."

"She's a strong woman," Mitch replied. "I wonder who she gets that from."

Alice laughed, just as he'd known she would. It was a well-known fact in the family that while she might look as soft as a marshmallow, when push came to shove she could be as tough as nails. "She's a chip off the old block and you know it!" she chuckled. "So how are things back in S.A.? Have you found anyone to help you with the Social Club until I get back?"

He couldn't lie to her, but neither did he intend to tell her more about Phoebe than he had to. "Actually, I did," he said, then expertly steered the conversation in a different direction. "You'll be happy to know that the Johnsons moved in without a hitch, so we've got a full house again. They seem like a nice couple. In fact, they're so quiet, you hardly know they're here."

"I knew they would be perfect for us," she said in satisfaction. Then with a skill that was every bit as sharp as his, she brought the discussion back to where *she* wanted it. "Now about this woman…"

"What woman?"

"The one you hired to help you with Social Club business."

"I don't remember saying I hired a woman."

She made an impatient sound, one he remembered all too well from his childhood when he would try to talk circles around her and get caught every time. "Mitchell Ryan, you stop that!" she scolded affectionately. "You know very well you hired a woman, and she must be a pretty one or you wouldn't be trying so hard to change the subject. What's her name?"

Trapped, Mitch hesitated. He could have refused to answer, but that would never stop Alice from finding out what she wanted to know. She'd just call her old friend, Elizabeth Kincaid, in 2D, who would be only too happy to tell her that her nephew was living with a woman in *her* apartment! And if she didn't learn the truth from Elizabeth, Phoebe herself would tell her if she happened to answer the phone when Alice called. He could hear it now.

Wondering how she had boxed him into a corner with so little effort, he swallowed a groan and grudgingly admitted defeat. "Her name is Phoebe Smith," he grumbled. "And I wouldn't know if she's pretty or not—I haven't noticed."

"Ha!" she laughed. "The day you don't notice a woman's looks, you'll be six feet under. So she must be something special if you don't want to talk about her. Will I like her?"

"Don't even think about going there," he warned silkily. "You might as well know now that she's living here, but only because she got thrown out of her apartment, and that's something I don't have time to go into now. Just take my word for it that everything is aboveboard and there's nothing going on here that shouldn't. Okay?"

Far from intimidated, she teased, "Oh, really? Is that due to lack of trying on your part or hers? Don't answer that," she said quickly when he muttered a curse. "I'm just pushing your buttons, dear. I'll find out myself when I meet her. Have you taken her out yet?"

Rolling his eyes, he counted to ten. It didn't come close

to helping. "Don't start planning the wedding, sweetheart. It's not going to happen. I'm going back to Dallas just as soon as you get home."

That sobered her, but not because he'd finally gotten through to her. "I'm sorry, dear, but that's one of the reasons I called. Glen's surgery was much more complicated than the doctors expected, so his recovery is going to take longer than anyone first thought. I'm sorry, but it looks like I may not be able to get back there until after the first of the year. I hope that's not going to be a problem."

Stunned, what could he say? *Of course it's a problem! You've got to get back here before I do something stupid...like forget all the reasons why I can't get involved with her and give in to this crazy need she stirs in me!*

He could just hear Alice's reaction to that! She'd think he'd lost his mind. And he couldn't say he'd blame her. Compared to the problems Glen and Emily were going through, how he was going to manage to keep his hands off Phoebe seemed a very trivial thing that only a selfish bastard would worry about when the rest of the family was caught in the throes of a crisis.

"I've got everything here under control," he assured her gruffly. "You stay with Glen and Em as long as you need to."

She was burning up...again. Checking on Phoebe as soon as he hung up after talking to Alice, Mitch found her moaning softly and kicking at the covers he'd tucked around her earlier to keep her from getting chilled. He only had to touch the back of her hand to know that her fever was back and hotter than before. Frowning, he glanced at the bedside clock and swore. He'd given her some aspirins right before the kids took their baths. He couldn't give her any more for another two hours.

Worried sick, he jerked the covers off her in the hope that that would at least make her more comfortable, but she was lost to everything but the fever that raged in her body like a forest fire. Tossing and turning, she searched for a cool spot on the bed without success.

Just watching her made him ache. There was, he told himself grimly, no way he was going to just stand by and let her suffer for the next two hours. Not when he could do something about it. He had to get her temperature down. The quickest way to do that was, of course, to give her a cool bath, but he was afraid that in her delirium, she would misunderstand his intentions. And if he was honest with himself, he didn't know if he could handle stripping her naked without going quietly out of his mind. He'd just have to find another way to cool her down.

Covering her gently with the blanket again, he turned and strode out. When he returned a few minutes later, he had a bowl of tepid water and a washcloth. Setting it on the nightstand, he pulled up a chair next to the bed, eased the covers back from her feverish body, and gently began to sponge her down with the dampened cloth.

Being able to touch her, feel her, stroke her face and throat and arms under such circumstances, was, he discovered, the worst kind of torture. At the first brush of the cool washcloth across her hot forehead, she turned her face toward him in her sleep like a flower lifting its petals to the sun and never knew how her quiet sigh of relief struck him right in the heart. Against all his better judgment, his touch turned caressing.

Ruthlessly, he reminded himself that she was sick, that she would have blindly turned to any stranger who could offer her relief from the raging heat that seared her body from the inside out. But he couldn't quite bring himself to believe it, not when *he* was the one she turned to with complete trust in her sleep. Not when it was his touch that calmed and soothed her and seemed to ease some of her restlessness. Not when the mysterious, unexpected attraction that had sparked between them right from the beginning was even now, when she was hardly aware of his presence, stronger than ever.

As if she read his thoughts, she stirred then, and before he could draw back, he found himself caught in the trap of her gaze. Through pain-dulled eyes, she looked up at him and didn't seem the least surprised to find his hands on her. Instead of protesting as he'd expected, she glanced over at the kids' bunk beds and struggled to sit up when she saw that they were empty. "The kids—they should be in bed. Becky—"

"Is just fine," he assured her, pressing her gently back down onto her pillow. "She seems to be over the worst of it—she even ate supper, and she hasn't had a fever in hours. Robby is still healthy as a horse, too. They're sleeping in my room tonight so they won't disturb you." Taking her arm before she could guess his intentions, he pushed the sleeve of her nightgown up past her elbow, then gently stroked the damp cloth down her forearm to her fingers and back up again. "You're hotter than a firecracker, sweetheart. We've got to get this fever down."

Her heart slamming against her ribs, Phoebe felt the heat inside her instantly flare to flashpoint and was helpless to do anything about it. He was, she told herself, only trying to help her. He would have done the same thing for any other poor soul who was alone and sick and had no one else to help her, and she would be a fool to read anything else into it.

She knew that, accepted it, should have been grateful that she could trust him to be a gentleman. But her defenses were down, her head felt like it had been split wide open with a battle-ax, and her emotions were in a tangle. Tears stung her eyes, and she couldn't for the life of her blink them away. Horrified, she turned her face away. "I'm sorry to be such a bother," she said thickly. "I don't know what's wrong with me. I'm not usually such a crybaby."

"So, here's your chance," he teased gently. "Go ahead. Let her rip."

She laughed weakly—she couldn't help herself—and felt immeasurably better. "Maybe later. I don't think I've got the energy right now."

"Tomorrow then. You'll be feeling better then."

She could have told him she was already feeling better, much better than she should have when her temperature was still hotter than hell. And it was all because of him. Because of the touch of his hands on her neck as he swept her hair out of the way and gently stroked the dampened washcloth over her hot skin. Because of the surprising tenderness he showed her, without even seeming to realize it. Her pulse jumped in the hollow of her throat, her eyes locked with his, and suddenly the silence that fell between them was electric.

She knew the exact moment he realized that they were alone together in her bedroom, it was late, and he was running his hands all over her. He froze, the breath seemed to still in his lungs, and his gaze dropped to where his fingers had moved to the buttons of her gown. Slowly, his eyes lifted to hers, and the heat in them was scorching. Her heart jerked in her breast, and for the life of her, she couldn't come up with a single word of protest. She wanted him to touch her.

And he wanted to touch her. She could see it in his eyes. Then, in the next instant, he was shoving the washcloth in her hand and jumping to his feet. "Since you're awake, you'd better do this," he said hoarsely. And before she could protest, he was striding out of the room.

Chapter 8

The door slammed shut behind him, leaving her alone with her thoughts and her pounding heart. Foolish tears stinging her eyes, she opened her mouth to call him back, only to shut it with a snap. No, she thought, sniffing. Some things were better off left alone, and whatever had just passed between her and Mitch was definitely one of those things. She didn't need him, didn't need the feelings he stirred in her so effortlessly, didn't need him to take care of her. She'd been on her own for a long time now and she didn't mind being alone. In fact, she liked her independence. She could go where she wanted, do as she wished, and not have to answer to anyone. So if Mitch was under the mistaken impression that she was one of those clingy, desperate women who thought she was no-body if she didn't have a man to make her feel beautiful and wanted, he could think again. She liked her life just fine the way it was.

Satisfied that she'd finally put her feelings for him into

perspective, she collapsed back against the pillow and weakly tossed the washcloth into the bowl of water he'd set on the nightstand. She was still hot—her muscles ached from the fever—and she needed to get up and change into a cooler nightgown, but she couldn't find the strength. Exhaustion dragged her down, making it impossible for her to keep her eyes open. She'd just rest for a minute, she told herself with a tired sigh. Ten seconds later, sleep pulled her down into oblivion, and she never even knew it.

The night, however, was not a peaceful one for her. Somewhere in the back of her mind, she knew she slept, but she couldn't have said when. Dreams warped by fever haunted her. She thought Mitch came to her sometime in the wee hours of the morning, murmuring to her, coaxing her to swallow some aspirins as he once again wiped her hot face with a cool washcloth; but the images were dark and hazy and she couldn't be sure. She drifted back to sleep and wasn't aware of when Mitch left.

Hours later, she woke to find the apartment bathed in silence and the morning sun streaming through the open curtains of the bedroom window, hitting her right in the face. Blinking, she brought her hand up to cover her eyes and was stunned by the effort it took. Half asleep, she frowned, wondering what was wrong with her. Then sharp, disjointed images from yesterday flashed before her eyes, and she groaned. No wonder she was weak as a newborn kitten. She'd been sick as a dog!

Her head groggy, she lay perfectly still, afraid that if she moved just the slightest bit, the nausea would come roaring back. But when she carefully shifted to a more comfortable position, her stomach was thankfully quiet. Relieved, she pushed back the covers and stumbled to the bathroom to wash her face and take stock of her condition.

One look in the mirror and she winced. With her eyes

sunk in her head and her cheeks as pale as Ivory soap, she looked as if she'd been dead for three days. No wonder Mitch's face had been so grave when he'd tended her in the middle of the night. A zombie would have had more color in its face.

Her energy quickly deserting her, she tugged on a robe and stepped out of the bedroom into the hallway. Hushed stillness engulfed her, broken only by the muffled chiming of the antique grandfather clock from the Social Club's entrance hall, and she knew that she was alone. She didn't have to count the sonorous strikes of the hour to know that Mitch must have taken the kids to school. It was too early in the morning on a weekday for them to be anywhere else.

She should have gone back to bed. She needed the rest if she was going to get back on her feet as soon as possible. But even as she told herself that, she made the mistake of stepping into the kitchen. She took one look, and any thought of going back to bed flew right out of her head.

He'd done yesterday's dishes, just as he'd told her he would, but he'd cooked while she was laid up in bed, then hadn't gotten around to cleaning up his mess. Considering the disaster she herself had left the kitchen in when Becky was sick, she couldn't blame him for that—and she was used to having the sole responsibility of the kids. Returning from a business trip to suddenly find himself saddled with the care of two kids and a sick woman would have thrown any man. Mitch, though, had handled it well, in spite of the condition of the kitchen.

He'd handled *her* well.

Even now, she could still feel his hands on her, caring for her, setting her heart thudding. If she'd had the energy, that would have worried her. Their relationship was strictly business and it was going to stay that way. He was her boss, nothing more, the man who had offered her shelter because he was in a bind and temporarily needed her services. Just because he had impulsively kissed her, just because he'd taken care of her while she was sick with a gentleness that brought tears to her eyes, it didn't mean that there was anything between them. Life had just thrown them together in unusual circumstances. Once things returned to normal, once they were back on a businesslike footing, they would both breathe easier.

And the quickest way to do that, she told herself as she slowly began to clean the kitchen, was to get back on her feet again as soon as possible.

Stepping in the open doorway of the kitchen, Mitch couldn't believe his eyes. When he'd last checked on her before taking the kids to school, she'd been out like a light, which wasn't any wonder. Not when she'd spent the night fighting a raging fever and troubled dreams. When her fever broke around six and she finally fell into a deep, dreamless sleep, he'd expected her to be out at least until noon. Instead, barely two hours later, she was not only up, she was cleaning house! She could barely stand up. He knew for a fact that nothing she had put in her stomach over the last twenty hours had stayed down. What was she trying to do? Kill herself?

Muttering curses, he headed straight for her. "Dammit, woman, what the devil do you think you're doing? Don't you know you should be in bed?"

Startled, she jumped guiltily and whirled to face him. "I was just cleaning up—"

That was as far as she got. Reaching her in three long strides, he leaned down and scooped her up in his arms.

"Mitch!"

She was still gasping when he headed for the bedroom. "Stubborn woman," he grumbled. "I knew I shouldn't have left you alone. Mrs. Sanchez offered to sit with you while I took the kids to school, and I should have let her. She used to be a deputy with the sheriff's department. She would have made sure you stayed in bed where you belong.''

"I'm not a child," she sniffed, even as she flung her arms around his neck to hang on. "I don't need a keeper."

"Tell that to someone who hasn't held your head while you tossed your cookies," he retorted, scowling down at her. "In case you haven't noticed, you couldn't swat a mosquito right now and do any damage. You need to rest."

"But that's all I've been doing!" she cried. "I'm so tired of lying in bed, I ache. My stomach feels like my throat's been cut, and I'm so thirsty I could drink a gallon of juice. Please, Mitch, let me stay up for a while. Just long enough to eat a piece of toast."

He should have insisted she go to bed and let him bring her a tray, but when she was caught so close in his arms, her face lifted to his, she could have asked to walk on the moon and he would have been hard-pressed to deny her. God, she was beautiful! Even pale and weak, her face totally devoid of makeup and her hair tousled from the restless night she'd had, she had a natural beauty that punched him right in the gut.

Instinctively, his arms tightened around her, drawing her higher on his chest. It was her eyes, he thought even as reason started to slip beyond his grasp. A mystifying hazel—sometimes brown, sometimes green—that reflected her every thought, they caught a man's interest at first glance. And then there was her mouth. Soft, sensuous, unconsciously pouty, it all but begged for a kiss. Just one, he told himself as his blood warmed, then heated. That was all he wanted. It seemed like forever since he'd tasted her, and he only just now realized that ever since that first time, the need had been silently eating away at him, lingering in the shadows of his thoughts, haunting him. It was enough to drive a sane man right over the edge.

Just one kiss, he promised himself again. That's all it would take to convince him that he'd imagined the heat and sizzle of the last one. Then he'd get her out of his system and he could sleep at night without reaching for her. In the scheme of things, he didn't think that was so very much to ask for.

But even as he slowly started to lower his mouth to hers, his gaze met hers and he knew one kiss was never going to be enough. Not when her lips were already parted in anticipation and the same emotions that tore at him were there in her eyes, darkening them with a need she couldn't hide. She wanted him as badly as he wanted her.

And that scared the hell out of him.

He never remembered moving, but suddenly he was depositing her in a chair at the old oak kitchen table and backing away like she had cooties or something. He saw hurt and confusion flash in her eyes and knew his behavior was asinine, but he couldn't do a damn thing about it. Abruptly turning away, he yanked open the door to the refrigerator.

"You're right," he said gruffly. "You need to eat something. How about a scrambled egg and toast? That shouldn't bother your stomach and it won't take me two seconds to fix it."

Not waiting for a yea or nay from her, he quickly assembled everything he needed to cook her breakfast, then moved to the stove. Shaken, Phoebe all but dissolved in a puddle in the chair. Close. That was close. He'd almost kissed her, and she'd wanted him to. So badly that even now, when he'd clearly changed his mind, she ached with longing for the feel and taste of his mouth moving over hers.

How? she thought wildly. How had this happened? She was the one who had laid down the ground rules and made it clear that there would be nothing physical between them. He'd kissed her once. *Once,* for God's sake! And even then, she'd convinced herself that the unexpected attraction he held for her was just a passing fancy, something she could easily control. But there was nothing fanciful—or easily controllable—about the emotions churning inside her now. And she couldn't for the life of her explain how the man had brought her to this when she'd known him just a matter of days, and part of that time, he'd been in Dallas.

But even as questions bombarded her, the answer was right there in the hazy images that flashed before her eyes. Mitch sitting on the side of her bed in the middle of the night, murmuring to her, stroking her aching brow, wiping a cool washcloth over her hot skin again and again. He'd only been trying to bring down her fever and make her feel better, and he'd done that. But he'd also, in the process, become much more intimate with her than she'd realized and taught her body to recognize his touch.

Hot color flooding her cheeks, she realized, stricken, that she never should have let him take care of her. If she'd been thinking clearly, she would have asked him to call Dana to come and stay with her. Then he could have gone to a hotel with a clear conscience. But she'd been so sick, and turning to him for help had, at the time, seemed so right. And now she was paying the price.

Her stomach tied in knots, the last thing she wanted to do was eat when he set a plate of fluffy scrambled eggs and toast in front of her a few minutes later. Especially when he took a seat opposite her at the table and looked as if he intended to stay a while. Forcing a weak smile, she said, ''It looks wonderful, but I'm really not very hungry.''

"Just a bite," he coaxed. "Just a taste to whet your appetite."

Caught in the trap of his watchful gaze, she dutifully picked up her fork and reminded herself that she had to eat if she was going to get her energy back. She just didn't know how she was going to do it, not with him watching her. Her throat was tight, her heart pounding, her mouth dry. Sure she'd never be able to swallow, she scooped up a forkful of eggs and was surprised at how good it tasted. She took another bite, then a third. Before she realized it, she'd cleaned her entire plate.

When she blinked in surprise, he teased, "And you thought you weren't hungry. Would you like something else? How about a cup of coffee?"

Another time, she would have loved one, but just eating had used up her last reserves of energy. Suddenly her eyes were heavy, and all she could think about was lying down. Just for a minute. "I think I'd better lie down instead," she said, yawning delicately behind her hand. "I've suddenly run out of gas."

"Then I'll carry you back to bed," he said easily, and pushed to his feet.

"Oh, no! You don't have to do that. I'm feeling much stronger. Really!" she insisted when he stepped purposefully toward her. "There's no reason for you to carry me around like I'm some kind of invalid. I can walk."

"You've been pretty sick," he retorted, his eyes dark with determination. "I wouldn't want you to fall."

"I won't." Jumping up, her heart already thumping at the thought of him sweeping her up into his arms again, she quickly glided around the table, keeping it between them. "See...I'm just fine. I may not be ready for a marathon, but I can certainly make it to my room under my own steam. So if you'll excuse me, I'll do just that."

She didn't give him a chance to reply, but simply scurried out of the kitchen like a skittish virgin running from the devil himself. She didn't look back, but she didn't have to to know that he found her antics highly amusing. His chuckle followed her all the way down the hall to her room.

She meant to lie down for fifteen or twenty minutes. Instead, she discovered when she finally woke up, she slept for three hours! Stunned, she hurriedly dressed in real clothes for the first time in what felt like days, then made her way back to the kitchen. She was determined to do the dishes whether Mitch liked it or not, but he had already taken care of the problem. There wasn't a dirty glass or dish in sight.

She should have been relieved—doing the dishes was one of those never-ending household chores that she detested—but it irritated her that he'd so easily outmaneuvered her. She wasn't sick anymore—she could carry her own weight when it came to her share of the chores. And the sooner he understood that, the better.

Her chin set at a stubborn angle, she marched into the living room to tell him just that, only to discover that he'd left a note for her on his desk while she was asleep, saying he'd gone to the grocery store. He didn't expect to be gone long, but even if it turned out to be only ten minutes, that was long enough for her to get started on some of the paperwork she'd had to let slide when Becky was sick. Sinking down into the chair at her work area, she went to work.

She had organized the sketches she'd made for the remodeling of the attic and was going through the notes she'd made on three of the city's best contractors when she heard Mitch's key in the door, then his muttered curse as he stepped into the apartment and saw her working.

Even from fifteen feet away, she could feel his disapproval.

But it wasn't his displeasure that had her heart doing wheelies in her chest. It was the memory of that almost-kiss earlier, when he'd scooped her up to carry her to bed, that still had the power to make her breathless. She thought she'd dismissed it from her mind, but the second her eyes met his, she felt as if she was right back in his arms, her lips parted for a kiss she had no business wanting.

Later, she never knew where she found the nerve to coolly look him in the eye when her heart was pounding so loudly she was sure he could hear it. "I made some sketches of the attic while you were in Dallas that I'd like you to take a look at when you get a chance. If you like the designs, I'll fax them to the architect. I've checked out contractors, and Kurt Elkins seems to be the best, but Tim Brown and Jason Kidd also have good reputations. Any one of them will do a good job, so just tell me who you want to go with and I'll set it up. We need to get started if the job's going to be finished by Christmas."

"I thought you were going to take a nap," he said accusingly.

"I did," she said simply. "Now I'm awake. Can you look at these now?"

Daring to hold the sketches out to him, she gave him no choice but to take them. He wasn't, however, happy about it. Muttering a curse about stubborn women under his breath, he snatched them out of her hand. "I don't even know why you're worrying about this today," he grumbled to himself. "You've got no business being out of bed—"

That was as far as he got. Glancing down at the beautifully detailed drawings she'd done, Mitch lifted narrowed eyes to hers. "You did these?"

At his sharp tone, Phoebe felt her spirits sink. She didn't often share her artwork with anyone but family and close friends, especially when it was unsolicited, and Mitch had certainly never asked her to submit her own ideas for the attic. Her job was to coordinate the remodeling, nothing more, and she'd have done well to remember that.

Reminding herself not to take his criticism personally—everyone had a right to their own likes and dislikes—she forced a weak smile and tried to take the sketches from him. "I know you wanted the architect to submit some designs, but I thought it would save time if I could give him an idea of what I thought you were looking for. Obviously, I was wrong—"

"Wrong?" he repeated, scowling. "What the devil are you talking about? These are great!"

Surprised, she blinked. "You like them?"

Taken aback that she even had to ask, he retorted, "*Like* them? Of course I like them! This is just the kind of thing Alice and I have been talking about doing for years. Something open and modern, but still somehow Victorian. How did you know? We never discussed it."

"I don't know," she said with a shrug. "I went upstairs with my sketch pad the other day, and suddenly I could just see this wonderful apartment. The next thing I knew, my pencil was flying across the page."

Mitch didn't know why he was surprised. For years, Alice had entertained him and the rest of the family with tales of ghosts and visions and soul mates who inexplicably found each other at the Social Club, long after they'd sworn off love. The stories were as fanciful and whimsical as the house itself, the kind that diehard romantics gobbled up with a spoon. He'd always enjoyed them, but he'd never put much stock in the house having any kind of special powers. If Phoebe was on his wavelength about the remodeling it was simply because, when she was in the attic, she'd been inspired by the setting. It certainly had nothing to do with any kind of mystical connection between them.

Not that she would believe that, of course. He'd read *Professor Rat,* and that single story of hers had told him everything about her he needed to know. She believed in chivalry and romance, white knights and the poetry of the soul. Given the choice, she would choose enchantment over logic any day of the week.

Which was just one more reason why he had to fight the attraction that she stirred in him just by breathing, he reminded himself grimly. Because a woman like Phoebe would always want the fairy tale, and it was his experience that it wasn't really the prince that Cinderella wanted; it was the security of the castle and all the treasures that went with it. He really should have put some distance between the two of them and insisted she take it easy for the rest of the day. But she had to be sick of lying in bed, and she did look better than she had earlier. What would it hurt to let her stay up a little longer, if that would eventually help her get back on her feet?

"This place has a way of inspiring people," he said, returning his attention to her sketches. "You did a good job. Alice is going to love these. Go ahead and fax them to the architect. And don't worry about getting bids. If Kurt Elkins is the best, then go ahead and contact him to see when he can do the work. Oh, and fax another set of the sketches out to L.A. so Alice can see them. The last couple of weeks have been pretty rough on her emotionally, and this'll help take her mind off Glen's condition for a while."

He found his cousin Emily's fax number in Alice's private telephone directory, then left Phoebe to that task. He settled at his desk with the pile of mail that had accumulated while he was in Dallas. The first letter he picked up was from an old college friend who had a business proposal for him. Caught up in the details, he didn't notice that Phoebe had completed the faxes, and called Kurt Elkins's office. She was setting up an appointment to meet with him when her low-pitched words finally caught Mitch's attention.

"This afternoon would be great, Mr. Elkins, if you don't mind the short notice," she said into the phone. "How about four o'clock? Just buzz the office when you get here and I'll let you in. I hope it's not going to be a problem that the architect hasn't drawn up the plans yet, but I can show you sketches of what Mr. Ryan wants."

Stunned, Mitch couldn't believe his ears. Four o'clock! She was talking about *this afternoon!* "What the hell!" She hardly had the energy to walk from one room to the next, and she was making appointments, as if she was strong as a horse!

His jaw rigid, he reached over and snatched the receiver from her before she could guess his intentions. When she gasped and made a move to grab it right back, he shot her a narrow-eyed look that warned her not to even think about it, and said pleasantly into the phone, "Mr. Elkins? This is Mitch Ryan. I apologize for interrupting your conversation with Phoebe, but something's come up and she's not going to be able to see you this afternoon. Could we postpone your meeting until tomorrow at the same time? Good. She'll see you then. Thanks."

The second he hung up, Phoebe shot up out of her chair like she'd been launched from a rocket. It was a mistake, of course. She was still weak and her knees didn't want to support the sudden move, but she stiffened them anyway and glared down at him in outrage. "How dare you! You had no right to do that!"

"The hell I didn't," he retorted, and pushed to his feet

to give her back glare for glare. "In case you've forgotten, you work for me, lady, which means I give the orders around here. I let you do a little bit of paperwork because I knew you were tired of being in bed, but I draw the line at you meeting with a contractor and traipsing up to the attic when you can barely stand up. As of now, you're on sick leave until I say you're well enough to go back to work, so you might as well go back to bed. You're through for the day."

"You can't do that!"

She knew the second the words left her mouth that it was the wrong thing to say. He was a man who relished a challenge and she'd all but waved a red flag in his face. "Watch me," he growled, and grabbed her hand to lead her back to the bedroom like she was a wayward two-year-old.

"Mitch! Damn you, let go of me!"

"The hell I will. You're going to bed even if I have to put you there myself."

If she'd been thinking clearer, she wouldn't have given him the satisfaction of a struggle. But her pulse was racing, her heart in her throat, and neither condition had anything to do with the fact that they were arguing. It was just him...his closeness, the feel of his fingers wrapped around hers, the rightness of his touch. It thrilled her and overwhelmed her and made her want to run for her life, and at the same time she wanted to cling to him and never let go.

"No!" she snapped, tugging at her hand. "I'm not a child to be sent off to bed just because you think that's where I should be. Let go!"

Her energy quickly deserting her, she gave one last tug against his hold and almost broke free. Swearing, he tightened his fingers and jerked back, and in the process, almost accidentally, pulled her off her feet. Suddenly they were hip to hip and chest to chest. Startled, their mouths just inches apart and their breathing ragged, they froze.

Move! a voice cried inside her head, as her heart began to slam against her ribs. But she was caught in the trap of his eyes and her own need, and she knew she wasn't going anywhere. Not this time. "Mitch..."

That was all she could manage in protest, just his name, and then she hardly recognized the soft, sultry voice as her own. What had he done to her? "You know we can't do this," she protested weakly. "You agreed."

He didn't deny it. "No touching, no kissing, no hanky-panky," he quoted in a rough growl. Slipping his arms around her, he drew her up on her toes and intimately close. "Have I left anything out?"

Her throat dry, she wanted to say, *"And no needing,"* but it was already too late for that and they both knew it. Desperately, she searched her mind for another reason why they couldn't do this and blurted out in relief, "The kids! School's going to be out in fifteen minutes. I need to go get them."

"I'll do it," he promised. "In a minute. After I break rule number two. That's the one about kissing," he informed her with a wicked glint in his eyes, then covered her mouth with his.

She expected him to tease, to flirt, to slowly drive her out of her mind, but the second his lips touched hers, he was deadly serious. His hands tangled in her hair, a low groan ripped from his throat, and suddenly he was kissing her like a man at the end of his patience who had waited a lifetime to get her in his arms. Desire grabbed him, his control shattered, and hunger raged like a living thing, threatening to devour them both.

Whimpering, Phoebe couldn't have protested if her life had depended on it. With a single-minded determination that nearly destroyed her, he kissed her fiercely with lips and teeth and tongue, holding nothing back. And she loved it. Her mind clouded, rules, the kids, *everything* fading from her thoughts. She crowded closer and moved against him, murmuring his name, needing him more than she needed her next breath.

With a groan of approval, he drew her tightly against him and let his hands roam over her, loving the feel of her and how she fit in his arms in a way no other woman ever had. Every time he touched her, he found it harder to walk away. With a will of their own, his hands measured the slimness of her waist, the curve of her hips, the perfect roundness of her breasts. He wanted her naked, skin to skin, stretched out under him on his bed. It seemed to him now that he had wanted that from the day he'd first met her.

And he could have her now, a voice whispered in his head. She wanted him as badly as he wanted her—he could feel it, taste it. And for once, the conditions were right. She was feeling better, and there was no one to interrupt them. It couldn't be the slow loving he'd promised himself, but they had a few minutes before he had to go pick up the kids at school—

Abruptly brought back to earth with a bone-jarring thud, he froze at the thought, cursing himself. What the hell was he doing? She was barely recovered from the flu and all he could think about was getting her in bed before the kids came home. Was he out of his mind? Not twenty minutes ago, he'd gone over all the reasons why he had no business touching her, then the first chance he got, he'd kissed her like he was starving for the taste of her. And he was, dammit! She was under his skin, in his blood, driving him crazy. If he didn't get a grip on his emotions, he was going to rush her off to bed before he even realized what he was doing, and then the fat really would be in the fire.

His gut fisted with need, he determinedly put her from him, but even then, he had to take a step back to keep from reaching for her again when she swayed toward him. "My mother always said I was going to get burned one of these days if I didn't quit breaking the rules," he said hoarsely. "Looks like she was right. Go back to bed, Phoebe. I'm going to pick up the kids at school."

She could have stopped him with a word. It shook him to admit it, but that was all it would have taken to destroy his good intentions. Just one word from her. But she didn't say it. Instead, she stood where he left her, a hand pressed to her mouth—whether to capture the heat of the kiss they'd just shared or to hold back a plea for him to stay, he couldn't say—and watched him head for the door. He walked out of the apartment and shut the door behind him, and she never said a word. He should have been relieved. He wasn't.

Her knees weak, her body hot with a fever that had nothing to do with the flu, Phoebe hugged herself and watched the door shut behind him. She couldn't, she told herself, deny any longer that she was in serious trouble where that man was concerned. He'd come close to breaking every rule she'd laid down before she'd agreed to move in with him, and what had she done? She'd whimpered in pleasure and all but begged for more.

And it had to stop. Before she lost her head completely and gave her heart to a man who really didn't want it. She would talk to him, explain that she couldn't be intimate with him without falling in love with him, and he would agree that it would be better for both of them if there were no more touchy-feely scenes like the one they'd just shared. Then nobody would get hurt.

But when the kids came flying through the front door twenty minutes later, with Mitch right behind them, she

saw that she might have already waited too long. Robby
and Becky had, in the past, always been open and friendly
with people, but since the death of their parents they'd
become much more reserved with anyone who wasn't
family. They hadn't yet dropped their guard with
Mitch…or at least they hadn't before Phoebe had gotten
sick. But now it was obvious that things had changed.

"We're having a Thanksgiving program next Wednesday, then we get Thursday and Friday off," Becky told
Mitch excitedly. "I'm an Indian. I get to wear feathers
and beads and everything. Are you going to come?"

"Well, I don't know about that, little bit," he teased.
"Do I have to play the turkey?"

"No, you get to *eat* turkey," Robby explained, grinning. "We have the program in the morning and everyone
gets to stay for lunch."

Not blinking an eye, Mitch nodded. "Sounds doable to
me, sport. Just tell me the time and I'll be there."

"Then Thursday's Thanksgiving, and Friday there's a
parade on the river when all the Christmas lights get lit,
and Santa's going to be there!" Becky said in one long
breath, her blue eyes dancing with excitement. "We can
stand right on the back porch and wave to him!"

"You sure can," Mitch said, chuckling at her enthusiasm. "Then maybe on Saturday we can go to the mall
and you can tell him what you want him to bring you. Of
course, it's so early, you may not have even thought about
that yet—"

"I want a mountain bike!"

"Me, too! And a Pooh. A great big one that's as big
as I am so I won't get scared in the dark!"

"And a computer—"

"With lots of games!"

Chattering eagerly, they named toys that Phoebe hadn't
even heard of, then told Mitch all about Christmas in New

Orleans with their parents, and how once they even heard the reindeer on the roof. Their eyes were lit with memories and excitement, their smiles wide, and when Mitch sat down on the couch and they gathered around him, Becky climbed right up in his lap.

Stunned, Phoebe couldn't believe it. Somehow, while she was sick, the kids had come to trust Mitch and accept him in their lives. She didn't know how it had happened; she just knew it worried her to death. They'd already lost enough people that they cared about. She couldn't stand by and let them make friends with Mitch, then be hurt when he went back to Dallas for good.

Chapter 9

She meant to discuss the situation with him the first chance she got, but she could hardly do that in front of the kids. So she held her tongue and bided her time and waited until bedtime, only to receive another shock.

It was a nightly ritual, checking under the bed and in the closet for monsters that might have snuck in when no one was looking. From the first night the kids had come to live with her, it had been Phoebe's job to rout out all the mythical beasts and cyclopes from their hiding places and slay them dead. It was a charge she dearly loved, one that always had her fighting back a smile. But when bedtime rolled around, she wasn't the one the kids turned to to help them fight their fears.

Surprised, Mitch glanced quickly at Phoebe and had to see the hurt she couldn't quite hide. "I don't know, guys," he said, hanging back when they tried to tug him into their room to search for things that go bump in the night. "Your Aunt Phoebe's the dragon-slayer around here. I just helped out last night because she was off her feed, but she's feeling much better now. You'd better ask her.''

"But you're much bigger than she is," Becky pointed out reasonably. "What if there's a really big monster under the bed? He could eat Aunt Phoebe in one bite."

His mouth twitched into a rueful grin as he looked down at her from his six-foot-two height. "So if he's going to eat somebody, you'd rather he eat me, huh? Is that what you're saying?"

"But he wouldn't," Robby argued, flashing his dimples at him. "How could he? One punch and you could knock him out of his shoes. Aunt Phoebe's a girl." He cast an apologetic look at Phoebe, but facts were facts. "She can't hit that hard."

Phoebe couldn't dispute that. She'd never developed a knockout punch. Then again, she'd never thought she needed one, especially for monsters that didn't even exist. But that, she realized, wasn't the issue here. The kids felt comfortable with Mitch and trusted him to protect them. To be hurt by that was ridiculous. After all, it wasn't as if they were choosing him over her. They just wanted to include him in their nightly ritual.

"Robby's right," she said quietly. "I'm better at handling gremlins and imps. And if it's all the same to you, Mitch, I'd just as soon you handle the big dragons and monsters. They've got fleas and really stinky breath, and it's a nasty job. Not that I can't do it," she assured him quickly. "But since I've been sick and everything, it would be nice if you could take over for me until I get my strength back."

Her gaze met his unflinchingly, and there was no doubting her sincerity. Still, he hesitated, his eyes searching hers before he finally nodded, a half smile curling his mouth. "Sure. I can do that—just until you get your strength back, of course. So who's going to back me up in case I get in trouble? Becky? How about you, Robby? You're not going to let me check out your closet all by myself, are you?''

Not the least afraid of being thought a coward, Becky took a quick step back. Robby, on the other hand, was more than willing to play the man of the family—as long as Mitch led the way. His chin up and his shoulders back, he was two steps behind him as they headed into the bedroom.

There were no dragons, of course. No monsters in hiding, waiting for the chance to jump out of the closet and grab a sleeping child in the middle of the night. Phoebe knew that deep down, the kids knew that, but after all that they had been through, they needed that extra little bit of reassurance that they were safe. Once they had that, they were always able to go to bed without a whimper of protest; and tonight was no different. As soon as Mitch gave the all-clear, they gave both him and Phoebe each a big hug and scampered off to bed as if they didn't have a care in the world.

As soon as the bedroom door shut behind them, Phoebe found herself alone with Mitch for the first time since he'd kissed her like he couldn't get enough of her, then left her to pick up the kids at school. And suddenly the apartment seemed too small, the living room too intimate. The air was humming with expectation and she couldn't for the life of her say why. Skittish, feeling like her heart was going to pound right out of her chest, she said quickly, ''I think I need a snack,'' and headed for the kitchen like the hounds of hell were after her.

Too late, she realized that she'd made a mistake. He followed her, of course, and seemed to take up all the air in the kitchen just by stepping across the threshold. ''I'll get it,'' he told her, and moved to intercept her when she reached for a bowl in the cabinet. His shoulder bumped hers, their hands collided, and without quite knowing how it happened, they were kissing-close.

Startled, Phoebe told herself to move, but there was no place to go. The L shape of the counter was at her side and back, and Mitch blocked any other escape. His eyes met hers, time ground to a stop, and all she wanted to do was step into his arms. Panicking, she blurted out, "We need to talk."

"All right," he agreed. "What's on your mind?"

She expected him to step back and give her some space, but instead, he planted a hand on the counter on either side of her and gave her his full, undivided attention. Effectively trapped, Phoebe not only forgot why she had come into the kitchen, but what she wanted to say to him, as well. "Mitch—"

With her heart thundering like a 747 racing down the runway for liftoff, that was all she could manage—just his name. Helplessly, she stared up at him, her mind blank, and watched as amusement spilled into his blue eyes, making them dance.

His lips twitching, he arched an eyebrow at her. "Well? What'd you want to talk about?"

She should have told him about the kids and her concern that they would grow to depend on him and then he would walk out of their life. But all she could think of was how close he was and kisses that never should have happened, so she said the one thing she shouldn't have said. "Us."

The minute the damning word popped out, she would have given anything to take it back. Dear God, what was she thinking of? There was no *us!* Not with Mitch.

Grinning broadly, he reached out and traced the blush that colored her cheeks. "Us, as in you and me? Why, Phoebe, I didn't know you cared."

He was teasing—she knew that—but still she couldn't stop from stuttering, "I—I don't! I mean—dammit, Mitch, you've got to stop that!"

"Stop what?" As innocent as a choir boy, he tucked a wayward curl behind her ear.

"That!"

Catching his hand, she pushed it away, only to have his fingers twine with hers as naturally as if they'd been holding hands all their life. God, why did it have to feel so right? As if he was a part of her that had always been missing until now? As if the whole world could be falling down around her ears and she would be all right as long as she had him to hold on to? What had he done to her? When? And how could it end in anything but heartbreak? He was an incredibly attractive, sexy man, but he'd told her himself that it was his money that women found irresistible. She wasn't looking for a man, but if she had been, why would he think she was any different from any of the other women who'd shown an interest in him over the years? Especially considering her financial situation. He knew better than anyone that she didn't have two nickels to rub together.

Unable to stop her fingers from clinging to his, she said huskily, "We had an agreement."

"True."

Agitated, she hardly heard him. "You promised—"

"That there would be no 'hanky-panky,'" he finished for her easily. "I know. And I'm a man of my word."

That was such an outrageous fabrication that Phoebe could do nothing but gape at him. "I can't believe you said that with a straight face! Just this afternoon you... you..."

"What?"

"Kissed me!" she blurted out, exasperated.

"So?"

"*So?* Dammit, Mitch, you promised!" She saw the laughter in his eyes then, the wicked mischief, and punched him in the shoulder. "Oh, you! Dammit, I'm serious! You can't just go around kissing me whenever you like."

Enjoying himself, he said baldly, "I don't know why not. You're a damn good kisser."

"But you agreed there'd be no hanky-panky!"

"And there hasn't been." Pretending confusion, he frowned and edged closer. "Maybe you'd better clear up just what you consider hanky-panky. It might have a different definition in Dallas."

"Mitch! You know perfectly well what it means."

He did, of course, but he couldn't pass up the opportunity to tease her a little more. Struggling to hold back a smile, he told her solemnly, "I know what I think it means, but you could have a different opinion. So just to make sure there are no misunderstandings later, we'd better get this cleared up right now. No," he said quickly when she looked as if she was going to object, "it's all right. I don't mind explaining myself. When two people make a deal, it's always best to make sure they're on the same page. Especially when they're living together."

Leaning down before she could guess his intentions, he nuzzled her neck playfully. "What about this? Is this hanky? Or panky? Hmmm? Whaddaya think?"

She should have pushed him away—he half expected her to—but when he trailed kisses down the side of her neck, her breath hitched in her throat and she just seemed to go boneless on him. Groaning, he gathered her closer. "God, I love it when you do that! It's so damn sexy."

Tilting her head to the side to give him better access, she couldn't keep her eyes open—or remember why this conversation was so important. "I can't…think. Maybe you shouldn't…"

"We'll go over that one again in a minute," he promised huskily, smiling as he took her hand. "What about touching? Nothing intimate," he assured her when she lifted eyes dazed with need to his. "Nothing dangerous. Just simple, innocent touching. The kind of thing strangers do every day of the week when they shake hands."

He made it sound easy and natural, uncomplicated, but there was nothing innocent about the way he lingered over her hand. Gazing into her palm as if it held the answer to every question he'd ever had about her, he stroked and caressed and seduced with a touch that was featherlight, setting every nerve ending in her body tingling. Then, when she was trembling, he did nothing more than slowly, gently trace the curve of her lifeline and her heart jumped in her breast. With a will of their own, her fingers curled around his.

"Mitch, please..."

Flushed, her throat tight and a need she couldn't control heating her blood, she meant to tell him he had to stop, but even as she opened her mouth to do just that, it was already too late. "And then there's kissing, of course," he murmured seriously, turning his attention to her mouth. "Most people would probably say that has to be hanky-panky, but there're all kinds of kisses. There are hello and goodbye kisses," he continued huskily, giving her two chaste kisses on the mouth. "And kisses on the cheek and forehead and even on the nose. People do it all the time and nobody thinks a thing of it."

He had a point, one she had to agree with. "I don't have a problem with that—"

"Then there are the kisses between a man and a woman," he growled softly. "The kind a man gives a woman when he first meets her and he's attracted to her, but he doesn't want to scare her off. You know the kind." Just to make sure there was no misunderstanding, he pressed a gentle, closed-mouth kiss to her lips, giving her just a touch of hunger, of heat. Murmuring her name, he lifted his mouth from hers, but only to change the angle of the kiss. Once, twice, as if he had all the time in the world, he caressed her lips with soft, nibbling kisses that teased and coaxed and seduced.

Her hands crawling up his chest to cling to him, her heart pounding and her head spinning, Phoebe knew she should have stopped him then, while she still could. But as he drew back just a fraction of an inch and his eyes, dark with intent, met hers, she knew it was already too late. He was going to kiss her, really kiss her, and this time there would be no holding back. Helplessly, she parted her lips in anticipation.

"And then, there's the kind that a man gives a woman when all he can think about is getting her in his bed," he whispered in a husky voice that had gone deep and rough with need. "The kind that turns the blood hot and sets the sheets on fire and makes you forget your own name. Most people would say that one goes way past hanky-panky, but I think it's an individual thing. What about you? Do you think this is going too far?"

As quick as a conquering knight would have claimed the damsel in distress as his prize, he buried his hands in her hair, turned her mouth up to his, and devoured her. There was no other way to describe it. His tongue dueled and played with hers, demanding a response that she couldn't have denied him if her life had depended on it. Moaning, she pressed closer and kissed him back until she did, indeed, forget her own name.

Time ceased to have meaning. Minutes passed, possibly hours, and she couldn't summon the strength to care. Then, before she was ready for him to release her, he slowly, reluctantly lifted his mouth from hers. Caught up in the taste and feel and wonder of him, she opened dazed eyes to discover that he'd been just as caught up in the kiss as she had. His usually neat hair was mussed from her hands, his cheeks were flushed with passion, giving him a boyish look that just turned her heart upside down in her chest. Lost to everything but her aching need for him, she tightened her arms around his neck and went up on her tiptoes to kiss him again.

Groaning, Mitch would have liked nothing more than to sweep her off to his bed and lose himself in her for the rest of the night. Just one night, dammit! That was all he asked for now. But in spite of his teasing, he hadn't forgotten that he had agreed to the conditions she had laid down before she moved in, and even if it killed him—and the way he felt right now, it just might—he was going to stand by his word.

But God, she didn't make it easy for him! She was soft and clingy in his arms, her mouth hot and hungry under his, and he wanted her so badly he could taste it. Desire clawing at him with sharpened claws, it took all his strength of will just to wrench his mouth from hers and put her from him.

When she moaned in protest and reached for him, he groaned, the sound that was torn from his throat midway between a strangled laugh and a growl of pain. "Sweetheart, you're killing me! We can't do this. In case you've forgotten, we have an agreement."

Confused, she frowned, struggling against his hold. "So? We don't have to talk about that now. I just want you to kiss me."

"You're the one who said no hanky-panky," he reminded her huskily. "If I keep kissing you, you're going to get a heck of a lot more than that, honey. You're going to end up in my bed. Is that what you want? If it's not, you'd better tell me now because I don't want you to have any regrets when I make love to you. The choice is yours, but you've got to tell me what you really want. I won't guess, not about this.''

He wouldn't sweep her off to bed in the heat of passion, not this first time, and he knew the second she realized it. The passion abruptly cleared from her eyes and a slow flush rose in her cheeks. She was embarrassed, and that was the last thing he wanted.

Cursing himself for not handling the situation better, he blocked her path before she could edge around him and escape into her room. "That doesn't mean I don't want you," he told her roughly. "You have to know I do. Hell, half the time, I can't keep my hands off you. But I won't take advantage of you, Phoebe. This has to be what you really want, not just something that happens in the heat of the moment."

He should have let her pass then, but he couldn't. Not yet. Pulling her close, he gave her one last heated kiss that left no doubt in either of their minds just how badly he wanted her. How he found the willpower to let her go after that, he never knew, but suddenly he was releasing her and turning her toward her bedroom. "Go think about it," he said hoarsely, giving her a gentle push. "We'll talk about it tomorrow."

If she'd have said one word, if she'd so much as hesitated, he never would have been able to let her go. But she didn't. Without ever looking back, she hurried out of the kitchen, and it was all he could do not to call her back. Whatever possessed him to turn her down?

Phoebe spent the rest of the night dreaming of him, aching for him, wondering how she was going to ever face him again in the morning. But thanks to the kids and the return to their normal routine, that was actually easier than she'd expected. Mornings were always a madhouse, and this one was no different. The phone started ringing at seven for Mitch, Becky couldn't find any bows for her hair, and Robby had misplaced his homework. As usual, both kids moved in slow motion, and it took a decided effort on Phoebe's part just to light a fire under them. Urging them to hurry, she found an appropriate bow for Becky in the kitchen pantry, of all places, dug Robby's homework out of the trash where he'd inadvertently thrown it, and still somehow managed to get breakfast down them and herself dressed before she had to rush them off to school. And all the while, thankfully, Mitch was on the phone.

She would, she knew, be unable to avoid working with him when she returned to the Social Club, and she was dreading it. How could she look him in the eye after last night? She'd all but begged him to make love to her, and it was only because he'd stuck to the original terms of their agreement—an agreement that *she* had insisted on!—that she hadn't woken up in his bed that morning. Dear God, what must he have thought of her?

I won't take advantage of you… This has to be what you really want, not just something that happens in the heat of the moment… Think about it. We'll talk in the morning.

His husky words echoing in her ear as she approached the front door to the Social Club, she felt her heart skip a beat and told herself that there was really nothing to talk about. Nothing had changed just because he'd kissed her senseless last night. He was still a man who didn't trust easily, still a man who was only in her life temporarily. If she didn't want him to break her heart, she'd do well to remember that.

Her shoulders back, she thought she was ready for anything when she stepped into the apartment. Then her eyes landed on the suitcase Mitch had set by the front door, and her heart jerked to a stop in midbeat. Surprised, she looked up and found him at his desk, packing contracts into his briefcase. "You're leaving?"

He nodded, grim-faced. "I've been getting calls all morning about Applebee. He found out one of my companies has been working on a way to extract oil from old, abandoned wells, and he's been buying up leases in West Texas as fast as he can snatch them up. If I don't get out there and damn quick, he's going to cost me a bundle."

"So where are you going?"

"Midland, Lubbock, El Paso. God knows where else. I left an itinerary on the desk with my cell number. If you can't reach me and something crops up that you don't know how to handle, call the office in Dallas. I may have to make a few trips back there anyway, depending on how things go. And even if I don't, Jennifer will know where I am at all times. She can track me down if you need me."

"It sounds like you're going to be gone a while."

His mind already on other things, he shrugged. "Probably a week, maybe longer. It just depends on how much trouble Applebee's caused," he replied as he shut and locked his briefcase. "Why? Is that a problem?"

Yes! she wanted to cry, and was stunned by the need to ask him to stay. What in the world was wrong with her? He'd hired her for this very reason—because he'd known business would crop up that would take him out of town—and considering what had happened between them last night, she should have been relieved that he'd be half a state away for at least a week. She wouldn't have to worry about him touching her, kissing her, making her want something she couldn't have.

But the emotion squeezing her heart had nothing to do with relief.

"No," she hedged. "It's just that I'm meeting with Kurt Elkins this afternoon to see about when he can start working on the attic. I thought you might want to be here. And then Thanksgiving is Thursday, and Friday night—''

"Is the lighting of the Christmas lights on the river,'' he finished for her, "and I promised the kids we'd watch it from the back porch. Damn!'' he swore softly. "I completely forgot!''

He sounded as disappointed as she knew the kids were going to be and found herself wishing that just this once, he would say to hell with business. But that wasn't going to happen. She and the kids weren't his family, and she couldn't expect him to turn his back on business just because the kids wanted to spend the holiday with him.

"I'll explain the situation to the kids,'' she said quietly. "They're old enough to understand that business can't always take a back seat to a holiday. They'll be okay with it. And their grandparents are going to fly over from New Orleans to see them if Ward is feeling up to it, so they'll be excited about that.''

"And what about you?'' he asked, studying her. "How do you feel about that? The kids lived with them before they moved in with you, didn't they? If the grandfather is feeling better, is there a possibility that he and the grandmother are going to want them back?''

"Oh, no. Louise and I discussed that when she sent the children to me, and considering Ward's heart condition, we both agreed that the kids needed to be with me. So, no, there's no tug-of-war between us for the kids. And since my parents both died before the kids were ever born, she and Ward are the only grandparents they've ever known. I'm thrilled they're coming, and so are the kids. They don't have much family left.''

"I'd still like to be here. And everything's going to be shut down on Thursday anyway, so it's not like I'm going to get any work done. Don't tell the kids in case I can't pull it off, but I may be able to juggle a few things and fly back in late Wednesday. I'll have to see how things go.''

"And what about Kurt Elkins? Did you want to meet with him?"

"No, you know what I want. Go ahead and schedule the work as soon as he can get to it."

With that cleared up, there was no longer any reason to linger. His suitcase and briefcase were packed and his corporate jet was scheduled to leave in a little less than an hour. He should have left for the airport ten minutes ago, but he couldn't bring himself to leave her. Not yet. They hadn't had time to talk, to discuss last night, to so much as touch this morning. And suddenly he knew he was never going to be able to walk out the door without touching her one more time.

"I have to leave," he said gruffly, and stood right where he was.

"Do you want me to take you to the airport?"

"No. I don't like public goodbyes."

Her eyes widened at that, her cheeks grew pink, and he had to hold her. Snatching up his briefcase, he set it next to his suitcase by the front door, then he was striding back to her to take her into his arms.

"Mitch!"

"I never expected it to be this hard to leave you," he growled, and gave her a hard, too-brief kiss that left them both wanting more. Then, while he still could, he released her, grabbed his bags, and walked out.

Forty-five minutes later, when his corporate jet lifted into the air, he could still taste her on his tongue. Trying to put her out of his head, he turned his attention to work and got on the phone with leaseholders and their lawyers in an effort to win them away from Applebee before the old goat cost him a small fortune. It was what he did best, making deals, and he usually thrived on it. But even as his jet raced toward Midland and he set up meetings within fifteen minutes of his estimated arrival time, Phoebe and the kids kept drifting into his thoughts.

And the situation only got worse as the day progressed. He hit the ground running and made what concessions he had to to get the leases he needed, but it wasn't easy. His concentration was shot, and at the most inopportune times, he found himself thinking about the feel of Phoebe in his arms, the kids and their reaction when they learned he probably wouldn't make it back in time for Thanksgiving, their faces when they talked about Christmas and what they wanted Santa to bring them.

When he met with Chase Walker, one of the biggest ranchers in the state, to discuss wells that had long since been abandoned because of their lack of productivity, he should have been thinking of nothing but profit margins and the bottom line. Instead, he couldn't forget the look on Becky's face when she'd solemnly asked him to check her closet for monsters. She'd trusted him to keep her safe, and in the process, she'd stolen his heart right out of his chest.

"Mitch? Are you with us? I thought you wanted the figures from the last year that the big well on Monument Hill was in production."

Jerking his attention back to Chase, he grimaced and took the computer printout the other man held out to him. "Sorry about that. My mind wandered there for a minute. Now, about Monument Hill…"

It was a long day. Although he never saw him, he knew Applebee was in the area—he was too good a businessman to be anywhere else—and he had to move fast if he was going to beat him at his own game. So he lined up meetings with a dozen ranchers, sealed deals with a handshake that was as good as a signed contract in that area of the country, and immediately moved on. By the time he finally checked into the airport La Quinta, it was going on nine o'clock at night and he couldn't remember the last meal he'd eaten. But he'd salvaged eight of the twelve leases that had been in jeopardy, and that was more than he'd expected to be able to save when he'd left San Antonio that morning.

All in all, he should have been happy with the day's work. Tomorrow morning, he would fly to Lubbock and the game would start all over again. There wasn't a doubt in his mind that he would win, but when he walked into his rented room and shut the door behind him, the satisfaction he should have felt in knowing that just wasn't there.

And for the life of him, he didn't know why. This was what he did, dammit! He'd been on a thousand such business trips, stayed in so many hotel rooms that they'd all begun to look alike. Normally, he would have gone over the figures he would need for the following day, then grabbed a shower and gone to bed without even thinking about it. But not tonight. Tonight, the room was too quiet, too empty, and it was the last place he wanted to be.

Restless, wondering what the hell was wrong with him, he turned on the TV, but the medical drama that was the hit of the fall season held little appeal. Disgusted, he was about to turn it off when the phone rang. Figuring it was his pilot calling to confirm what time he wanted to leave in the morning, he picked it up and said, "Get us out of here by seven-thirty if you can, Joe. I've got a nine-o'clock meeting in Lubbock and I can't be late."

The caller, however, wasn't his pilot. Sudden silence echoed with surprise, then a sweet, childish voice said hesitantly, "Mitch? Is that you?"

Stunned, he almost dropped the phone. "Becky?"

"Yes," she giggled. "Are you surprised?"

That was putting it mildly. "You knocked me right out of my shoes, honey. How'd you know where I was?"

"Aunt Phoebe has your i-ten…i-ten-ry," she finally managed. "You know—that piece of paper that says where you're supposed to be. She showed me the numbers to punch so I could call you and tell you good-night. Did you check your closet for monsters?"

"Actually, I didn't," he said, grinning. "But I'll be sure and do that before I go to bed. Did Phoebe scare off all of yours for you?"

"Yep," she said happily. "She told them all to leave, and they did. Just like that! That's 'cause she's the boss. Did you know that? They have to do what she says."

"They'd better if they know what's good for them," he chuckled. "She won't take any nonsense from them now that she's feeling better. Is everything else okay?"

She told him about school and the Christmas program she and the rest of the kindergartners were already practicing, then, in the background, he heard Phoebe tell her it was time for bed. "I have to go now. Nighty-night, Mitch. Don't let the bedbugs bite."

"I won't, sweetheart. You sleep tight."

He half expected Phoebe to come on the line then, but Becky hung up, and he figured it was just as well. Because the second he heard Phoebe call out that it was bedtime, he knew why he was so restless. He missed her—and the kids—like hell.

And the situation didn't improve with the passage of time. For the next three days, he barely had a moment when he wasn't meeting with someone or racing to keep an appointment. He should have been too busy to think of anything but work, but Phoebe and the kids were right there with him every step of the way. Then, when he checked into another La Quinta, this time in El Paso,

Robby called just to tell him that they missed him and hoped he'd be home soon.

And it tore him up. If things continued the way they were, this would be the most successful business trip he'd ever taken, but he couldn't remember the last time he'd been so miserable. He was doing the right thing, the responsible thing as far as business was concerned, but for reasons he refused to examine too closely, he didn't care if he won or lost to Applebee. He just wanted to go home, and he didn't mean Dallas.

He still had business to conduct, however, and though he'd tried to arrange things differently, meetings were scheduled for as early as nine o'clock the Friday morning after Thanksgiving. He told himself it would be stupid to fly to San Antonio just for a meal, then turn around and fly right back to West Texas that evening. The practical thing would be to stay and try to wrap things up early on Friday so he could make it back to town for the river-lighting festival. Then, with business out of the way, he could spend the entire weekend with Phoebe and the kids.

The decision made, he spent Wednesday morning in meetings, just as he'd planned. But as the day lengthened, he knew he wasn't going to be able to do it. He couldn't go back on his word to the kids. This might be the only holiday he could have with them, and he wasn't spending it halfway across the state from them. Not when he could negotiate some of the leases over the phone and handle the rest in whatever meetings he was able to cram into the rest of the day. He would get into San Antonio late, but better late than never.

He told himself he was doing it for the kids, but when he reached for the phone and started rescheduling meetings, he knew it was Phoebe he wanted to surprise.

Chapter 10

He wasn't going to make it.

Listening to the grandfather clock in the foyer strike twelve Wednesday night, Phoebe accepted the inevitable. Mitch had warned her that he might not be able to make it back by Thursday, but deep down inside, she'd secretly hoped that he would. She'd told herself it was for the kids' sake—she hated for them to be disappointed—but now, as each slow, deep strike of the clock echoed hollowly throughout the sleeping house, she was forced to admit that she'd stayed up because she hadn't been able to let go of the hope that he might blow in with the norther that swept through the city an hour ago.

She should have known better. She had his initial itinerary; she knew he'd planned to canvas whole sections of West Texas and the panhandle. But there were some meetings that he wasn't able to schedule before he left, and those might have to wait until after the holiday. Then there was the weather to consider. The norther that had sent the temperature plummeting in San Antonio had brought ice and dangerous travel conditions to North and West Texas. According to the last weather report she'd caught on TV, airports in that part of the state were forced to shut down hours ago. Even if Mitch had intended to make it back, he couldn't have.

It wasn't the end of the world, she told herself as she switched off the living-room lights and made her way to bed in the dark. As they'd hoped, Ward and Louise were flying in from New Orleans in the morning, and the kids were thrilled. There would be a lot of love and laughter and the stuff memories were made of, not to mention enough food to feed an army. The only thing missing would be Mitch.

She tried to convince herself she'd be too busy to even notice that he wasn't there, but the ache that lodged where her heart normally was told her it was too late to lie to herself. Somehow the man had become much more important to her than she ever should have allowed, and there didn't seem to be a thing she could do about it. Except hurt.

An hour after she slipped between the sheets, she was dreaming of him when she woke with a start, her heart, for no explicable reason, pounding wildly. Still half asleep, she rolled over and buried her face in her pillow. A split second later, something fell with a soft thud in the living room.

She froze, her blood suddenly cold in her veins. It was just her imagination, she told herself. But, much as she wanted to believe that, she knew she hadn't imagined anything...especially the muffled curse that sounded like a shout in the quiet of the night. Someone was in the living room, and it wasn't the kids.

Trembling, she soundlessly sat up in the darkness, her widened eyes trained on the closed bedroom door. She had to do something! But what? The phone was in the living room, so she couldn't call the police, and she'd never be able to get the kids out of the apartment without alerting the intruder to the fact that he didn't have the place to himself. And right now, that was the best weapon she had. If she could surprise him, catch him off guard in the dark, she might be able to run him off before he realized that the only thing standing between him and an apartment full of treasures, most of which belonged to Alice, was a terrified woman dressed in nothing but a Mickey Mouse nightshirt who didn't have a single brave bone in her body.

Searching her mind for anything she could use as a weapon, the only thing she could come up with was Robby's baseball bat. Solid wood, it could, she knew, do serious damage if she swung it with all her strength; and he kept it propped right in the corner, next to his bed. Soundlessly, she slipped out from beneath the covers and reached for it in the dark. When she encountered nothing but emptiness at first, she started to panic, but then her fingers closed around the familiar, reassuring weight of it, and she sighed in relief. Thank God! If Robby had moved it, she didn't know what she would have done.

Holding her breath, the bat clutched tightly in her hands, she cautiously approached the closed bedroom door and pressed her ear against it, listening. In the living room, nothing moved. Her heart thundering, Phoebe didn't fool herself into thinking that the intruder had left. He was out there—she could almost feel him in the hushed expectancy that vibrated on the night air. She hoped he was enjoying himself, whoever he was, because in about ten seconds flat, she was going to make him regret he'd ever even heard of the Lone Star Social Club, let alone that he'd broken into it.

Later, she never remembered easing open the bedroom

door or slipping out into the shadowy hallway. Suddenly she was standing in the living room without any memory of how she got there, her eyes locked in growing horror on the huge, towering shadow of a man who appeared to be heading right for her in the dark. Instinctively, she lifted the bat and drew it back for a full, no-holds-barred swing.

In the next instant, the lights flared on, the bat was jerked out of her hands, and Mitch was glaring at her incredulously. "What the hell are you doing?" he growled. "Trying to take my head off?"

Stunned, she went weak with relief. A split second later, his accusing tone registered. "What am *I* doing?" she echoed indignantly. "What does it look like I'm doing? I heard someone moving around out here in the dark, knocking things over, and I came out to brain them one! Dammit, you scared me to death!"

"I scared *you?* You weren't the one who was almost on the wrong end of that bat! Dammit, woman, were you trying to get yourself killed? What if I really had been a burglar? I could have had a gun!"

"You didn't."

"But you didn't know that when you came out here with that damn bat. You could have been hurt! Why didn't you call the police?"

"How? There's no phone in the bedroom!"

"So call the phone company and have one put in!"

"I wouldn't need to if you'd let a person know you were coming."

"I told you I'd try—"

"Then didn't bother to speak to me the rest of the week. The kids called you and you didn't even ask about me. I thought you might have decided that it would be better if we didn't see each other for a while. It hurt, dammit!"

"Why would you even think such a thing? I missed you like hell!"

Standing toe to toe, their voices raised in anger, they threw the words at each other like darts and didn't realize what they were both admitting to until it was too late. Hearts stopped in midbeat, and suddenly, the silence was deafening.

His eyes locked with hers, Mitch asked cautiously, "Did I just say what I thought I said?"

She nodded. "I think so. Did I?"

For an answer, he reached for her. "You're driving me crazy," he growled roughly as he pulled her into his arms. "You know that, don't you? No matter how hard I try, I can't get you out of my head."

That was an admission that he knew he was going to regret later, but for now, he didn't give a damn. Nothing mattered but holding her, getting his hands and mouth on her, giving in to the need that had been with him so long now that he couldn't remember a time when he *hadn't* wanted her. Groaning her name, he tightened his arms around her, lifted her completely off her feet, and laid a kiss on her that curled her toes.

"We shouldn't—"

"I know. Just let me—"

Wrenching his mouth from hers, he trailed slow kisses down her neck and loved the way she shuddered in his arms. Moaning, she clung to him. "I can't think—"

"Don't," he murmured thickly, and turned his attention back to her mouth. "Don't think. Not yet."

Not now. Not when he finally had her back in his arms and his bedroom was only steps away. It seemed like he'd been waiting for this moment from the second he first laid eyes on her, and tonight, nothing was getting in their way. No house rules, no business, nothing.

Caught up in the taste and feel and heat of her, he

would have sworn Phoebe was just as lost to reason as he was. But one second, she was kissing him back with a hunger that matched his own, and the next, she was five steps away. Swearing, he instinctively reached for her.

Behind her, her bedroom door quietly swung open, and it was only then that he realized that she'd heard the kids stirring. And before he could blink the passion from his eyes, the kids were rushing into the living room, both of them excitedly talking at once.

"Mitch! You came!"

"I knew you would. I knew it! Robby said only Santa can fly in the ice, but you said you'd come back if you could, and you did!" Shooting her brother an I-told-you-so look, she grinned cheekily at Mitch. "Boys think they know everything."

Chuckling, he scooped both kids up for a monster hug. "Actually, for a while there, I thought I was going to be stuck in Amarillo for the rest of the week. The airport was closed, and I almost had to call Santa for a lift."

Drawing back, Robby looked up at him, wide-eyed. "You have Santa's phone number?"

"Well, no, I don't have it, personally," he admitted. "But I know some people with some pretty high connections. One of them could get it for me."

"Can you call them? Could we talk to Santa tonight?"

"Please?"

Trapped, Mitch hedged, "Well, I don't know about that, guys. It's awfully late."

"And Santa likes to communicate through the mail," Phoebe reminded them. "Letter-writing's a lost art. Anyway, you squirts are supposed to be in bed asleep. Tomorrow's a big day, and we don't want any grumpy grapes because you didn't get enough sleep. So go on—off to bed with you. Scoot."

Her expression as innocent as a cherub's, Becky stared

up at the two adults guilelessly. "Can't Mitch read us a story first? Just a little, tiny, baby one?"

The little minx knew she only had to smile at him to wrap him around her little finger. Fighting a grin, Mitch looked at Phoebe. "It's your call. Do they get a story or not?"

She should have said no—tomorrow was going to be a long day and if they didn't get enough rest they'd be picking at each other by noon. But if she sent the kids back to bed, she and Mitch would be alone again, and she wasn't ready for that just yet, not when her heart hadn't stopped racing from the moment he'd told her how much he'd missed her. If the kids hadn't come in when they had…

Shying away from completing that thought, she said quickly, "All right. You can have fifteen minutes, but that's it. Then it's lights out."

"Then I'd better hustle," he said promptly. "Come on, kids. Grab a book, then into bed with you."

He didn't have to tell them twice. Laughing, Becky snatched a book from the bookcase, then raced with Robby into the bedroom. Within seconds, Mitch's low murmur and the kids' muffled chuckles floated back into the living room. Entranced, Phoebe should have stayed right where she was and waited for him to finish before even approaching the bedroom. But the sound of his voice drew her like a pied piper. Unable to resist, she found herself moving to the open bedroom doorway to listen.

He sat perched on the side of the lower bunk, a half smile curling the corner of his mouth in a crooked grin as he read a story about two boys on a treasure hunt. The kids had heard the tale so many times that they knew it by heart, but you would have never known that from their faces. Spellbound, they crowded close and stared up at Mitch with rapt attention, hanging on every word.

Just watching the three of them together, Phoebe felt her heart lurch. He was a man who should have had children. Why hadn't she realized that before? Why hadn't she seen that under the ruthless, cynical businessman image he presented to the rest of the world was a softy—when it came to a couple of rug rats who just happened to be crazy about him?

Lost in her reflections, she didn't realize he'd reached the end of the story until he suddenly leaned down, kissed the kids good-night, then hoisted Robby up into the top bunk. "All right, monster children," he said teasingly, "not another peep out of you till morning. Okay?"

"Okeydokey," Becky said happily as he switched out the bedside light. Snuggling down under the covers, she watched him head for the door, where Phoebe stood in the light that streamed in from the hall. "Are you going to kiss Aunt Phoebe, too?" the little voice called out. "She's going to bed, too. Aren't you, Aunt Phoebe?"

Leaning against the doorjamb, Phoebe straightened like a poker, heat flaming into her face. "I think there's been enough kissing for one night," she began stiffly, only to realize what she'd said. Mortified, she added hastily, "I mean...of you kids!"

That only sounded like she hadn't gotten her share of kisses. Cursing her wayward tongue, she wanted to sink right through the floor. "It's late," she said in a strangled voice. "It's time everyone was in bed."

His blue eyes twinkling with devilment as he approached where she stood in the doorway, Mitch murmured, "I agree completely. Good night, Phoebe." And before she could step back out of the way, he placed his hands on her shoulders and leaned down to plant a soft, tantalizing kiss on either side of her mouth. Then he propped her back against the doorjamb, stepped around her and headed for his own room. She was still standing where he'd left her when she heard him softly shut his bedroom door. Watching from their bed, the kids giggled.

How she slept after that, Phoebe never knew. But the next thing she knew, the alarm was going off and it was time to put the turkey in the oven. After that, the day just seemed to fly. The kids were up with the sun, so excited that they could barely stand still long enough to get dressed. If it hadn't been for Mitch, they would have been bouncing off the walls. While Phoebe bustled around gathering the ingredients for the pies she planned to make, he rounded up the kids for breakfast, cleaned up after them, helped them set the dining-room table with Alice's holiday china, then took them with him to the airport to pick up their grandparents.

While they were gone, Phoebe put the last pie in the oven, checked the turkey, and made the cornbread for the dressing. She just had time to change into a holiday sweater and black slacks, then tie on an apron before the kids were back, bursting through the front door with wide grins on their faces and their grandparents in tow.

Up until then, she'd been nervous about the meal and her ability to pull it off—she was a decent cook, but she'd never attempted to roast a turkey before. But with the Mallorys' arrival, she realized that it wasn't the food that was important, but the fact that they were all together. They weren't her family—their only connection to her was the kids—but they greeted her like a daughter, with hugs and kisses, and just that easily, the day became the holiday that it was meant to be.

Caught up in greeting them, with everyone talking and laughing at once, Phoebe completely forgot about the pie she had in the oven until Louise sniffed and said suddenly, "Is something burning?"

"Oh, my God! My pie!"

Rushing into the kitchen, Phoebe grabbed hot pads and quickly pulled out a cherry pie that was bubbling over and just on the verge of burning. "Oh, no!"

Following her into the kitchen, Louise chuckled and patted her on the shoulder in sympathy. "It's not that bad, dear. When you serve it, just put a scoop of ice cream on top, and everyone will rave about it. Now, what can I do to help?"

"Oh, nothing! You came to visit with the kids."

"And I will," the older woman said, grabbing a spare apron from the hook hanging by the back door and tying it on. "But there's plenty of time to do that later—Ward and I don't fly back home until Sunday evening. In the meantime, you look like you could use some help. If I had to guess, I would say this is the first time you've cooked a turkey."

Phoebe couldn't have denied it if she'd wanted to—the kitchen was a disaster area and anyone with eyes could see that she wasn't quite sure what she was doing. Grimacing, she had to laugh at herself. "Is it that obvious?"

"Only to another woman who's tried to do it all by herself," she retorted with a grin. "Believe me, it's no fun. So let me help, and you can tell me about the kids and how they're getting along. They look wonderful. Happy."

There wasn't so much as a smidgen of envy in her voice, no trace of regret that the children were no longer with her and Ward in New Orleans, and for that, Phoebe was extremely grateful. The kids had become such a big part of her life that she couldn't imagine what she would do if the Mallorys ever decided that they wanted them back.

Reading her thoughts, Louise said, "You'll never know how much comfort we take in knowing they're with you. You're good for them, and it's obvious that you love them like they were your own. The three of you belong together.''

Touched, tears stinging her eyes, Phoebe hugged her. ''Thank you. You don't know how much that means to me.''

Her own eyes watery, Louise hugged her back and laughed. ''Lord, look at the two of us! It's a holiday. We should be laughing. Tell me what the kids have been up to. Knowing Robby and the way he likes to get into mischief, your life hasn't been dull the last couple of weeks.''

''Well, he did flush a puffer fish down the toilet,'' Phoebe admitted, grinning, as Louise sat down at the kitchen table to peel potatoes. ''He thought it was dead...until it puffed up in the pipes and stopped up the toilet.''

''He didn't!''

''Oh, yes, he did. That was when we were living in the other apartment. The next day, we were politely asked to leave.''

''I bet you wanted to kill him,'' Louise laughed. ''Wasn't that the apartment where children weren't allowed?''

Phoebe nodded. ''After that little escapade, I could see why. I didn't think the plumber was ever going to get that fish out of the pipes.''

With Louise's help, getting the rest of the meal together was a piece of cake. While they laughed and talked and cooked in the kitchen, the kids played a new video game with Ward and Mitch in the living room. Tantalizing scents floated on the air, stirring appetites, and more then once, both the kids and the men wandered into the kitchen with their noses in the air. Then Phoebe was putting the food on the table, and everyone couldn't get into the dining room fast enough.

''I want to sit next to Grandma.''

"But she told me I could!"

Scowling at each other, the kids had the first cross words of the day until Louise stepped in and separated them. "Goodness," she chuckled, "I didn't know I was so popular. What do you say I sit between the two of you? How's that?"

The skirmish settled, everyone took their seats, and moments later, Phoebe asked Robby to say the prayer. "You're seven now," she told him with a smile when he looked doubtful. "You can do it."

Encouraged, he solemnly took Phoebe's hand and his grandmother's, and hands were joined around the table. It wasn't until Phoebe felt Mitch's fingers close around hers that she realized he'd taken the seat on her other side. It was the first time he had touched her all day. Her heart skipping a beat, she glanced over to find him smiling at her, then she quickly lowered her gaze as Robby began the prayer.

"Thank You, God, for this food. And for taking care of us and making Grandpa Ward better. And for Mitch and whoever gave him Santa's number," he added quickly. "We're going to call him for Christmas because we lost the art of letter-writing. Amen."

Phoebe choked back a laugh and swore she wasn't going to reward the little devil with so much as a grin. But then she made the mistake of looking at Mitch, who was still holding her hand and struggling to look serious, and they both burst out laughing.

"Robby! Shame on you!"

All innocence, he said, "What? I was just thanking God for our blessings. Wasn't that what I was supposed to do?"

He had them there and he knew it. Chuckling, his grandfather said, "You did very well, son. Now how about some of that turkey we've been smelling all morning? You want white meat or dark?''

Dinner wasn't a Hallmark card, but it turned out better than Phoebe had hoped. If the turkey was a little dry and the potatoes more than a little lumpy, no one seemed to notice or care. And when it was over, the men insisted on doing the dishes! Sitting at the dining-room table with Louise, lingering over pie and coffee, Phoebe could hear Ward and Mitch talking and laughing as they tried to figure out how to load the dishwasher, then the occasional sharp sound of glassware nearly breaking from too rough handling.

Wincing, she started to get up to help—and save Alice's dishes before they were completely destroyed—when Louise stopped her. ''They'll manage, dear,'' she said with a chuckle. ''If you go rushing in right now, they'll step back and let you do the job, which is what they're secretly hoping for.''

''But I didn't ask them to do the dishes. They volunteered!''

''Of course they did. It was the right thing to do, especially after you spent all morning in the kitchen cooking. But if they make enough racket in there, and you insist on taking over for them, I can guarantee you, they won't fight you on it. Then they can go back to playing games with the kids with a clear conscience while you—and I—do all the work.''

''Are you kidding me? That's why they keep banging the glasses together?''

Her blue eyes twinkling, Louise laughed softly. ''I'm not saying they're consciously doing it. But Ward's mother warned me about that little trick the day I married him and told me not to fall for it. If a man can take a motor apart and put it back together again, he can surely do a few dishes once in a while. So…what are your plans for tonight and this weekend?''

Blinking at the sudden change in subject, Phoebe said, ''I don't have any, actually. Except to watch the river parade tomorrow night and the lighting of the lights with the kids. Why?''

''Ward and I were hoping you'd let us have the kids for the weekend,'' she replied. ''We have a suite, so there will be plenty of room. I know I should have called you last week and discussed it with you, but with Ward's health the way it is, we didn't know until the last minute if we were really going to be able to come.'' Disappointed, she forced a smile. ''Of course, if you've already made plans…''

''It's not anything that was carved in stone,'' Phoebe assured her. ''The kids do want to see the parade, though. As long as they get to do that, I don't have a problem with them spending the weekend with you. They've missed you. It'll be good for them.''

The kids were, in fact, thrilled at the idea of spending the entire weekend with their grandparents. By the time Mitch and Ward finished the dishes, they had their overnight bags packed with enough clothes to last them a week, and they were chomping at the bit to leave. They hardly took time to give Phoebe a couple of quick, distracted kisses before they were rushing out of the apartment with their grandparents, beside themselves with excitement at the unexpected treat.

When the door shut behind them and her eyes met Mitch's in the sudden silence that fell with a crash in the apartment, only then did Phoebe realize she'd just arranged for the two of them to spend the weekend together. Alone. Dear God, what had she done?

Her heart thudding, she quickly moved to straighten the living room, chattering as nervously as an old maid on her first blind date. "Well, that was a surprise, wasn't it? I imagine you've got to get back to Amarillo and get back to work tomorrow, so it looks like I'm going to have the place to myself. When's your flight? Tonight or in the morning?"

Humor glinting in his eyes, he moved into her path and smiled slightly when she immediately changed course to avoid coming anywhere near him. "Actually, I hadn't planned on going anywhere until Sunday night, and maybe not even then if I can get some things done on the phone," he said lightly as she skirted around the far end of the couch. "Are you okay? You seem a little... jumpy."

Jumpy? Of course she was jumpy! She'd only had a few hours' sleep, the day had been wonderful but hectic, and even though the length of the couch was between them, he was too close. Especially when he had that wicked sparkle in his eyes. The one that always made her heart race. The one that always warmed his eyes whenever he was just about to kiss her.

"Jumpy?" she said hoarsely. "No, I'm fine. Just a little...tired. It seems like I've been moving in fast-forward all day. I think I'll go take a nap."

Her chin up, she headed for her bedroom and told herself she wasn't acting like a scared rabbit. She was just retreating until she had a better handle on her suddenly raging hormones. But she'd only taken two steps when he suddenly reached out and grabbed her.

"Mitch! What do you think you're doing?"

Even as he reeled her into his arms, he asked himself the same thing. He knew he had no business touching her. Not now. Not today. Not after he'd spent what was left of the night last night aching for her and fighting the need to go to her. He wanted her too damn much, and if he had any sense, he would get his butt to the airport and take the next flight out, and to hell with where it was headed. It was the right thing to do, the *smart* thing to do, and he prided himself on being an intelligent man. But brains didn't count for a hill of beans, he was discovering, when he had the chance to have her all to himself for the entire holiday weekend.

"Give me five minutes," he coaxed thickly, suddenly starving for the taste of her. "If you still want me to let you go then, I will."

He covered her mouth with his before she could say another word and wouldn't have blamed her if she'd hauled off and punched him one. He deserved it. He was rough, his control nearly nonexistent, his arms too tight around her. If she'd insisted he let her go right then and there, he didn't know where he would have found the strength. Not when he wanted her so badly.

But although she immediately stiffened in his arms, she didn't push him away. For what seemed like an eternity, she just stood there, and he could feel the struggle going on inside her, the fight against an attraction that had been inescapable from the moment they'd met. But she wanted him as badly as he wanted her—he knew she did!—and she couldn't fight the need any more than he could. Moaning softly, she wrapped her arms around his neck and kissed him, holding nothing back.

He wanted her then more than he'd ever wanted any woman in his life, in his bed, under him, loving him like there was no tomorrow. But he hadn't forgotten that he'd promised her that he would never take advantage of her—if they made love, it had to be because she wanted it as much as he did, not because she was caught up in the heat of the moment.

Capturing her face in his hands, he pulled back a fraction, just far enough that he could see her eyes. "I couldn't think of anything but you the entire time I was gone," he said huskily. "Make love with me, Phoebe. I want you in my bed."

Her heart turning over in her chest, Phoebe couldn't have protested if her life had depended on it. This was what she wanted, what she'd dreamed of and thought would never happen... Mitch holding her, loving her, showing her just how much he needed her. Later, there would be time for words, for declarations of the heart, for talk of the future, but for now, those things could wait. Nothing else mattered but being in his arms, loving him.

Her smile coming straight from her heart, she went up on tiptoe to brush a soft kiss to his mouth and said simply, "Yes."

It wasn't until then that she realized that he'd expected her to say no. Surprise flared in his eyes, and then he was walking her backwards toward his room, kissing her all the while.

She couldn't count the number of times she'd dreamed of making love with him, but when he laid her in a muted patch of sunlight on his bed, nothing was as she'd thought it would be. There was no darkness to conceal him from her or her from him as they slowly undressed each other, no starlight to set the scene with romance. Naked, skin to skin, there was just the two of them, alone in a golden glow of sunlight, and it couldn't have been more beautiful.

His eyes met hers, the heat in the dark blue depths stealing the very air from her lungs as he leaned over her. And then he smiled. A slow, intimate smile full of promise, just for her. And just that easily, the last, lingering doubts she had about giving herself to him vanished in a heartbeat. She wanted this, wanted *him*.

With the sun shining down on them, the rest of a lazy afternoon stretched out before them. They had hours to slowly drive each other out of their minds, but the second he kissed her, fires that had been banked ever since the kids broke them apart last night sprang to life. Gasping, Phoebe clung to him, breathless, as his hands raced over her breasts, her hips, her belly, stroking and caressing and teasing until she shuddered and whimpered with need.

She'd thought she knew what passion was, thought she knew her own body, but no one had ever taken her out of herself and given her what he did. She couldn't think for the pounding of her heart, couldn't breathe for the feel of his mouth pressing kisses to her breast, then latching on to her nipple to suckle strongly. Desire knotted like a fist low in her belly, and she cried out softly, clinging to him.

With his mouth alone, he drove her up one peak and over the edge before she could do anything but gasp. Shuddering, pleasure rippling through her in waves, she was sure she was spent. But with a murmur of praise, he settled between her thighs and eased into her, and just that quickly, her heart was pounding, her blood hot. He moved, her hips lifted to his, and what she knew about loving took on a whole new meaning. His eyes, midnight blue with need, locked with hers, and then they were both racing for the stars, wanting, needing nothing but each other.

Chapter 11

He couldn't seem to stop touching her. Even after he'd made love to her—again—and he should have been sated, he couldn't get enough of her. And he couldn't for the life of him understand why. He'd had his share of women, though not as many as reported, and a wise man knew how to keep a tight rein on his emotions. He'd never had a problem sticking to that in the past—he shouldn't have now. But there was something about her...the softness of her skin, the feel of her arms around him, the way she cried out his name when she shattered under him...that left him reeling in a way he'd never expected. Somehow, she'd reached right inside his chest and turned his heart upside down; and he didn't have a clue how she'd managed it. He just knew he wanted, needed, more than a day, a night, a week, with her.

Tightening his arms around her, his only thought to keep her with him, he said impulsively, "When Alice gets back from L.A., I want you to come with me to Dallas."

Sprawled across his chest, she snuggled against him and pressed a kiss to his pounding heart. "You mean to visit?"

"No," he murmured, loving the feel of her in his arms. "For good. I want you with me."

"But I can't just take off for Dallas. The kids are in school. And once Alice comes back, I'll be out of a job. I have to find something—"

"No, you don't. I have enough money to support you and the kids. And they can go to school anywhere. We'll enroll them in Dallas in January, and the three of you can move into my condo. There's plenty of room, and then you can write to your heart's content."

Caught up in the fantasy, he didn't notice that she'd gone stiff in his arms until she abruptly drew back. Her face pale, she said carefully, "Let me get this straight. Are you asking me to live with you?"

There was a look in her eye that told him she wasn't overjoyed with the offer, and he knew why. In this day and age, a woman had to look after her own interests, especially when she had children to consider. He knew that, accepted that, but deep down inside, he was disappointed that she didn't trust him to look after her and the kids even when they ended their arrangement. Hadn't he looked out for her so far?

"I'll take care of you, honey," he promised gruffly. "You don't have to worry about me throwing you and the kids out in the cold if things don't work out. I'll arrange a nice settlement for you, enough for you to come back to San Antonio, if you that's what you want, and take your time looking for a job. Money won't be a problem."

It was, he thought, a generous offer. One that any one of the women he'd dated in the past would have jumped at because it was a well-known fact that he was not a stingy man—especially when it came to ex-lovers. He was promising her security, and wasn't that what all women were looking for? He thought she'd be relieved.

But the woman who extracted herself from his arms and stiffly pulled the sheet up to shield her naked breasts from his eyes was anything but pleased. In fact, she looked like he'd just stabbed her in the heart. Concerned, he started to reach for her. "Honey, what is it? I thought—"

Lightning-quick, she scrambled out of the bed, dragging the sheet with her. "Don't!" she choked. "You don't have to draw me a picture—I know exactly what you thought. It isn't as if you've ever tried to hide your opinion of me. Right from the first, you thought I was just like all the other women who have chased you over the years, wanting to get their fingers on your pocketbook."

"I never—"

"Oh, *please!* Save it! I can't believe I've been such a fool! I actually thought you were starting to care for me. What a joke! You don't care about anything but your precious money and keeping it out of the hands of greedy little gold diggers—like me. Well, congratulations! You succeeded. You can take your bank account and everything else you own and stuff it where the sun don't shine! *I don't want it!*"

But just to be sure there were no misunderstandings, she grabbed pen and paper from the nightstand and hastily scribbled a disclaimer. "*I, Phoebe Smith, swear on my parents' grave that I want nothing from Mitch Ryan, now or at any time in the future.* There," she said, shoving it under his nose. "Have I made myself clear enough? You're safe from me. You haven't got a damn thing I want."

That was an out-and-out lie—she wanted his heart—

but a woman had her pride. And what was left of hers was badly bruised and hurting. How could he think… Not even able to finish the thought, she was so furious, she whirled away from him and started snatching up her clothes.

"Phoebe, if you'll just be rational—"

It was the wrong thing to say. Straightening, she shot him a look that could have melted lead. "You want rational? I'll give you rational. You stay away from me! Just leave me alone and we'll get along fine."

She didn't give him time to say another word, but simply stormed out, her chin in the air and her clothes clutched in her arms, too angry to care that she was magnificently naked. Just let him try and stop her, she fumed. She just dared him!

But whatever else Mitch was, he liked to think he wasn't a stupid man. He let her go. He couldn't for the life of him, however, understand what she was so upset about. She acted like he'd just insulted her when all he was really trying to do was protect her interests. All he had to do was give her a little time to cool down and she would see that. Then she'd apologize, they'd make up, then spend the rest of the weekend making love and discussing everything that would need to be done to make her and the kids' move to Dallas a smooth one.

Wisely, he gave her the rest of the day to herself. It wasn't easy. When she couldn't manage to avoid him outright, she gave him the cold shoulder and barely spoke to him. Tension in the apartment was interminable, the temperature downright chilly. Frustrated, Mitch told himself that she couldn't stay mad at him forever. She was too warm, too loving, and what they had shared was right there in her eyes every time she looked at him. Tomorrow, she would talk to him and they would work this out.

But after a restless night, he woke to find her already

up and packing. Stunned, he stood in the open doorway of her bedroom, sleep still in his eyes, and scowled at her in disbelief. "What the hell are you doing?"

"What does it look like?" she retorted, not bothering to look up from her task as she packed the kids' toys and books in a sturdy box. "We obviously can't stay here any longer, so I'm packing our things. As soon as the kids get back Sunday afternoon, we'll get out of your hair."

She was serious. She was going to leave, just walk out like nothing had ever happened between them! Stunned, he couldn't understand how they had come to this. Had he hurt her that badly that she couldn't wait to get away from him? He hadn't meant to, dammit! Couldn't she see that? He cared about her. Didn't she realize that he never would have asked her to move in with him if he hadn't? And he couldn't just let her walk away. Not after what they'd shared yesterday afternoon. Even now, hours later, he was still reeling from it, and just the thought of losing her sent him into a panic. She had to give him a chance to explain, to make her understand and make things right between them, and he'd never be able to do that if she moved out.

"Just because we had a misunderstanding doesn't mean you have to move out," he told her quietly. "Where would you go, anyway? Apartments are expensive—at least, the better ones are—and the kids like living here. You won't be able to find anything comparable that you can afford."

If he'd wanted to touch a nerve, he couldn't have found a better way. Her eyes narrowing dangerously, she leveled a chilly glance at him. "My finances aren't your concern. The only thing you have to be worried about is whether I get to work on time, and I can assure you I will."

"But that wasn't part of our agreement," he argued. "You were hired to take over for Alice while she was gone, to be here for the tenants day or night. You can't do that if you're living somewhere else.''

"So you're firing me?" she demanded, outraged. "Is that what you're saying?"

There was no way in hell he would have fired her, but that was something she didn't need to know. If that was playing dirty, then so be it. When a man's back was to the wall, he did what he had to do. "With Alice gone, I need someone here around the clock to deal with whatever problems crop up. If you can't do that, I'll have to find someone who can."

"I'll have a phone. The tenants can call me at the new place if something happens after hours—"

"That's not good enough," he said ruthlessly. "You either live here, or you'll have to find another job. It shouldn't be too hard—you're very well qualified. Of course, there may not be anything available until January. That could make things pretty tight."

"I'll manage," she said stiffly.

"I'm sure you will if you get a cheap apartment. They're out there—you just have to look for them. Of course, the low-rent districts aren't always the safest, and the Mallorys probably won't like the idea of the kids living in such a dangerous area, but you can only do so much when you're out of work. Once you explain the situation, I'm sure they'll understand. Hell, they might even loan you enough money to get a better place. They know you're good for it," he continued blithely. "You're raising their grandchildren. If they can't trust you, who can they trust, right?"

She was going to kill him, Phoebe thought, seething. Dammit, why was he doing this to her? He'd stabbed her right in the heart yesterday, and it felt as if she'd been crying ever since. She'd thought he knew her, knew the type of woman she was. But how could he if he thought her first concern when it came to living with him was how much of his money she was going to get when she moved out?

That thought had nagged at her all night, tearing her apart, and with the coming of the dawn, she'd known what she had to do. She could work for him because she couldn't walk away from a paying job when Christmas was right around the corner, but there was no way she could continue to share an apartment with him. Not after yesterday.

"Louise and Ward know I would never do anything to put the kids in jeopardy," she said through her teeth, glaring at him. "But you're right—it would be difficult for me to find another job this time of year. So the children and I will stay. But not here," she said quickly, before he could get the mistaken idea that he'd bested her. "We'll move upstairs to the attic—"

"The hell you will!"

"There's a bathroom up there already," she continued as if he hadn't spoken, "and we really just need a place to sleep."

"I thought the contractor was starting the remodeling Monday. You and the kids can't stay up there in all that dust and construction."

"We're not going to be up there in the middle of the day," she retorted. "The kids'll be in school and I'll be down here working. I'm just talking about spending the nights up there. We have sleeping bags—"

"No!"

"What do you mean…*no?* Dammit, Mitch, you can't have it both ways! You insist that I have to live here if I want to keep my job. I'm willing to do that—if we can stay in the attic. We'll still continue to use the kitchen facilities down here, of course, until the kitchen is built, but we're sleeping upstairs," she warned, "or you really can find someone to replace me. Those are my conditions. Take 'em or leave 'em.''

She meant it. She'd walk out if he didn't agree. At a stalemate, they glared at each other, and something in her eyes must have convinced him that she wasn't going to bend. Not this time. Swearing softly, he said, "You don't have to sleep in the attic. *I will.* There! Now are you happy?''

"But—"

"This isn't negotiable, Phoebe," he told her flatly. "The kids are happy and secure here, and that's where they're staying. It's not going to hurt me to bunk down in the attic. But my computer stays down here—you can't expect me to do business in a construction zone.''

"Of course not—"

"Then it's settled," he said quickly, before she could object. "Now that we've got that cleared up, I've got some work to catch up on, so I'll be here to look after things if you want to go shopping. The malls will be packed, but since the kids aren't here, I thought you might want a chance to go through the stores by yourself. Go ahead," he said when she hesitated. "Most of the rest of the world is shopping today anyway, so you might as well go, too. I can handle things here until you get back.''

It would still be several weeks before she'd saved enough of her salary to even think about buying the kids anything, but just the thought of staying there in the apartment with him all day, sharing the quiet, being aware of his every move, had her jumping at the chance to get away. "If you're sure you don't mind, I think I will," she said coolly. "The kids have already given me their Christmas lists and I need to price things.''

Out of all the shopping days in the year, the day after Thanksgiving was her favorite. The malls were packed,

Christmas decorations that had been up since Halloween finally fit the season, and the sound of holiday music was in the air. She loved it. She very seldom bought anything, but spending money had never been what made the day special to her. It was the crowds that were fun, being caught up in the rush and excitement, and wandering from store to store, just looking. She could happily browse for hours.

Or at least, she had in the past. But this year, the ringing of the Salvation Army bell held little joy for her, and watching other shoppers scramble for a bargain when there was plenty for all didn't so much as stir a smile. She'd never been so miserable, and it was all Mitch's fault.

She shouldn't have let him pressure her into staying. He was going to hurt her more than any man ever had—she knew that as surely as she knew that he had already stolen her heart—and there didn't seem to be anything she could do about it. She had to have money to make sure there were presents from Santa under the tree on Christmas morning, and she only had a limited number of ways of making it. One was working for Mitch. The other was selling her manuscript to a publisher in New York. And since she had nothing but a drawer full of rejection slips to show for that creative effort, she wasn't exactly holding out hope that that was going to happen—especially in time for Christmas.

No, she had to stay where she was for now, she decided as she headed home hours later. But it was only a temporary situation, just until after Christmas. Because her future wasn't with Mitch. If yesterday had shown her anything, it was that. He'd kissed her, held her, made love to her with a tenderness that had nearly destroyed her, and, for a while, made her forget why she didn't want a man.

Her memory returned soon enough when he opened his mouth and stabbed her right in the heart.

But that was something she didn't want to think about, not now. Her feet were firmly planted in the real world again, her priorities straight. She had two goals—to support the kids and get published. If the manuscript she was currently circulating in New York didn't sell, then the one she was working on now would. She had to believe that. And in the meantime, she would keep things between her and Mitch strictly business. There would be no more kisses, no more lovemaking, no more romance. Maybe then when Alice returned and he walked out of her life for good, she wouldn't be completely destroyed.

She thought she had her emotions under tight control by the time she let herself into the apartment, but nothing was that simple. Mitch had just finished making himself a turkey sandwich in the kitchen when she walked in. Her eyes met his, and all the feelings he stirred in her when they made love welled up in her heart. It was all she could do not to walk into his arms.

But she couldn't. If he touched her now, all her fine resolves just might crumble, and then she'd really be in trouble. But Lord, it was hard. She'd never known that her heart could really, physically hurt until she'd met him, and just being in the same room with him made her want to cry. But that wasn't allowed either. Not if she was going to work with him.

"Are you hungry?" he asked quietly, breaking the silence that stretched between them like a chasm. "I just made myself a sandwich. You want one?"

"No…thanks. I ate at the mall, but you go ahead." She had, in fact, only picked at a salad that had held little appeal, but that was something he didn't need to know. "When you're finished, I'd like to use the kitchen table if you don't mind. With the kids gone, this is a good time for me to work on their Christmas stories.''

"Oh…sure," he said, surprised. "You can have it now if you like. I don't need the whole table just for a sandwich. I've got to work anyway. I'll just sit at my desk.''

"You don't have to—''

"It's no problem. Go ahead.''

Their conversation couldn't have been more stilted. Phoebe hated it, but if she was going to keep things strictly business between them, this was the way it had to be. Without a word, she went to her room to collect her art supplies, and within minutes, she was bent over her work at the kitchen table and appeared to be totally engrossed. Only she knew she couldn't even see what she was doing for the tears in her eyes.

Seated at his desk, chewing on a sandwich that tasted like cardboard, Mitch stared at her through the open kitchen door and wanted to throw something. How could she ignore him so easily? Less than a little over twenty-four hours ago, she'd been in his arms, his bed, and nothing had ever felt so right. They'd been so close that he'd have sworn that nothing could ever come between them again. Then it had all blown up in their faces, and there was no question that he was to blame.

He'd had all day to think about it, to relive again and again the conversation they'd had in his bed. He'd been so caught up in the wonder of her that all he'd been able to think about was keeping her with him and making her happy. He'd said something about transferring the kids to a school in Dallas and her staying home so she could write, and the next thing he knew, they were talking about money, and suddenly everything began to unravel. He didn't even know how it had happened. He just knew he didn't want to lose her or ever see that look in her eyes again. She couldn't have looked more wounded if he'd actually stabbed her in the heart.

He'd hurt her. He certainly hadn't intended to, but he'd hurt her badly. While he'd hung around the apartment all day waiting for her to return, he'd hoped that after some time to herself she might have cooled off enough for them to talk when she got home. Now he could see that that wasn't going to happen, and for the first time, he began to realize the extent of her hurt and anger.

And it shook him. She wasn't like any other woman he knew. Why had it taken him so long to see that and realize how much he liked that difference? With any other woman, he would have already gone out and bought a diamond bracelet or some other pricey piece of jewelry, and that's all it would have taken to convince her to kiss and make up. Phoebe, though, was a whole other kettle of fish. If he tried that with her, she'd probably cram it down his throat.

He couldn't, he thought in disgust, say he blamed her. He wasn't normally insensitive to others' feelings. He should have realized that with her pride, offering her any kind of settlement was a slap in the face. He'd reduced their relationship to dollars and cents, and in the process, thoughtlessly ruined things between them. She hadn't, however, walked out. And as long as she stuck around, he had a chance of earning her forgiveness.

He didn't fool himself that she would make it easy for him. The silence in the apartment was as thick as mud, but it didn't seem to bother her at all. Every time he looked up from his work, she was right in the middle of his field of vision, but she never once looked his way.

And it frustrated him no end. Hours passed. Outside, the sudden strains of holiday music announced the beginning of the river parade and the lighting of the Christmas lights, an event they had planned to watch together with the kids. But although Phoebe stiffened, she didn't look up from her work. He told himself that she wouldn't be able to keep it up—there would come a point when she would have to glance out the window at the crowds partying on the river or at least say *something*—but the lady was nothing if not stubborn. She eventually took a break—she even got up and stretched and cut herself a piece of pie—but she never went near the window or acknowledged his presence in the living room in any way. For all practical purposes, she could have been completely alone.

Irritated, he finally said, "It's getting late. I guess I'll go to bed."

He hadn't forgotten that since she refused to share an apartment with him any longer, he'd agreed to sleep in the attic. He'd hoped she'd relent, especially since it was such a cold night and the only heat up there was whatever managed to float up the stairs, but when she spoke for the first time in hours, it wasn't to tell him that she'd changed her mind.

"You can use my sleeping bag," she told him coldly. "It's in the hall closet."

"She speaks," he muttered under his breath as he retrieved the sleeping bag and a pillow from the closet.

He could feel her eyes on him and knew she was watching him as he headed for the front door. When she got up from the table and followed him, he was sure it was to tell him she'd changed her mind. She wasn't a vengeful woman; she wouldn't really condemn him to a cold night in the attic.

But that's exactly what she did. When he stepped out into the central hall, she not only shut the door in his face, the little witch threw the dead bolt.

He liked to think he had a sense of humor. Another time, he would have laughed at the thought of sleeping on the cold, hard floor in the attic when he had a perfectly good bed in *his* apartment. But as he started up the stairs, he realized that there was only one reason why he had ever agreed to such a ridiculous arrangement, and there was nothing the least bit funny about it. He was nuts about the woman. It was the only explanation.

The attic was dark as pitch and colder than the bowels of hell. Muttering curses about the lengths he would go to to make this one particular woman happy, Mitch tossed and turned and tried in vain to get comfortable. Outside, a strong wind whistled around the eaves, searching for a way to get inside. If Alice had been there, she would have said the ghosts that haunted the place were restless. Punching his pillow, he snorted at the thought. There were no spirits, nothing supernatural or unusual about the house. If it seemed to moan and groan at times, it was just because it was old, and the mansion's foundation had a tendency to shift slightly in the rocky South Texas soil.

Deliberately closing his eyes, he accepted that he wasn't going to get much rest. Not on a floor that was harder than granite, in a sleeping bag that had about as much padding as a tissue. But he hadn't slept much the night before, and exhaustion hit him like a ton of bricks. Sleep dragged him under, and almost immediately, he began to dream.

Later, he couldn't have said what he dreamed about. The images were too vague, too fleeting. He thought Phoebe was there, in his head, but he couldn't be sure. The woman had her face, her smile, but the clothes were all wrong. She wore a beautiful, old-fashioned ball gown with a hoop skirt, and a necklace that for some reason struck a chord in a memory he didn't even have. And in her eyes was a love that came straight from the soul.

Transfixed, he reached for her in his dream, needing to

hold her almost more than he could bear, but she drifted away and he woke with a start, his heart slamming against his ribs. It was then that he heard the music. Light and airy and beautiful, the strains of a waltz floated on the night air just as it had over a hundred years before.

Stunned, Mitch lay perfectly still and tried to come up with a logical explanation for the phenomenon. There had to be one. Just about every nightspot on the river played some sort of music, he reminded himself. Even though it was well past the hour when most places closed, the music could conceivably be coming from there. Or maybe one of the tenants on the second floor had his radio tuned to an easy-listening station, and didn't realize it was too loud. He'd have to hunt him down tomorrow and ask him to keep it down next time.

It sounded good, but even as he tried to convince himself that that was where the music was coming from, Mitch knew he wasn't fooling anyone, least of all himself. He couldn't remember the last time he'd heard a waltz on an easy-listening station, and the music wasn't coming from downstairs or the river. It was softly seeping out of the walls and swirling over his head, and there was only one explanation for it. He'd been working too hard.

For the rest of the weekend, the apartment was an armed camp. Mitch was in a bear of a mood and walked around with a scowl on his face most of the time. Phoebe suspected he wasn't sleeping well, but the current sleeping arrangements were something they didn't talk about. They kept their conversations limited to business and avoided each other as much as they could in the small apartment, but it wasn't easy when they had to share a bathroom and a kitchen, not to mention work space. Phoebe had never been so miserable in her life.

On Sunday, the kids burst into the apartment like a

breath of fresh air, shattering the silence that had fallen all too often over the weekend. Dressed in new clothes, their smiles wide and their eyes bright with excitement, they launched themselves first at Phoebe, then at Mitch, both of them talking at once.

"We talked to Santa at the mall!"

"And at the parade. He threw us some candy from his float!"

"He said he knew we'd been really, *really* good, and Christmas morning there'd be a big surprise for us under the tree!"

"Do you think he's going to bring me a bike, Aunt Phoebe? I told him just what I wanted so he wouldn't bring me the wrong kind. You know—one of those cool mountain bikes that I showed you in the Toys 'R' Us ad? It's awesome!"

"Whoa, guys!" Louise laughed as she and Ward followed the kids into the apartment. "Give Phoebe a chance to catch her breath. She can't hear you with both of you talking at once."

Laughing, Phoebe hugged them again and told their grandmother, "Actually, I'm getting pretty good at carrying on two conversations at once. I guess I don't have to ask if they had a good time."

"It was the best!"

"Super!"

"It really was wonderful," Ward spoke up, grinning affectionately at the kids. "They kept us hopping, but it was fun. I can't remember the last time I laughed so much."

"Then you'll just have to come back for Christmas and stay with us," Phoebe said. "I know the kids would love to have you and so would I."

"Oh, we'd love to!" Louise said. "But are you sure there'll be room? We don't mind going to a hotel."

"The attic apartment should be ready by then," Mitch replied, "and Phoebe and the kids'll be living up there. There'll be plenty of room for all of you."

"And it'll be much more fun if we're all together," Phoebe added. "Please say you'll come."

She didn't have to ask twice. Thrilled, the Mallorys graciously accepted the invitation and would have loved to stay longer to discuss what they needed to bring, but they had a cab waiting for them downstairs to take them to the airport for their flight back to New Orleans. Quickly kissing the kids, they then each hugged Phoebe and Mitch, then rushed out with a promise to be in touch.

With their leavetaking, silence threatened to once again invade the apartment. Afraid that the kids would notice she and Mitch were barely speaking to each other and start asking questions she wasn't prepared to answer, Phoebe quickly pulled them down to the couch with her. "Okay, let's hear more about this visit with Santa. I know you told me about the bike you wanted, but tell me again. Is it really neat?"

"It's awesome, Aunt Phoebe! It's black, with these really thick tires that can go over anything. Tommy Heartfield has one just like it, and he rides it all over the place." Frowning, he looked up at Phoebe hopefully. "Do you think Santa'll really bring me one?"

Slipping her arm around him to hug him close, Phoebe would have loved to assure him that she could pretty much guarantee Santa would make sure there was a mountain bike under the tree Christmas morning, but she just didn't see how that was possible. Not when she'd already priced one and almost dropped her teeth in shock.

Then Becky piped up and added her two cents. "You can have your silly old bike," she told her brother. "*I* want a computer. Grandpa showed me one in the mall, and you can play games on it and everything. That's better than a bike any old day.''

"Is not!''

"Is so!''

"You're just saying that because you can't ride a real bike. You have to have training wheels.''

"I do not! Aunt Phoebe, tell him—''

"If I were you two, I think I'd watch what I say the next couple of weeks,'' Phoebe cut in firmly. "Santa has really sharp ears, and if he hears you arguing, he just might not bring you anything.''

Startled, Becky immediately lowered her voice to a cautious whisper. "He wouldn't really do that, would he, Aunt Phoebe? You'd tell him we're really good kids. Sometimes we just…forget.''

"Forget what?'' she teased. "That you're good kids? I'm pretty sure Santa knows that.''

But knowing and being able to do something about it were two different things. Listening to the kids eagerly go on about the newest got-to-have toys, she laughed and talked with them and encouraged them to tell her their hearts' desire. And though her smile never faltered, deep inside, the knot of worry in her stomach tightened painfully. Her paycheck was enough for her and the kids to get by, but since living at the Social Club and storage for her things was considered part of her salary, the actual money she received each week wasn't even close to what she'd made as a secretary at Wainwright. She'd managed to save a little, but it was a pitiful amount, and Christmas was less than a month away. What was she going to do?

Chapter 12

Watching her with the kids, Mitch couldn't have said when he first noticed the tension in her smile as she teased the kids about the bundle of toys they were expecting Santa to bring them. She seemed all right after the Mallorys left, but as the kids talked more and more about Christmas and all the things their friends at school were getting, her smile became tight, her laughter slightly strained. And when Robby retrieved the toy-store ads from the Sunday paper and pointed out the latest high-priced, technical gadgets that most kids nowadays thought they couldn't live without, Mitch would have sworn he caught the glint of tears in her eyes before she quickly blinked them away.

It was then it hit him. She didn't have the money to buy the kids Christmas presents.

Swallowing a curse, he wanted to kick himself for not realizing sooner just how bad a bind she was in. He knew how much she made—he paid her salary, for God's sake!

And most of it went for her and the kids' share of the daily living expenses and keeping the kids supplied with the things they needed. She didn't spend so much as a nickel frivolously—and never anything on herself—but it didn't matter how tight she was with her money, it only stretched so far. And with her savings wiped out by the rent money she'd been conned out of, she had no reserves to fall back on. Considering all that, he didn't see how she was going to be able to give the kids anything but the most inexpensive of presents, and even then, she'd have to find some real bargains.

Just the thought of her worrying herself sick over how she was going to manage made him want to snatch her up into his arms and assure her she had nothing to worry about. He could pay for a whole roomful of toys from Santa, and he'd do it in a heartbeat if she'd let him. But she wouldn't. She had too much pride to take anything from him, especially after the way he'd botched things between them when he'd asked her to move in with him. He could try to give her a raise, but she wasn't stupid and would no doubt know immediately what he was up to.

No, she wouldn't take money from him, not even for the kids, so he would just have to find another way to help her. He didn't fool himself into thinking it would be easy. The lady was nothing if not sharp. If she thought that he was in any way, shape, or form responsible for any sudden good fortune that came her way, she'd reject it in an instant.

Unless it was something so wonderful, so close to her heart, that she couldn't possibly turn her back on it. And he could think of only one thing besides the kids that meant that much to her. Her writing.

He didn't know why he hadn't thought of it sooner, he thought, as the kids announced that they were hungry and pulled Phoebe into the kitchen to make them a snack.

Quinn Thompson, one of his best friends from college, was a senior editor with Hudson Publishing in New York. He was always looking for new talent, and Mitch knew he would be more than happy to look at Phoebe's work if he asked him. The trick was getting something to him without Phoebe being aware of it. Because if she had even an inkling that he was pulling strings for her, she'd never go for it.

That immediately ruled out the murder mystery she was currently working on. And her other manuscript, the first one she'd written, was in the mail, probably sitting in a slush pile somewhere waiting for a junior editor to get around to reading it. He didn't doubt that both manuscripts were good, but he hadn't read either of them; and it was really *Professor Rat and the Case of the Missing Glasses* that he wanted Quinn to see. If he didn't snap it up the second he read it, Mitch would be shocked. He wasn't an expert on what appealed to children, of course, but he knew when he liked something, and he'd been damned impressed with that little book. Now all he had to do was get his hands on it when Phoebe wasn't looking and send it off to New York without her knowing it.

The opportunity presented itself the next morning when she took the kids to school. Mitch sometimes took them for her, but he used the excuse that he had to make an important business call, so Phoebe drove them instead. Becky and Robby gave him quick hugs, then they were rushing out the door with Phoebe right behind them. Seconds later, Mitch was hunting through the bookcase in the hallway for *Professor Rat.*

When he couldn't find it, he swore softly and had no choice but to search Phoebe and the kids' bedroom.

If Phoebe had walked in then, he would have been hard-pressed to explain what he was doing, but she didn't, and he finally found the book at the bottom of a stack piled on the nightstand next to the bunk beds. Quickly packaging it up, he slipped out of the apartment to the post office around the corner and mailed it before Phoebe got back.

He'd already called Quinn to tell him he was sending it, and he'd definitely been interested in looking at it. Quinn couldn't, of course, make any promises except to give the book a fair reading, and that was all Mitch could ask for. If it sold, Phoebe might not have the money before Christmas, but just knowing it was coming would make it possible for her to use her credit cards without worry about how she was going to pay the bills when they came in. And if *Professor Rat* didn't sell, then he'd have to come up with another way to help her without her knowing it. Either way, he wasn't letting her or the kids miss Christmas.

When Phoebe returned from taking the kids to school, she expected to find Mitch packing to leave again. He'd only come back from his business trip because he'd promised the kids he'd be there for the holiday, and now that that was past, she'd assumed he had more pressing issues to get back to in West Texas. It was, she told herself, for the best. By unspoken agreement, they'd both tried to act as if nothing was wrong in front of the kids, but it was a pretense that she knew she wouldn't be able to keep up for long. Not when her heart ached every time her eyes met his.

Steeling herself to tell him goodbye—possibly for the last time—she walked into the apartment and wouldn't have been surprised to find him already gone. Instead, he was at his desk, still dressed in the jeans and sweatshirt he'd had on when she left to take the kids to school, hammering out a deal on the phone with someone in El Paso.

"You don't have to tell me about Applebee, Mr. Scarsdale," he said into the phone. "I know how the old warhorse works. He'll throw numbers at you and double-talk you until you don't even know what you're agreeing to. That's not the way I operate. You've got my numbers in writing, and I won't try to change them on you. If you want to deal, we can do it right now. Just sign the contract and fax it to me here in San Antonio. Sure, you can think about it. If you've got any questions, just call me."

Surprised, Phoebe felt her heart lurch in her breast. For a man who could have easily come up with an excuse to be somewhere else, he didn't sound like he was going anywhere.

When he hung up, he quirked an eyebrow at her when he found her frowning at him in confusion. "What? Why are you looking at me like that?"

"I thought you still had business you had to get back to in West Texas," she blurted out.

"And you were hoping I was leaving?"

She was, of course, but she had no intention of telling him that. "It makes no difference to me one way or the other," she said stiffly. "But Kurt Elkins is starting the remodeling of the attic this morning, and he and his crew should be here any second to start work again. It could get pretty noisy, even down here, and at some point, the electricity will have to be turned off, so you won't be able to use the computer. You probably won't be able to get much work done."

If he needed an excuse to leave, she'd just given him one, but he only said, "Then maybe I should use this time to wrap up the rest of the oil leases in person. I'll think about it and let you know."

But he didn't leave that day or the next. And when the middle of the week came and went and he was still there, Phoebe began to suspect that he wasn't going anywhere.

Every time she turned around, he was right there, watching her, making her aware of his presence. And, try as she might, she couldn't forget the feel of his arms around her, the heat of his mouth on hers, the way he'd made love to her, as if she was the most precious thing in the world.

But a man didn't offer to make a cash settlement on a woman he held dear, she reminded herself every night when she lay alone in her empty bed. She'd done the right thing by breaking things off with him. But knowing she was right offered little comfort when she ached for him in the dark of the night.

And still, he stayed. Frustrated, she'd never been so confused in her life. Why was he still there? What did he want from her? He hadn't tried to so much as touch her since she'd turned down his unflattering proposal. In fact, he seemed to have completely lost interest in having any kind of a physical relationship with her. He teased and joked with her, and generally treated her like a big brother, and it was driving her crazy. Didn't he know that they'd gone way past the point where she could just be friends with him now?

She wanted, needed him to leave. Not only for her sake, but for the kids'. They'd become so close to him, and she knew he was genuinely fond of them. But it couldn't last. He had to see that, had to realize that they would be devastated when he walked out of their lives. Which was why when they pressed her to buy a Christmas tree, she put them off with the excuse that it was too soon—Christmas was still weeks away, and anything they bought now would dry out long before Santa slid down the chimney.

That wasn't a complete fabrication, but it wasn't the real reason why she didn't want to get a tree right now. She knew the kids would want Mitch to go along, and she couldn't let that happen. Picking out the perfect

Christmas tree was a family affair, something special that was a lot more involved than going to a lot and buying the first fir that crossed your path. If Mitch went with her and the kids, she knew that memory would be with her every Christmas for the rest of her life. And she already had too many memories of him as it was.

So she put the kids off—again—and waited for Mitch to leave on another business trip. He wouldn't stick around long, she assured herself. He couldn't afford to, not with Applebee stirring up trouble for him every time he got the chance. Any day now, he would get a call from his secretary about a new crisis that required his personal attention, and before she could blink, he'd be gone.

But Jennifer never called, and by the time the weekend rolled around, Mitch was still there. And the kids, counting the days until Christmas, refused to be put off any longer about a tree. "All right, we'll go Saturday morning," she said, giving in, and secretly prayed that it would rain. It didn't.

Mitch not only went with them, he drove. And it was a beautiful morning, perfect for looking at Christmas trees. The sky was crystal clear, the scent of firs and Scotch pine heavenly on the cool air. The kids, however, wouldn't have cared if it was overcast and dreary. The second Mitch pulled into the tree lot parking lot and cut the engine, they were out of the car and rushing into the trees.

"Look at this one. It's huge!"

"I like this one better. It's bigger than Mitch!"

"Can we have this one, Aunt Phoebe? Please?"

"No, this one! Please, Mitch? Tell Aunt Phoebe this is the best one."

Laughing, Mitch held up a hand. "Hey, guys, slow down a little. We just got here. We don't have to make a decision right this second. Let's look over here."

He coaxed them over to a row of smaller trees, and Phoebe let out a silent sigh of relief. When she'd told the kids they could get the tree, she'd pictured a Charlie Brown tree, something small and cheap that could be decorated with popcorn and construction paper decorations. But that didn't seem to exist—at least not on this lot. Most of the trees were huge, well over six feet, with price tags that were staggering. And the few that were smaller weren't that much cheaper.

Mentally counting the cash in her wallet, she winced. She had just enough for one of the smaller trees, but it would take part of the money she'd planned to use for decorations. They could, she supposed, skimp on the lights and use more homemade ornaments. The tree would probably still look a little bare, but at least the kids would have one that was theirs, and that was what was important.

"Aunt Phoebe, come quick! We found it!" Robby called out suddenly from the trees one row over.

"It's *beeeutiful!*" Becky added excitedly as Phoebe pushed through the trees to join them. "Mitch says it has our names all over it, but I don't see them."

Grinning, Phoebe said, "He means it's just perfect for you, sweetie. So where is it?"

"Right here," Mitch said, and stepped aside to reveal a blue spruce that was a foot taller than he was.

There was no question that it was, indeed, beautiful. Full and healthy, it had nice thick, evenly spaced branches that would easily support a ton of ornaments. Phoebe could see it set up in the bay window of Alice's living room, glittering with lights that sparkled like diamonds.

There was only one problem. It carried a price tag that rivaled the national debt.

She took one look at it and felt her heart sink. "It's gorgeous," she began regretfully, "but—"

"Then we're all in agreement," Mitch cut in smoothly. "This one's on me."

Startled, her eyes flew to his. "Oh, no! You can't—"

"Of course I can. It's my treat to the rug rats." The kids let out a cheer at that, and with a grin, Mitch said, "Why don't you guys go get us a cart so we can get this monster back up to the front and pay for it? Watch where you're going," he called after them as they took off like a shot. "Don't run into anybody."

Neatly outmaneuvered, Phoebe frowned, miffed, as the kids disappeared into the trees. "Dammit, Mitch, I can't let you do this!" she hissed. "It's too expensive."

Not the least disturbed by the price, he drawled, "One Christmas tree isn't going to break me, sweetheart. It's a gift. Didn't your mother ever tell you that when someone gives you something, you're just supposed to smile sweetly and say thank you? It's the polite thing to do."

"I don't think a Christmas tree qualifies as a gift—"

"Sure it does. It's a plant, isn't it? So technically, it's not any different than if I gave you flowers."

Frustrated, she seriously considered strangling him. "It's not the same thing at all and you know it."

"So sue me," he said, grinning. "It's a done deal. Say thank you."

Her lips twitched, but she wasn't about to give him the satisfaction of smiling. Giving him a withering look, she retorted, "I wouldn't push my luck if I were you. You're skating on thin ice as it is."

It was the wrong thing to say to a man who liked a challenge. "I always did like living on the edge," he murmured, and swept her into his arms.

"Mitch! What do you think you're doing?"

"Just accepting your invitation, sweetheart." Devilment dancing in his eyes, he motioned for her to look up.

"From where I'm standing, it looks like you're just begging to be kissed."

Too late, Phoebe realized she was standing directly under one of the sprigs of mistletoe that had been strategically hung around the Christmas tree lot. Her heart starting to pound with traitorous anticipation, she stiffened. "Oh, no you don't, Mitch Ryan! Don't you even think about—"

"Too late," he growled, and covered her mouth with his.

He just meant to tease her, to give her a playful smack that would bring the color to her cheeks and make her laugh. But the second his lips touched hers, he completely forgot his good intentions. Gathering her closer, uncaring that they were right out in the open and anyone could chance upon them, he indulged himself and took the kiss deeper.

He might have kept his head if she hadn't kissed him back. But she melted against him and met his passion with her own, and just that quickly, he was as caught up in the moment as she was. Vaguely, he heard what sounded like a metal cart coming toward them, but it could have been an invading army and he still wouldn't have been able to let her go.

Then he heard the kids giggle.

He laughed—he couldn't help it—and set a dazed Phoebe away from him. "That mistletoe's powerful stuff," he teased huskily, grinning down at the kids. "Every time I see somebody standing under it, I've just got to kiss them. Oops, you two are in the danger zone. Watch out!" And with no more warning than that, he scooped down, wrapped his arms around both of them for a fierce bear hug, and nuzzled their necks, making them squirm and laugh.

Her pulse racing, her head still spinning, Phoebe

watched Mitch with the kids and felt her heart swell with emotion. If she wasn't very, very careful, she warned herself, he was going to destroy her. Oh, he wouldn't mean to, but it would happen just the same. Because she wouldn't be able to stop herself from getting caught up in the season, in passionate kisses under the mistletoe that stole her breath and left her aching for something she couldn't have.

She tried. But how was she supposed to resist the man when he not only paid for the tree and lugged it inside once they got back to the social club, but also dug out Alice's decorations when he realized that she didn't have enough of her own to decorate the monster fir properly? Becky wanted to put the star on the top, so he lifted her up, making her giggle, and soon, he was knee-deep in tinsel and ornaments with the rest of them.

Later, she didn't know how she would have gotten along without his help. When she started stringing the lights, he was right there with the ladder, holding her steady while she climbed to the fourth rung and carefully leaned over to drape the lights around the uppermost branches. If his hands lingered longer than they should have, she told herself it was just because he was afraid she was going to fall. He released her quickly enough when she stepped down from the ladder, then moved back to give her room to do the bottom half of the tree. The limbs were very large, though, and she didn't want the lights just on the end of the branches, so she needed help getting the long string of lights deep inside the thick bows. Once again, Mitch was there to help her.

This time when his fingers brushed hers, it seemed almost too deliberate to be an accident. Suspicious, she shot him a quick look, but he glanced away just then to tease Robby about something, and she convinced herself she was just imagining things. When it happened again a few minutes later, she was on to the man.

Waiting until she got him alone on the opposite side of the tree from the kids, she turned on him, her eyes sparking fire. "What do you think you're doing?" she hissed.

As innocent as a five-year-old up to mischief, he gave her a guileless look he'd probably perfected at his mother's knee. "What? What are you talking about?"

"Oh, don't give me that," she snapped in a low voice that wouldn't carry to the kids. "You know very well what I'm talking about, and you'd better stop it right now, Mitch Ryan. You keep your paws to yourself!"

He didn't, of course. He took every opportunity to touch her, to accidentally brush up against her, to ever-so-slightly bring his body into contact with hers. Like some kind of animal mating dance, he swayed and dipped and feinted as they decorated the tree, moving counterpoint to her, yet still somehow always finding a way to caress her without seeming to touch her at all.

And every time his fingers trailed across her skin, every time a hip gently nudged hers, her breath would catch in her lungs and her heart would skip a beat. He was slowly seducing her right in front of the kids, and there didn't seem to be a thing she could do about it. Oh, she could have gotten angry and told him off, but anger was the last thing she was feeling. She was bewitched and captivated and more frustrated than she had ever been in her life, but angry? No. How could she be angry when the wicked amusement in his eyes dared her to give him back a taste of his own?

Oh, how she wanted to! She wanted to touch him and caress him and drive him slowly out of his mind, and it had nothing to do with payback. She needed to know that she could make his breath catch in his lungs and his blood warm with passion at just a touch from her, that she could, with delightful ease, make him as crazy for her as she was for him. Because she loved him.

The truth came to her so easily that she didn't know why she hadn't seen it before. Now that she had time to think about it, it seemed as if she had always known it. She would never have let a man become such an important part of her and the kids' lives if she hadn't cared about him. And she would never have been so hurt when he asked her to move in with him after they made love if he hadn't already owned a piece of her heart. She wanted the fairy tale, happily ever after, the dreams that her heart made, and he'd offered her money instead—to cushion the blow when they broke up.

And it still hurt. She'd fallen in love with a man who didn't believe in love, and she could see nothing but heartache ahead. Commitment didn't mean the same thing in his world as it did in hers, and she wouldn't make the mistake of living with him. Because if she couldn't have his love, if he didn't trust her enough to give her his heart the way she was willing to give him hers, she didn't want anything from him. It had to be all or nothing.

Too late, she realized that she should have found somewhere else to stay weeks ago, before she fell in love with him, before she set herself up for a heartache that was never going to go away. She'd waited too late, and now she couldn't leave. The tree was up and even though most of the decorations on it belonged to Alice, the kids claimed it as theirs. They'd written Santa to tell him that they'd moved, and they were expecting him to show up at the Lone Star Social Club with his bag full of presents on Christmas morning. Even if she could somehow come up with the money to rent a new apartment, she couldn't just pack them up and haul them off to someplace new when they were expecting to spend Christmas right where they were. Not only would they not understand—they'd never forgive her.

Stuck, she had no choice but to make the best of things and somehow get through Christmas. How she was going to do that, she didn't know. She couldn't even get through the decorating of the tree without almost losing her mind. Just a few teasing touches from him, and all she could think about was her own almost desperate need to feel his arms around her again. And it was still three long weeks until Christmas. How would she be able to bear it?

Things would have been easier if he'd been called away on business at least for a couple of days, but he wasn't. An entire week went by, and with each passing day, she lost more of her heart to him. And for the life of her, she couldn't understand why. It wasn't as if he was constantly trying to seduce her. They hardly saw each other. He spent the nights in the attic, and during the day, they were both working. He handled more and more of his business on the phone, and the remodeling of the attic took much more of her time than she'd expected. When she wasn't running upstairs to confer with the contractor, she was making trips to the hardware store to choose paint and wallpaper and molding. The tenants seemed to have a host of problems that only she could deal with, and whenever she could manage it, she worked on the kids' Christmas stories while they were in school. And every day, there seemed to be less time to do everything.

And always there was the threat of Christmas hanging over her head. It was all the kids talked about; the decorations were a constant reminder, and there was no way to get away from it. With every passing day, it drew closer, and money was as tight as ever. She still didn't have a clue how she was going to be able to manage to buy anything for the kids, and she readily admitted that she was starting to panic. And with good reason. She was running out of time.

Her stomach tight with worry, she pulled out her typewriter every evening and worked on her murder mystery, determined to finish it before Christmas, come hell or high water. She knew she was grasping at straws—even if she could get it in the mail and into the hands of an editor who wanted to buy it immediately, there was no way she would have a contract or any money on the deal before the end of the year. From what she'd heard, the publishing world didn't work that fast. Still, it was the only hope she had at the moment.

So while the kids had a snack before going to bed, she pounded away at the keys while worry ate away at her stomach. *Fourteen days. Fourteen days until Christmas.* Over and over again, the refrain echoed in her head to the clatter of the typewriter keys, teasing her, taunting her, frustrating her until every nerve ending she had was tied in a knot. And still she wrote, though God only knew how. What was she going to do? That was all she could think about.

Caught up in her own private nightmare, she didn't notice that the kids were picking at each other until Becky whined, "Make Robby leave my cupcake alone, Aunt Phoebe. He ate his and now he's trying to snitch mine—"

"I am not! She's waving it in front of my face—"

"'Cause you did that to me!"

"Did not!"

"Did so!"

Frowning, Phoebe glanced up from the last line she'd typed and began, "All right, kids, that's enough—"

Glaring at her brother, Becky chose that moment to once again taunt Robby with her virtually untouched cupcake. It was the wrong thing to do. Snarling at her, he made a move as if to knock her hand away, she jerked back, and someone hit the glass of chocolate milk sitting between them on the table. Gasping, they both froze, but it was too late. The glass fell over, and like a flash flood that came out of nowhere, chocolate milk went everywhere.

It happened so fast, Phoebe didn't have time to do anything but watch in horror as the milk raced across the table and swept over the chapter she'd been working on all week. In the time it took to blink, twenty typed, hard-wrought pages were soaked in chocolate milk.

"Oh, no!" Jumping up, she grabbed the manuscript, but it was too late. The pages were ruined.

After a roller-coaster week, it was too much. She never meant to cry, but suddenly her eyes were stinging, and she was horrified. It was just twenty pages, she tried telling herself. And it wasn't as if a week's worth of work had gone up in smoke. When the pages dried, they would still be legible—she'd just have to retype them before she could send the finished manuscript to a publisher. It was no big deal. But still, her eyes burned.

In the sudden stunned silence, Robby said tremulously, "We're sorry, Aunt Phoebe."

"We didn't mean to make you cry," Becky added, puckering. "Are you mad at us?"

Surprised that she would think such a thing, she said, "Of course not! It was an accident. These things happen. It's nothing to get mad about. We just have to be more careful next time. Okay? So come here and give me a hug. It's getting late and you guys need to be in bed."

More subdued than usual, they each gave her a fierce hug, then begged her to read them a story, one of the ones she'd written especially for them. She wasn't really in the mood, but they looked so pitiful that she didn't have the heart to tell them no. "Okay," she said, giving in. "But just *one!*"

She was chuckling as the kids pulled her off to the bedroom, but Mitch knew she wasn't nearly as unconcerned about her ruined manuscript pages as she pretended. She'd been working on her novel every spare moment, and although she hadn't said anything, he knew she was desperately trying to finish it so she could sell it before Christmas. Considering the strain she was under to come up with money for the kids' presents, it was no wonder she'd almost cried.

He'd seen the entire incident from the living room, and when she'd snatched up her ruined chapter, all he'd wanted to do was take her into his arms and assure her that everything was going to be all right. She didn't have to live like this, scrimping and saving and worrying about every little dime. Didn't she know he could make things easier for her if she'd just let him?

But she wouldn't, and that was the only thing that had kept him from going to her. He'd never in his life met such an independent woman, and it was driving him crazy. He didn't want anything but for her to be happy. Why couldn't she see that instead of constantly throwing roadblocks in his path? He just wanted to help her.

And dammit, he didn't always need her permission to do that! Enough was enough. He wasn't going to stand around with his hands in his pockets and watch her try to hold things together when nothing that had happened to her had been her fault.

Making a snap decision, he retrieved Phoebe's blow drier from the bathroom and strode into the kitchen. Separating the pages of her manuscript so that they wouldn't stick together, he quickly blew them dry, then carried the lot into the living room where he had his office set up and scanned them into the computer. By the time Phoebe finished reading to the kids and returned to the kitchen, he'd run the entire chapter out on his printer and the new pages were waiting for her on the now clean kitchen table.

She took one look at them and frowned in confusion. "How—"

"I dried them and scanned them into my computer," he said from the living room doorway. "I didn't read it, if that's what you're worried about. I just couldn't see you spending hours retyping the whole thing when I could do it in a matter of minutes on the computer."

He half expected a protest from her, but it was tears that he got instead. She tried to hide them from him by quickly glancing away, but her voice gave her away as she said thickly, "No, I wasn't worried about you reading it. I just hadn't thought of trying that. Thank you."

"You're welcome," he said gruffly, and had to fight the urge to take her into his arms. Afraid of scaring her off and losing her for good, he said, "Well, I guess I'll let you get back to work. If you need to use the computer again, feel free."

If she'd have looked at him just once, offered one word of protest at being left to her work, he didn't know if he'd have been able to walk away from her. But she didn't, and he had no choice but to return to his own work. But as he stared unseeingly at some figures Jennifer had faxed to him earlier, all he saw was the panic Phoebe was able to hide less and less as Christmas drew closer. If something didn't give soon, she was going to crack, and that was something he was determined wasn't going to happen. She'd worried enough. Tomorrow, he was going to play Santa. If Phoebe didn't like it, that was just too damn bad!

Chapter 13

He did, he admitted later, get carried away. But how could he have known that buying Christmas presents for Becky and Robby could be so much fun? He'd just meant to get them a few things so they wouldn't be disappointed on Christmas morning, but it had been years since he'd been in a toy store, and the second he stepped through the front door, he was hooked. By the time he wandered up and down all the aisles, he had a basketful of toys to pay for and a mountain bike waiting for him at package pickup. And he was just getting started. From the toy store, he headed to Computer Warehouse. He'd specifically heard both kids ask for a PC, and he didn't see any reason why they couldn't have one. Phoebe would be upset, but once she saw how happy the kids were, hopefully she'd relax and not worry about the cost. This was something he wanted to do, and he could afford it.

Loaded for bear, he returned to the Social Club with enough presents for a small army but didn't have a clue where he was going to hide them until Christmas Day. The kids would immediately notice the packages if he brought them into the apartment, and he couldn't risk leaving them in the car. Alice had a storage area out in the garage, but the last time he'd checked it, it was crammed full of family keepsakes. He couldn't clean that out without risking her ire, which meant the only other available space was the attic.

His first instinct was to reject that, too. With carpenters and workmen traipsing in and out all day with the remodelling job, it wasn't all that secure. But there was a closet in the old bathroom that had a dead bolt on it. Not only did he have the key, but it wasn't a place that the kids were likely to wander into, not as long as the attic was off-limits to them until the remodeling was finished. That made it perfect.

Picturing the kids' faces when they got up Christmas morning, he had to make three trips from the car to get the packages inside the entrance hall of the Social Club. Then he started up the stairs. Everything was carted up to the attic closet except Robby's bike, and he was in the process of wheeling that up the stairs when Phoebe stepped out of the apartment to see what all the racket was about.

This wasn't the way Mitch had intended to break the news to her. He'd known, of course, that he would have to tell her what he'd done, but he hadn't planned on doing it quite so soon. Or exactly in this way. But she took one look at the bike, and she knew.

"What have you done?"

"Now, Phoebe, there's no reason to get upset. This is no big deal, okay? I know I should have probably discussed this with you first, but I just couldn't stand by any longer and watch you worry about where you were going to get the money to buy the kids anything for Christmas.

So I took care of the problem for you and did a little shopping.''

She frowned at that. ''You call a mountain bike a *little* shopping?''

''Well…yeah.'' Figuring he might as well spill the whole story now that he'd been caught red-handed, he said reluctantly, ''Actually, I got a little carried away. The rest of the stuff is up in the attic.''

''The rest of— My God, Mitch, what did you buy?''

Wincing at her alarm, he decided it would be best to start with the things he considered fairly inexpensive. When her eyes widened at that, he added defiantly, ''And a PC. And I'm not taking it back. It'll help the kids in school and they need it.''

Reeling, Phoebe couldn't manage anything but a faint, ''I see.''

''I guess you're mad, huh?''

She should have been. She should have been furious with him for taking matters into his own hands without so much as a by-your-leave. From the very beginning, he'd classed her with other women he'd known in the past, the ones who saw dollar signs every time they looked at him, and for no other reason than that, she should have insisted that he take everything back.

But he seemed truly concerned about her, and she couldn't deny that there wasn't a night that went by that she didn't lie in her room and worry herself sick about money. She kept having a nightmare vision of the kids racing into the living room Christmas morning and finding nothing there but the tree. And in every horrible dream, when she tried to explain why Santa had failed to put in an appearance for the first time in their lives, the kids looked up at her with eyes full of betrayal.

And it hurt. There was so much she wanted to give them and so little that was within her reach right now.

Next year, after she got another job and she was able to recover from the financial hit she'd taken when she'd been scammed out of her rent money, things would be better and she would be able to give them a wonderful Christmas. But to a six- and seven-year-old, next year was a hundred years away. And they only believed in Santa for so long before someone ruined the fantasy for them.

That wouldn't happen this year. Thanks to Mitch. Even though he'd known he was overstepping his bounds, he'd done it anyway...simply because he hadn't wanted to see her worry any more or the kids do without. How could she possibly be angry about that?

Emotion squeezing her heart, she said huskily, "No, I'm not mad. I'm overwhelmed. I don't know when I'll be able to pay you back, but you'll get every penny back, plus interest."

"Honey, I'm not asking for a payment plan. It's just money, and I won't even miss it. I just want to see the kids' faces Christmas morning when they wake up and see what Santa brought them."

If she hadn't loved him before, she would have fallen head over heels right then. He was such a wonderful man, and she would have given anything to tell him at that moment how much he meant to her. But she couldn't. He didn't want love from her, just a physical relationship, and it broke her heart.

Sudden tears flooded her eyes, horrifying her, and she knew she was going to make a complete fool of herself if she didn't get out of there. "I don't know how to thank you—" She couldn't manage any more than that. Swallowing a sob, she turned and fled back into Alice's apartment.

"Phoebe, wait!"

She never checked her pace, never even looked back. She headed straight for her bedroom, her only thought to get inside and shut the door before the tears she'd been holding off for days washed over her. But she never got that far. Caught up in her own misery, she didn't realize Mitch was right behind her. Quickly propping the new bike against the couch, he caught up with her right in front of the Christmas tree.

"Let me go!" she gasped.

"The hell I will," he growled, pulling her into his arms. "Not until you tell me what I did to make you cry."

"You didn't," she sniffed. "It's just—"

She couldn't finish, couldn't tell him that she was only just now realizing the depth of her love for him, and that it hurt. It hurt to realize that he didn't want what she wanted, that one day soon, he would walk away from her as if the last few weeks had never happened, and that was all there would ever be between them. How, dear God, was she ever going to be able to stand the pain?

Feeling like her heart was breaking, her tears overflowing, she tried to push her way free of his arms, but he only pulled her closer, and with a sob, she buried her face against his neck. "I'm sorry," she choked. "I'm just kind of emotional right now."

"It's all right, honey," he murmured, tightening his arms around her and pressing a kiss to her hair. "You don't have to apologize. I know the last couple of weeks have been rough on you. Just let me hold you a second."

That was all he meant to do...just hold her, comfort her, and kiss away her tears. But it seemed like forever since he'd had her alone and in his arms, and the feel of her against him went straight to his head. He kissed her wet cheeks and couldn't resist the lure of her soft, trembling mouth.

"Mitch..."

"I know, sweetheart," he groaned. "It's okay. I just want to kiss you."

But one kiss led to another, then another. She was too close, the need that tore at him too fierce, and all he could think about was that he wanted, needed to love her. His very bones ached with it, and he had to believe that hers did, too. When she could have pushed him away, she pulled him close. When she could have turned her mouth away from his, she kissed him back with a hunger that matched his own.

His blood roaring in his ears, he tore his mouth from hers, but only to drop short, fierce kisses on the curve of her cheek, her nose, the sweep of her brow. "I want you," he rasped, making her shudder just kissing his way down the side of her neck. "Right now. Right here. Don't say no, sweetheart. Let me love you."

Her heart pounding, every nerve ending in her body crying out for his touch, his kiss, Phoebe couldn't have denied him if her life had depended on it. Not when this would probably be the last chance that she would ever have to hold him, to love him. Without a word, she reached for the buttons of his shirt.

She had dreamed about making love with him again. Even after he had hurt her and she'd accepted the fact that they were never going to have any more than what they already did, she'd fantasized about where and when they would give in to the maddening, crazy need they had for each other. And never in her wildest dreams had she thought it would be like this...in the living room, right in front of the Christmas tree.

But no place could have been more appropriate. Right from the beginning, he had been a surprise, a gift in her life when that was the last thing she was expecting. Even as he pulled her down to the braided rug with him, she knew she'd never again think of Christmas without thinking of him.

This was all she would ever have of him—just these

few precious memories. And she wanted it to last forever. But this last time was like the first time—hot and fierce and desperate—and any chance she had of any kind of control ended the second he touched her. Clothes melted away, his hands rushed over her, caressing, trailing liquid fire over her breasts and hips and thighs, and she turned into a woman she didn't know. A woman with needs and wants and demands of her own. A woman who wasn't afraid to ask for what she wanted, show what she needed.

Pushing him to his back, she rolled over on top of him, and it was her turn to make him burn and groan and shudder. And she loved it. She loved the freedom of exploring every hard inch of his body, of driving him wild, of knowing that every thought he had began and ended with her. Just her. It was her name he called out, her body he couldn't get enough of. Under her hands, her mouth, she could feel the thunder of his heartbeat, a primal rhythm that throbbed and hummed, the tension that tightened in him with every flick of her hands, her tongue, and she took fierce satisfaction in knowing that she had brought him to this. She might not have him forever, but for this moment stolen out of time, he was hers, and for now, that was enough.

But it couldn't last. As much as she longed to hang on to the moment, to the magic that they had found together, it couldn't last. Balanced on a razor-sharp edge of desire, they strained together, hearts pounding, in a fast-paced dance as old as time. Then, with no warning, she cried out as the passion gripping her shattered. With a hoarse cry, he followed, taking her with him over the edge into ecstasy.

For a long time afterwards, Mitch lay with Phoebe cradled limply in his arms, unable to let her go. Staggered by the depth of emotions she had pulled from him so effortlessly, he tried to convince himself that what they had just shared was nothing more than sex. But he'd had just sex before, and this wasn't it. This wasn't anything that he'd ever experienced before.

Because you've never been in love before, you idiot.

Like a bullet from a sniper's gun, the truth came out of nowhere to strike him right in the heart, knocking him senseless. Love? It had always been a four-letter word to him, a weakness that left a man wide open to a woman looking to feather her nest. He'd sworn there would never come a time when he would want a part of anything remotely resembling that kind of vulnerability, and he'd meant it. But that was before he'd met Phoebe.

She was unlike any woman he'd ever known. She'd been cheated, fired, thrown out of her apartment, all while trying to support two children who weren't even hers. Just because they were her niece and nephew didn't mean she had to take them in. She could have refused. Or when things got dicey, she could have looked around for a man to support her. It would have been the easiest thing to do. She could have taken one look at him and seen dollar signs, but she'd wanted nothing more from him than what she could earn. She was proud and strong and gutsy and she'd slipped under his guard without him even realizing it. She was everything he thought he'd never find, and now that he had, he couldn't imagine his life without her.

God, he loved her! How had it happened? When? He felt like the hero in a fairy tale, a modern-day Prince Charming who wanted to sweep her up in his arms and carry her off to his castle, where she'd never have to worry about anything again. And that scared him spitless. He was thinking marriage. Forever. Till death do us part. And for a man who had perfected the art of avoiding commitment, that was enough to stop his heart dead in his chest.

Panic hit him then, right in the gut, and all he could think about was getting away. He needed to think, to work this out in his head, to deal with the emotions churning inside him. And to do that, he had to be alone.

Easing her gently from his arms, he quickly pulled the afghan from the end of the couch and draped it over her, then started pulling on his clothes. Not proud of himself, he pretended he'd just now noticed the time. "Damn! I hate to leave you, sweetheart, but I've got an appointment with a banker in fifteen minutes on the north side, and I'm not going to make it if I don't leave right now. Can you take Robby's bike upstairs for me?"

"Yes, of course," she said, hugging the afghan to her breast. "But—"

"Thanks! I'm not sure when I'll be back, but it should be before supper. Don't bother cooking. I'll stop and pick up a pizza on the way home."

"You don't have to do that—"

"It's no problem," he assured her, dropping a quick kiss on her mouth. "The kids like pepperoni, right? I'll get an extra large, then they can really pig out."

He was gone before she could say another word, shutting the door behind him and almost running out of the Social Club like the miserable coward that he was. There was no meeting, nowhere that he had to be, which was probably a good thing. Dazed, his thoughts chasing themselves in circles, he got in his car and just drove. Later, he couldn't have said where he went—it didn't matter. All he could think of was Phoebe.

He loved her. Just how much still stunned him. No one's happiness had ever meant so much to him, and it was daunting. He'd cared about women before—he was thirty-six years old, for God's sake! But caring was a whole different feeling from loving, and he was only just now realizing that. It explained so much. Like why he'd gone so far as to volunteer to sleep on the floor in the attic just to keep her close. He was a man who liked his creature comforts—he didn't rough it for anyone. But he would have slept on the roof if that's what it would have taken to convince her to stay.

Because he loved her. Because he would have moved heaven and earth to make her happy. Because he couldn't even contemplate the thought of losing her. Not now. Not ever. She was his. Why had it taken him so long to see that?

His car phone rang suddenly, cutting into his thoughts. Frowning, he almost ignored it. It was probably business, and he didn't feel like talking. But the thing kept ringing, and with a muttered curse he jerked it up. "What?"

As a greeting, it was a damn rude one, but his caller only returned it in kind. "I want to know what the hell you think you're doing, Ryan," Applebee growled in his familiar gravelly voice. "I had a verbal contract for every one of those leases you stole out from under me in the Permian Basin, and if you try to get so much as a drop of oil out of those wells, I'll tie your ass up in court for the next ten years. If you don't believe me, you just start pumping and we'll see who blinks first."

At any other time, Mitch him would have told him to do whatever he thought he was big enough to do—he could handle whatever he dished out. But today he didn't give a damn about business. And if that didn't tell him just how crazy in love he was, nothing else would.

"You want the leases back? Fine, they're yours," he said flatly. "Take them. I don't care anymore."

For a second, there was nothing but stunned silence. He could almost hear the wheels turning in the old man's head. Then he said suspiciously, "My daddy taught me to always look a gift horse in the mouth. Especially when it comes from a tricky bastard like you. What are you up to?''

"Not a damn thing," Mitch retorted, scowling. "Unlike you, I just have more important things on my mind right now. So if that's the only reason you called, you can rest easy. You win, okay?''

"No, it's not okay," he snapped irritably. "It's no fun trying to beat you at your own game if you're going to *let* me win, dammit! What's wrong with you?''

"Nothing!''

"The hell there isn't. You're sick, aren't you? What is it? One of those bugs or something more serious?''

His patience almost at an end, Mitch clenched his teeth on an oath. "I'm *not* sick, all right? I'm healthy as a horse.''

"Then what the devil's wrong with you? In all the years I've known you, you've never given up on a deal. Something's wrong, and don't try to tell me it's not. I know you too well to fall for that kind of a snow job.''

Goaded, Mitch never intended to tell him, but the words just popped out. "All right," he said through his teeth, "you want to know what's going on, I'll tell you, you old goat. I just realized I'm nuts about someone. There! I told you. Are you happy now?''

He expected a sarcastic remark, but Applebee surprised him. "The question is…are you?''

He didn't even have to think twice about it. "Yeah, I am. Of course, I'll be even happier when I know the lady feels the same way.''

He had to believe that she did, but what if she didn't? Just the possibility that she might not sent a cold chill rippling through his blood. And suddenly he understood how Applebee's granddaughter, Lisa, must have felt when he'd had to tell her that he didn't love her. No wonder her entire family had hated his guts after that. Until then

they'd been close friends, but Applebee had been so outraged that he'd hurt his granddaughter that he'd been trying to make him pay ever since. And Mitch couldn't say
he blamed him. He'd never set out to hurt Lisa, but he
had, and he regretted that.

"I know it's a little late for apologies," he said gruffly,
"but I really hate that I hurt Lisa. She's a wonderful
woman. I never wanted anything but the best for her."

"You sound like you really mean that," the old man
said, surprised.

"I do. I just wasn't what she needed. She didn't want
to believe that at the time, but obviously I was right. I
heard she was getting married to Wesley St. John's son.
She'll be happy with him. She wouldn't have been with
me."

It was the simple truth and Applebee was wise enough
to know it. "I didn't agree with your methods at the
time," he said grudgingly, "but looking back on things,
I'd have to say you did her a favor. And if you want to
do yourself one, you'd better snatch up this gal you're
crazy about before someone else comes along and steals
her away from you. Good women are in short supply this
day and age, and you don't want to lose her."

Just that easily, peace was made between them. Grinning, Mitch said, "I plan to do that just as soon as I can
get her a ring. Now about those leases. You still think you
want to take me to court over them?"

They both knew that yesterday, Applebee would have
gone for his throat if the opportunity had presented itself.
Today, since they'd found a way to bury the hatchet, he
only chuckled and said, "I was only trying to get your
goat, anyway. Call me after you get things worked out
with your lady friend. I've got a joint venture I'd like to
talk to you about."

* * *

Phoebe waited as long as she dared for Mitch to return with the pizza he'd promised for supper, but the kids were hungry and it was getting late. Hurriedly throwing together spaghetti and meat sauce, she glanced at the clock for the third time in as many minutes and tried to convince herself there was no reason to be concerned just because Mitch had been gone for hours. He'd told her he was meeting with a banker, and any discussion that involved money could always be expected to run long. There was certainly nothing to be worried about. Any second now, he'd stroll in with a pizza box and she'd wonder why she had ever been worried.

But ten minutes passed, then another ten, and there was still no sign of Mitch. She fed the kids, but she couldn't eat herself. Not when she remembered Mitch's face when he'd practically run out of the apartment.

He knew, she thought, shaken. She must have given herself away when they'd made love, and somehow he'd figured out that she loved him. That was why he hadn't come back. He didn't know how he was going to break it to her that he didn't love her back.

No! her heart cried. She was just being paranoid. He couldn't possibly know for sure that she loved him—she'd never said so much as a word about her feelings. If he was late, it had nothing to do with her. He'd just gotten held up by business.

As if in response to her troubled thoughts, the phone rang at that moment, and she went weak with relief. He'd probably just realized he was running late and was calling to let her know that he wasn't going to be able to make it home in time for supper after all.

She grabbed the phone on the third ring, but it was Alice, not Mitch, on the other end. Disappointed, she said, "Oh, hello, Alice. I'm sorry, but Mitch isn't here right now. He's in a business meeting. Would you like him to call you when he gets back?''

''Oh, no, dear,'' she assured her. ''You can just give him a message for me, if you wouldn't mind. I just wanted him to know that since his surgery, Glen has made a remarkable recovery, and it looks like he's going to be released from the hospital much sooner than expected. So I may be able to come home by the end of the week. Isn't that wonderful?!''

Stunned, Phoebe reached for a chair and didn't even remember sinking into it. ''Y-yes, wonderful,'' she echoed faintly. ''I know you must be thrilled.''

''Oh, I am!'' the older woman exclaimed happily. ''Emily and I have been so worried about him. Then when the doctors said today how well he was doing, we both just broke down and cried. It'll still be a while before he's back on his feet, of course,'' she added, ''but just knowing that it's only a matter of time before he's completely recovered has been a tremendous boost for him and Emily. This has been a nightmare for both of them, and now that the end is in sight, they know they're going to get through it just fine.''

She was coming home. She'd be there by the end of the week, and Mitch would leave because there was no longer any reason to stay.

Devastated, hardly hearing the older woman as she chatted about the excellent health insurance her son-in-law had, and the in-home health care that would be provided once he left the hospital, Phoebe said all the right things at all the right places. But inside, her heart was breaking. This was it, then. The end. By the time Alice returned, the remodeling of the attic would be far enough along for Phoebe and the kids to move upstairs. Mitch wouldn't stick around, of course—why would he? He had a life back in Dallas, and with Alice back to oversee the last of the remodeling, not to mention any problems that cropped up with the Social Club, he would no longer be needed in San Antonio. In all likelihood, he wouldn't even come back for Christmas.

Her throat tight with emotion, she said huskily, "I'll give Mitch the message when he gets back. I'm sure he'll be thrilled."

Heartbroken, she told herself she wasn't going to cry. Not in front of the kids. They wouldn't understand, and it would just upset them. So she cleared off the table after they'd eaten, then with forced cheerfulness, helped them with their homework. They were just finishing up when she heard Mitch's key in the lock and he walked in.

He'd forgotten the pizza, and he looked like he'd been running his hands through his hair, but he offered no explanation of why he was late. And she didn't ask. She couldn't. The second her eyes met his, her heart started to pound, and she knew she couldn't tell him about Alice's call. Not yet. She'd have to tell him goodbye soon enough—she couldn't do it then.

Turning her attention back to the kids' homework, she tried to concentrate, but she was fighting a losing battle. He came into the kitchen to greet the kids and ask them about their day, and although he didn't so much as touch her, she was aware of his nearness, the brush of his eyes on her, his every little move. And it hurt. Afraid the tears stinging her eyes would spill over her lashes, she quickly rushed the kids through the rest of their homework, and then escaped to the bedroom to lay out their clothes for the next morning while they took their baths.

She couldn't hide in the bedroom forever, though, and all too soon, she was doling out good-night kisses and hugs, and then she was alone with Mitch in the living room. In the sudden silence, she would have sworn he could hear the pounding of her heart.

"Alice called," she blurted out, and didn't even realize she was going to tell him then until the words popped out. And then it was too late to take them back. Resigned, she gave him a rundown of Glen's prognosis. "Since he's doing so much better, and Emily will have a LVN to help her once he goes home, she doesn't need Alice. So she'll be home by the end of the week—barring any complications, of course," she quickly added.

"Alice is coming home?" he repeated sharply. "*This* week?"

Forcing a smile that never reached her eyes, she nodded. "She can't wait to get here. If it's okay with you, the kids and I will move into the attic early. The remodeling's ahead of schedule and should be finished sometime next week anyway, so that shouldn't be a problem.

"I don't know what I'm going to do about the Christmas tree, though," she added, knowing she was chattering but unable to stop herself. "We might be able to move it upstairs, but we did use a lot of Alice's decorations, and the kids won't understand how Santa's going to find them if we start moving things around at this late date. I'll talk to Alice when she gets here and see what she thinks about leaving it where it is. That might be better anyway since you'll be heading back to Dallas. Then we can spend Christmas with her, and she won't be alone."

The news hit Mitch like a blow to the stomach. He was happy for Glen and Emily, glad they were going to be able to rebuild their lives faster than they'd thought they could. And now that the crisis was over, he knew a huge weight had been lifted from Alice's shoulders. But all he could think of was that he wasn't ready for her to come home. Not yet. He had to tell Phoebe how he felt, had to work the words out in his head, had to set the scene for a romantic proposal. It was what she deserved, what he wanted for her, for them. But the clock had just run out, and he didn't have a clue how to begin.

"Phoebe—" For a man who didn't know what it was to lack confidence, he suddenly felt like a shy sixteen-year-old about to bare his soul to the prettiest girl in the school. "Sweetheart, I'm not going back to Dallas. At least, not without you."

He meant to tell her he loved her, but before he could get the words out, hurt flashed in her eyes and she shot him a wounded look that stabbed him right in the heart. "I can't believe that you would bring that up now. You think just because I've got to get out of here by the end of the week that I'm going to change my mind and live with you?"

"No, of course not!" he exclaimed, shocked that she had so misunderstood him. "I never meant for you to think—I want you to live with me, but—" Suddenly realizing how that sounded, he winced. Damn his stumbling tongue! Why couldn't he just get the words out? She meant so much to him. Couldn't she see that? If he lost her now, he didn't think he'd be able to stand it.

So tell her! a voice retorted from deep in his soul. What are you waiting for? Christmas?

"I love you!" He never meant to just blurt it out like that, but suddenly the words were spilling out of him. "Can't you see that I'm crazy about you? Of course I want you to live with me! As my wife, sweetheart. I love you."

Surprise bloomed in her eyes, and for what seemed like an eternity, she didn't do anything but stare at him. When she finally did manage to find her voice, it was little more that a hoarse whisper. "You want to marry me? But I thought—"

"I know," he groaned. "Don't remind me what an idiot I was to ever ask you to move in with me. I thought you were like other women and just looking for someone to take care of you. I knew I was wrong almost as soon as the words were out of my mouth, but you have to understand the women I was used to dealing with, honey. They were out for what they could get out of me, and you weren't. I couldn't believe you were for real.

"Now I wonder how I could have been so blind," he said with a simple honesty that brought tears to her eyes. "You're everything I never thought I would find, and I love you and the kids with all my heart. I don't want to ever risk losing you again. Say you'll marry me and make me the happiest man on earth."

He meant it. She only had to look into his steady, loving gaze to know that he meant every word. He loved her…completely, without reservation. The last feeble barriers protecting her heart fell away, and with a cry of joy, she flew into his arms, words tumbling from her lips as he caught her close against his heart. "I was so afraid that you would leave when Alice came home and I would never see you again. I didn't know how I was going to bear it. I love you! So much. I can't even find the words."

Chuckling, he crushed her close. "I just need one right now, sweetheart. Yes. You're killing me. Are you going to marry me or not?"

She didn't even have to think twice. Slipping her arms around his neck, she pulled his mouth down to hers and kissed him fiercely. "Yes, Mitch Ryan, I'll marry you. Today. Tomorrow. For the rest of my life." Pulling back slightly, her eyes sparkled up into his. "How was that?"

"Perfect," he growled, tugging her close again for another kiss. "Just perfect."

Epilogue

Santa had come, the presents had all been opened, and the living room of Alice's apartment looked as if it had been hit by a tornado. Torn wrapping paper and bows were strewn everywhere, not to mention unwrapped presents stacked haphazardly on every available space. The kids were busy checking out the games on the computer that Santa had brought them, while their grandparents and Alice raved about the Christmas stories Phoebe had done for everyone.

"They really are the most incredible little books, Phoebe," Louise told her as she carefully examined the one she'd been given. "How in the world did you possibly find time to do them all by yourself? It must have taken forever."

Seated on the floor next to Mitch among the paper, Phoebe stretched her legs out in front of her, crossed her ankles and smiled. "The stories just sort of come to me, and the artwork isn't that complicated. And they're not all that long,'' she reminded her. ''Anybody could probably do it if they just sat down and thought about it.''

''Anybody with talent, maybe,'' Mitch agreed. ''And you definitely have talent, honey. And I know at least one editor who agrees with me.'' Retrieving a letter from under the tree, where it had been hidden under the presents, he took a seat beside her on the floor and held out the white envelope to her. ''Merry Christmas, sweetheart.''

Confused, she frowned. ''What's this?''

''Another Christmas present,'' he said, grinning. ''Go ahead. Open it.''

''But I already got my present.'' Holding up her left hand to show him the antique diamond solitaire he'd placed on her ring finger just last night, she said, ''I don't need anything else.''

Smiling, he kissed her fingers, then closed them around the letter. ''Trust me—you need this. Read it.''

Something in his eyes set her heart pounding, and she glanced down at the envelope again, only to frown. ''This is from Hudson Publishing. I just got a rejection letter from one of their subsidiaries yesterday turning down my murder mystery. Why would they send me a second rejection letter? Don't they think I got the message the first time?''

''Read it,'' he said again, chuckling. ''What's it going to hurt to see what they have to say?''

She would have liked to throw it out on sheer principle, but everyone was watching, and with a shrug, she tore it open and began to read.

Dear Ms. Smith,
My name is Quinn Thompson, and I recently had the pleasure of reading your children's story—*Professor Rat and the Case of the Lost Glasses.* It was a delightful story, one that we feel sure our readers will

also enjoy. Therefore, I would like to offer you a contract—

Gasping, she lifted stunned eyes to Mitch. "They want to buy one of my children's stories! But how—"

"I sent it to Quinn," he confessed. "He's an old friend, and I knew he would be as impressed as I was when he read it. All I did was ask him to take a look at it," he quickly assured her. "He didn't pull any strings for me except to read it when he got the chance. If he hadn't liked it, I wasn't even going to mention it to you. I hope you're not upset."

"Upset?" she echoed, still dazed. "No, of course not. I just never thought anyone would be interested in the children's stuff."

"Why?" he teased. "Because you love doing it and it comes easy to you? Honey, I can't speak for your murder mystery since I haven't read it, but the stories you did for the kids are outstanding. They should be published. They're wonderful."

There was no doubting his sincerity, no doubting that Alice and the Mallorys all agreed. Stunned, she finished reading the letter Quinn Thompson had sent her, her eyes widening at the sizable advance the company was going to pay her, and then it hit her. She had everything she loved right there within reach—Mitch, the kids, Alice and the Mallorys, who had become like family, and an honest-to-God writing career. Life didn't get any better than that. Tears glistening in her eyes, she threw herself into Mitch's arms.

* * * * *

invites you to go West to

Margaret Watson's exhilarating new miniseries.

FOR THE CHILDREN...IM #886, October 1998:
Embittered agent Damien Kane was responsible for protecting beautiful Abby Markham and her twin nieces. But it was Abby who saved him as she showed him the redeeming power of home and family.

COWBOY WITH A BADGE...IM #904, January 1999:
Journalist Carly Fitzpatrick had come to Cameron determined to clear her dead brother's name. But it's the local sheriff—the son of the very man she believed was responsible—who ends up safeguarding her from the real murderer and giving her the family she's always wanted.

Available at your favorite retail outlet.

Take 2 bestselling love stories FREE

Plus get a FREE surprise gift!

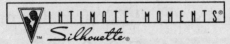

For a limited time, Harlequin and Silhouette have an offer you just can't refuse.

In November and December 1998:

BUY **ANY** TWO HARLEQUIN
OR SILHOUETTE BOOKS and
SAVE $10.00
off future purchases

OR BUY ANY THREE HARLEQUIN OR SILHOUETTE BOOKS
AND **SAVE $20.00** OFF FUTURE PURCHASES!

(each coupon is good for $1.00 off the purchase of two
Harlequin or Silhouette books)

••

JUST BUY 2 HARLEQUIN OR SILHOUETTE BOOKS, SEND US YOUR
NAME, ADDRESS AND 2 PROOFS OF PURCHASE (CASH REGISTER
RECEIPTS) AND HARLEQUIN WILL SEND YOU A COUPON BOOKLET
WORTH $10.00 OFF FUTURE PURCHASES OF HARLEQUIN OR
SILHOUETTE BOOKS IN 1999. SEND US 3 PROOFS OF PURCHASE AND
WE WILL SEND YOU 2 COUPON BOOKLETS WITH A TOTAL SAVING OF
$20.00. (ALLOW 4-6 WEEKS DELIVERY) OFFER EXPIRES
DECEMBER 31, 1998.

••

I accept your offer! Please send me a coupon booklet(s), to:

NAME: _____

ADDRESS: _____

CITY: _____ STATE/PROV.: _____ POSTAL/ZIP CODE: _____

**Send your name and address, along with your cash register
receipts for proofs of purchase, to:**

In the U.S.
Harlequin Books
P.O. Box 9057
Buffalo, NY
14269

In Canada
Harlequin Books
P.O. Box 622
Fort Erie, Ontario
L2A 5X3

PHQ4982

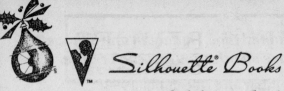

**The Fortune family requests
the honor of your presence at the weddings of**

Silhouette Desire's scintillating new miniseries,
featuring the beloved Fortune family
and five of your favorite authors.

The Honor Bound Groom—**January 1999**
by Jennifer Greene (SD #1190)

Society Bride—**February 1999**
by Elizabeth Bevarly (SD #1196)

And look for more **FORTUNE'S CHILDREN:
THE BRIDES** installments by Leanne Banks,
Susan Crosby and Merline Lovelace,
coming in spring 1999.

Available at your favorite retail outlet.

INTIMATE MOMENTS®

™ Silhouette®

COMING NEXT MONTH